FOXWEPT ARRAY

BOOK 1

PINE, ALIVE

A FUTURISTIC ROMANCE RETELLING OF PINOCCHIO

A.W. CROSS

GLORY BOX PRESS

Pine, Alive

Published by Glory Box Press
British Columbia, Canada.
gloryboxpress@gmail.com

First edition, 2019

ISBN 978-1-9995711-4-6

Cover design by Danielle Fine
Interior design and formatting by Glory Box Press
Editing by Danielle Fine

FOR MY LITTLE
WOODEN-HEAD

PINE,
ALIVE

PART ONE

ONE

Rain broke against the car window then slid down the smoky pane to disappear into the coming darkness.

If only I could do the same.

Envy at the water's liberty squeezed Pine's chest, a familiar, unpleasant ache. She pressed closer to the glass, willing herself to pass through it.

As though he could read her mind, Antonio Carpenter patted her shoulder from the next seat as their vehicle navigated itself from the seaport toward the bright lights of inner Portfade. The touch was supposed to be pleasant, a gesture humans used to comfort one another. Pine's skin crawled. If only she could slap his hand away, tear off the synthetic hair they'd stitched to her head and smash her feet through the windscreen before vanishing into the night. She'd return to the ocean, to see if any of her kind still lingered, or perhaps she would go to one of the hundreds of islands off the coast of Foxwept, where no human would ever find her.

"It's going to be okay," Antonio said. "You'll like Joseph." He dabbed at the cherry-red tip of his nose with a handkerchief.

How can I? He's a stranger. A stranger who now owns me. Pine fingered the barcode tattooed on her wrist, an unmistakable mark of what she was.

"What do you think of your new clothes?"

Pine glanced down. Her luminescent wetsuit had been replaced with what Antonio called "street clothes"—skinny-legged jeans and a shiny, buttoned-up blouse. They were ridiculous. The jeans were suffocating, the stiff material bunching intolerably behind her knees and chafing her groin, and the slippery silver of the blouse echoed the pale skin of the dead fish that had once floated past her on their way to the surface, their bodies bloated and peeling. Her fingers itched to rip off the buttons, to rend the shirt from her body.

"They're fine."

Her hair was the worst part. She'd always been bald and had once admired from a distance women with long, silky hair that bounced and shimmered as they walked. Imagined having hair like that, gathering it up and twisting it into shining plaits, like the ship figureheads she'd found half-buried in the sand, their arms flung behind their backs and their pointed breasts arched toward freedom.

But that wasn't the hair they'd given her, with its fashionable asymmetrical shape and garish cerise streaks. Again, the urge to wrench the outrageous mop from her head and throw it in Antonio's surprised face washed over her.

"You'll find your own style in time, I'm sure," Antonio said in the soothing voice that burrowed into her mind like a crab. "I don't know much about young women's fashion, but the girls in the office said this is what the kids are wearing these days." He gave her what he probably thought was a winning grin.

She hated him.

No, that wasn't fair. Shame flooded her, laced with guilt. Antonio *was* only trying his best to make her comfortable. It wasn't his fault. None of this was. Pine gave him the sincerest smile she could muster and gazed out the window again, carefully avoiding the ghostly reflection that peered back at her, imploring her to do *something*.

The view outside the car was just as foreign as her clothes. Houses—real houses, not just barracks—and cars filled with all kinds of passengers multiplied as she and Antonio drew closer to the heart of the city. Pine had never seen so many. In fact, she'd never seen much of anything they passed—stores, schools, trees just now in bloom. Even the open air itself was strange. *Especially* the air. It threatened to dissolve her.

Down in the depths of the Ghostlight sea, close to the Foxwept shoreline, the warm weight of the water had been comforting. Now, sea and sky had switched places, and the air, though heavy with moisture and tangy with salt, seemed thin and insubstantial, displacing Pine. Making her as fragile as the raindrops shattering on the glass outside, so far from home.

But the Ghostlight wasn't home, not anymore. That was here now, in a place she'd never been, with people she'd never met. It was no less surreal now than when Mrs. Hayes had first told her she was being relieved of her duties, explaining that there'd been protests, court cases, and grand speeches made on wallscreens across the region— and that Pine, like all other sentient androids, had been emancipated.

Emancipation. Pine snorted. All it was was going from one owner to the next. Synadroids like her still had no legal standing or rights. All emancipation had done for Pine was force her to leave her friends and everything she'd ever known. Some freedom. What would she do now, if not what she'd been created for? The storm of anger and fear inside her threatened to short her circuits out. Whoever had insisted on emancipation hadn't seemed concerned with how the synadroids themselves would feel about it.

Mrs. Hayes had told Pine that she was lucky, that the man who now owned her was kind and would treat her like a daughter. Just like that. As though humans were the ones programmed with emotions. Just flick a switch and, "You're my daughter, as real as if you'd been born to me." Until the next flick, when she was once more property, to be sold on to the next buyer.

But, as bitter a pill as it was, Pine didn't have a choice in the matter. It was done. Her only option now was to play along, to wait and watch for her opportunity. Then, when the time came, she would make her escape to that remote island, and live alone or among others who'd suffered the same fate of being not quite human, not quite a machine.

There, she would be free.

TWO

James Cruicéad balanced awkwardly on the edge of a too-small chair, forearms resting on his gangly thighs. He was trying to seem relaxed, as though his closest friend wasn't about to make the biggest mistake of his life.

"Are you sure I'm not keeping you? You can always come by tomorrow to meet her if you have business to take care of." Joseph Polendina glanced at the digital numbers in the corner of the wallscreen.

"No, I'm happy to stay." James also eyed the clock. 8 p.m.

Antonio was nearly an hour late—as usual—but there was no way James was leaving his friend alone now. Not until he was sure he was safe. No, he was staying put, and he wasn't going to do it quietly.

"I think you're crazy, if you want my honest opinion." Joseph, in fact, *hadn't* asked for his opinion, but he was going to get it anyway. "There are too many uncertainties. I understand there's a huge sentimental value to you, but—"

"It's not *just* sentimental value." The older man paced the room. "Not that I have to justify myself, but I believe we have a responsibility toward these synadroids. We built them, gave them human emotions, and designed their lives for them. We can't simply abandon them now we've decided it's morally unconscionable." He crooked his head in sympathy. "James, I know you've had some bad experiences with—"

"That's an understatement." James's time as a soldier on the Perimeter had marked him in more ways than one. "I understand all that, Joseph, I really do. What I *don't* understand is why you're insisting on taking one into your home. I mean, I know you designed them, helped build them, but look at how Sonder treated you. And now they've palmed one—"

"The company didn't *palm* her off on me. When Antonio told me what was happening, that the synadroids were being replaced by non-sentient droids, I—"

"Replaced? I thought they'd been 'liberated.'" James shook his head in contempt. "Isn't that what all the protests were about?" He'd watched the rallies from the fringes, biting back the temptation to tell the naïve campaigners the truth about the synadroids they were trying so hard to free.

"They were," Joseph agreed. "But do you really think a corporation as big as Sonder would've given in to a handful of synadroid sympathizers, no matter how loudly they shouted? No, the synadroids were already on their way out. But this way, the corporation got to unload them while looking magnanimous. Great optics, and a public relations success all round."

"But why would they replace them? I thought the synadroids were Sonder's greatest accomplishment." The day the synadroids had been announced, Robert Smythe, the head of Sonder, had nearly fallen off the stage, light-headed as he was with pride. Even then, James had been skeptical.

"They were. But give a being complicated human emotions…" Joseph shrugged. "They react like humans. Which is ironic, given that emotional instability was one of the things they were supposed to replace."

"But then why give them human emotions in the first place?" It seemed so obvious. "Surely Sonder foresaw the complications? And considering the risk and expense—" Joseph had shown him once just how intricate the synadroid's physiology was. Though they were completely synthetic, they'd been constructed to mimic humans in every way—skeletal structure, muscles, skin, even a fully functional nervous system complete with synthetic hormones. *That* James had seen firsthand. An overwhelming rush of adrenalin through a physically superior body… He shuddered. It had been a stupid, foolhardy venture. Thank goodness the experiment had been short-lived.

Joseph stopped pacing and stood before a large picture on the far wall of the living room. Within the frame, a dozen men and women grinned back at him, their faces unlined and buoyant. "Robert had a very romantic view of sentient androids and what they would mean to humankind. He had a vision of man and machine, separated only by birth, working together, hand-in-hand, toward a better future. The synadroids having the same emotions and physiology as us was fundamental to that equality."

"He sounds like a lunatic to me." James rose and examined the picture over Joseph's shoulder, fascinated as always by the younger version of his mentor. He couldn't reconcile the open brightness of the face in the portrait with the weary wisdom of the man he now knew.

"Perhaps he was, but I shared his vision, as did the government at the time. And there was enough funding to make it come true. So we did. Now, we need to take responsibility for that and protect them."

"By *adopting* one?"

"I know you don't approve." Joseph turned away from the picture.

Frustration swelled in James. How could he make Joseph understand? James was only trying to protect the most important person in his life. Why couldn't Joseph see that? "I just think there are other ways—"

"It's not just about taking responsibility. I have selfish reasons, too." Joseph wandered across the room to another image on the wall, a portrait of a middle-aged woman with rosy cheeks and a screwdriver in her fist, her expression caught between concentration and excitement as she tinkered with a tiny robotic hand, the fingers opening and closing as she manipulated the controls. She looked up at the cameraman and smiled before returning to her work, captured forever in an eternal loop.

Joseph's smile was gentle. "Mara and I always hoped we'd have children... She wanted a daughter, but working on these androids was as close as she ever got, and she loved them like her own. This is what she would've wanted." He reached out and traced his finger over her image. "We're going to have a daughter, Mara," he whispered.

James looked away, uncomfortable with the intimacy. He understood. Really, he did. He lived with loneliness and loss and the need to fill that awful void every day. But to relieve it by putting your own life at risk? That was something else.

It's not your decision, James. The best he could do was make sure it didn't end badly for his old friend, no matter what he had to do to shield him. Resolution filled him. He would see this charade through to the end.

"Aaah, there they are," Joseph said as a swathe of light cut across the bay window. He rubbed his hands together in anticipation, and his steps toward the front door were lighter than James had ever seen them.

Joseph flung the door open. Antonio stood on the doorstep, blinking at the sudden rush of light, his hand hovering in front of the doorbell.

"Come in, come in." Joseph beckoned with trembling fingers that hurt James's heart. "Get yourselves out of the rain."

Antonio eagerly obeyed, and after a moment's hesitation, a smaller, slighter figure followed him through.

And there she was. The sentient android Joseph was so ready to embrace as his flesh and blood.

She kept close to the door, skittish, a wild animal poised to flee. What could she possibly have to be afraid of? If anyone was in danger, it was the three men. Maybe it was all an act, playing the scared little synadroid so Joseph wouldn't realize just how threatening she was.

James had to admit, it was a good disguise. She looked like any other attractive young woman, her fashionable hair and clothes making her as chic as those who sauntered through the downtown sectors on their way to vape overpriced, flavored oxygen at those ridiculous bars.

Except that, unlike those young men and women, she stood self-consciously inside her clothes, an imposter. Despite the trendy cut and expensive fabric, the outfit was alien on her petite frame, inelegant and wrong. She kept her eyes downcast. He had to hand it to her: she was playing the role of vulnerable outsider perfectly.

"Joseph, James, this is Pine. Pine, Joseph and James." Antonio placed a bolstering hand on her arm and gestured toward the two men with the other.

Pine finally raised her eyes to meet theirs, and it was like someone had punched James in the gut.

Her eyes were definitely *not* human. They had all the elements of a human eye framed by sweeping eyelashes, but the color was decidedly alien, the black, bottomless pupils surrounded by an iris that rippled from dark copper in the center to golden peridot edged with ivory. They reminded him of a brown cup coral, or perhaps the ocean where it met the shore during the first burning after the Goldhare Horizon disaster, when smoke had covered the sky and turned the sun a bloody crimson.

She was all at once beautiful and disturbing, and something stirred in James. He couldn't look away. *This is how they get you.* Joseph had also told him how their appearance had been carefully fashioned to make them attractive to humans—all the better to integrate them.

"James? Are you all right?" Joseph asked, breaking the thrall.

Quiet had descended on the room, and two pairs of human eyes peered at James. *Hers* were again focused elsewhere.

He shook himself. Now *he* was the wild animal. But was he predator or prey? "I'm fine. It's just been a long day." He considered the synadroid. "Pine. That's an interesting name. Did you choose it yourself?"

She raised her strange gaze to his, her expression solemn. "No. They don't let us choose our names." Her voice held a bitter edge. "I think it was a joke."

"A joke? What do you mean?" Joseph frowned.

"We spend our lives underwater. Or would have," she replied. "So they named us after things they knew we would never see."

Joseph cleared his throat in the following silence. "Well, I think it's a lovely name. And don't you worry, I'll take to you see your namesake—and anywhere else you'd like to go."

Pine nodded, her attention fixed now on the wood-tiled floor.

"Joseph, Antonio? Could I see you in the other room?" James couldn't wait any longer. Seeing Pine in the flesh had only cemented his doubts—if Joseph insisted on going through with this, he could do so *after* James had said his piece. His conscience wouldn't be able to rest otherwise. "Pine, would you excuse us for a moment, please?"

This time, she didn't even nod.

The three men passed through the living room and into the smaller one Joseph used as his office. James waited until the door had been shut tightly behind them. Free of Pine's presence, he finally regained some of his composure.

"What do you think, James?" Joseph asked, his eyes gleaming. His cheeks had more color in them than James had seen for a long time. *Damn.* Joseph was already getting attached to this strange being, just as James feared he would.

"I'm sorry, but I just don't think this is a good idea. I think she needs to go." *There. No point tip-toeing around it.*

"Pine? Why? She seems fine." Joseph twisted his head, as though he could glimpse her through the closed door.

"I know she's a bit quiet," Antonio said. "But she'll get over that in time. She seems like a lovely young woman—"

"That's just it," James interrupted. "She's *not* a young woman. She's a *machine*."

"She's a *sentient* android, James," Joseph reminded him. "Even if her body isn't human, her mind is."

"But it's not the same. Her emotions aren't real—they're a *program*." He clenched his hands at his sides.

"And what are yours, James? Your emotions—all human emotions—are encoded into you by nature. These synadroids were programmed using the same mechanisms."

"It's not the same."

"Enough. I understand how you feel after what happened at the Perimeter, but you can't put that on Pine. She stays." Joseph's voice was unyielding.

"Antonio…" James turned to the other man. Surely Antonio would support him. As cheerful as he seemed, synadroids made him nervous too.

He held up his hands. "This doesn't have anything to do with me. Joseph is a grown man. You have to trust he knows what he's doing."

"But he doesn't," James flared. "He's— Joseph, I'm sorry. I know you miss Mara, and that you want some kind of connection to her, but Pine is not that connection. She—" The exasperation threatened to choke him.

"I think you should leave."

The older man might as well have slapped him. "What? Joseph, I just—"

"Please, James, *now*. You know I think of you like a son, and I don't know if that's where this is coming from, but—"

"You think I'm *jealous*?" Incredulity rushed through him. How could Joseph think that? Like James was some kind of spoiled child?

Joseph sighed, deflated. "I don't know. I just can't understand why you're so against Pine being here." He laid his hand on the younger man's arm. "Please go for now, James. We'll both sleep on it and talk tomorrow."

Stunned, James could only shake his head. He stalked away from the two men and pushed the door open with a fist, revealing Pine, still rooted to the spot. Her gaze was averted, but James swore resentment rolled off her in waves, a mirror image of his own.

He strode past her without a word and stomped out into the night, oblivious to the temperate rain that plastered his hair to his head before he'd even reached the curb. Sliding into his car, he issued directions to the vehicle in a terse voice.

"Home." He didn't say please, petty as it was.

Pine's peculiar eyes were branded into his memory. Why had she rattled him so much? He'd spent months working alongside synadroids. And yes, he was biased. But he had his reasons, and Joseph damn well knew it. All the resentment, anger, distrust—and admittedly, fear—Pine roused in him had a very real cause.

James pushed all thoughts of the synadroid from his mind as his car pulled into its parking spot under his apartment complex. Joseph was right. A good night's sleep was in order. He could apologize tomorrow, when he'd had time to think things over.

The car door slid shut with a soft click, and James stood for a moment, staring at the sleek metal and his distorted reflection on the surface before heading toward the exit.

Just before he typed his code to request entry, he turned back.

No. He wasn't going to do it. It was ridiculous, thanking a machine. Why had it even crossed his mind?

It was Pine. Even in that short time, she'd managed to get under his skin. She probably had Joseph wrapped around her little finger by now. She was dangerous, and despite what Joseph had said, no more human than his car. The fact that she'd stirred something in *him*, something unnerving, proved just how threatening she was.

His throat tight with irritation, he turned off the light and slammed the door behind him.

THREE

Pine was miserable. She'd resisted the urge to push past James and run through the open door and into the night where she could lose herself. But that was exactly what would happen—she would get lost. She had no clue how to navigate the warren of streets, no idea what direction to go. She was still determined to get away, but if she didn't do it properly, they would only drag her back. Humans didn't like it when their property wandered off.

Besides, if she followed James, she'd have to endure the antipathy in his eyes again. She'd seen that look too many times in the last few days. Many people were fine with synadroids, but more were troubled by their sentience. Like James, those critics regarded her with distrust and apprehension mingled with a curiosity they often found as disturbing as her presence.

And yet, part of her *wanted* to see him again. He wasn't like the men she was used to. He was...exotic. The blue-so-pale-it-was-almost-silver of his eyes reminded her of the sun shining down through the deeper blue of the ocean, its filtered light promising a different kind of life.

The male synadroids she'd worked alongside or

had brief flings with all looked similar, since, like the females, most were the same model. Their skin was perfect, like hers, their heads smooth, their bodies as leanly built as her own.

James, on the other hand, had broad shoulders, and his body was corded with solid muscle. The skin on his arms and face was anything but smooth, marred by scars, weathered by the sun and air. What would those ridges feel like under her fingertips?

It doesn't matter what he looks like or how attractive he is. He's horrible.

And he obviously couldn't stand the sight of her. Well, he didn't have to worry. She would avoid him as much as possible.

"Pine? Are you all right?" Joseph's voice broke her reverie, and all thoughts of James's pale eyes fled.

She nodded mutely.

Antonio held out a hand to her and smiled. "Well, Pine, I've got to get going. It was nice to meet you. I think you'll be happy here, and I know that Joseph," he inclined his head toward the older man, "is glad to have you."

Despite how much he'd annoyed her on the ride here, Pine was sorry to see him go, but a small flicker of hope kindled in her at the affectionate expression on Joseph's face. He seemed like he would be kind enough.

Antonio squeezed her fingers then turned back to Joseph. "I'll bring you the paperwork tomorrow—the license and everything."

The license. The piece of paper that gave Joseph ownership of her. That brief hope sputtered and went out.

Antonio gave Pine one last wave then went out

into the cool evening. As the door snicked shut behind him, Joseph rubbed his hands together and paced the room.

"Right. I know you don't have much with you, so when you've adjusted to being here, we'll go downtown, and you can choose some clothes and things for your room, which is just up these stairs and down the hallway, by the way. James and I spent—"

Pine couldn't help herself. "Why doesn't James like me?"

"I—" Joseph stopped and turned toward her, a frown deepening the creases in his forehead. "He does," was all he could muster.

"He didn't *look* like he did." Pine's hand tightened on the banister. "And I heard what he said when you all left the room." Her hearing was better than a human's, something they all should've known. But maybe that was the point—they *wanted* her to hear. That hurt even more than what James had said.

Joseph ran his fingers through his coarse gray hair, making it stand on end. "It's not you, Pine, it's— Cricket used to be a soldier on the Perimeter. He headed a team of synadroids like you. There was an incident, and, well, I'm afraid it's colored his feelings toward your kind somewhat."

"What happened?" Had they refused to jump when he told them to? Hadn't saluted fast enough?

"It's not my story to tell." Joseph rubbed his beard. "He doesn't really talk about it, and I don't like to pry too much. Regardless, he was different when he came back. He was discharged from the military and became my assistant after I began freelancing as a consultant."

"Why did you call him Cricket?"

"Did I?" Joseph chuckled softly. "Yes, I guess I did. It's a nickname."

Pine frowned. That didn't make sense. Wasn't a cricket a tiny insect? "I don't understand."

"Because of his height," Joseph explained. "He's all legs, like a cricket." He grinned at the image. "There may be other reasons as well, but I don't know them. He was already called that when I met him."

Well, he *did* have long legs. Pine still didn't quite get it, but Joseph was waiting for her to respond so she simply nodded and smiled at him, as though sharing the joke.

Satisfied, Joseph started down the hall again, indicating for her to follow. At the far end, he opened a freshly painted door to reveal a moderately sized room, furnished with a queen-sized bed, a nightstand, and a simple dresser, all in replica dark wood. The single window looked out from the back of the house onto a small patch of snarled weeds cradling an empty, round pond overgrown with algae.

Joseph visibly held his breath as she took in the personal touches he'd added. He'd painted the walls an undulating palette of gold-tinged blues and greens in a deepening ombre from ceiling to floor. On the dresser was a large mirror rimmed with mother-of-pearl, standing behind a grooming set made from luminous abalone shell. Throw pillows and blankets the vibrant rose, honey, and ivory of coral were placed carefully around the room. On the bed, leaning against the abundance of pillows, was a stuffed whale, its stitched mouth drawn back in a companionable grin.

For the first time since she'd left the Ghostlight, a swell of something other than resentment and bitterness rolled over Pine. A cozy sensation warmed her as though Joseph had reached through her ribcage and patted her heart gently. When she opened her mouth to speak, her voice caught in her throat. Everything he'd done for her, everything she was feeling, was overwhelming.

"It's— It's beautiful," she finally managed. "Thank you."

Joseph beamed at her. Why did her happiness mean so much to him? What was he getting in return by going to such lengths? To cover her confusion, she asked him, "Did you do this yourself?"

He nodded, but added, "James helped. I'm great with electronics, but not so much with the DIY."

"Oh." The thought of James, with his dark hair and pale eyes, painstakingly coaxing the underwater scene into life for her was disconcerting. He'd been in here, *her* room, had touched these walls with those seasoned hands...those *human* hands that had twitched convulsively when he saw her. The room lost some of its beauty. Had he resented it the entire time?

Joseph smiled. "Don't worry about James. He'll get over it. Your kind is still somewhat...novel, especially given the recent protests. In a few months, you'll be walking around town and nobody will bat an eye—James included."

"Do you really think so?" Her eyes darted back and forth over his face as she waited for his answer. She wanted so badly to believe him.

"I do," he said warmly. "I really do. I know you've been somewhat isolated, but in cosmopolitan cities such as Portfade, synadroids have had a presence, albeit a small one, for a couple of years. They're finding their niche in our society, and so will you. But," he raised his eyebrows in warning, "that doesn't mean it's...*safe*, for lack of a better word."

"What do you mean?" Where Pine was from, *safe* meant staying away from ocean predators and the whims of nature. But the subtly sheepish look on Joseph's face told her that the danger here was more serious than anything underwater.

"Well, because of your uncommonness and your...similarity to a biological human, you are...at risk from certain interested parties."

Pine flinched. She knew what *that* meant. Mrs. Hayes had warned her. "But you have laws that prevent assault, don't you?"

Joseph took a sudden interest in something outside the window. "We do, but— They apply only to *biological* humans, Pine, not constructed ones."

What? She'd known she would be considered Joseph's property—legally, at least. But surely she had some civil rights, *some* level of the protection that humans gave so vocally to one another? "They're *allowed* to hurt me?"

"No, Pine, of course, not," Joseph said swiftly. "But...but they would be charged and punished according to the laws of *property*, not of a crime against a person." He sat down at the foot of her bed. "Do you understand?"

Of course I do. I have the same rights as that bed you're sitting on. Pine nodded curtly then turned toward the tangled garden. She wished Joseph would just go and leave her alone.

He didn't. "You're very valuable, Pine, and so the government thought these laws were the best way to protect you."

"Valuable," she repeated. "You mean I have a

price."

At first, Joseph looked like he was going to deny it. But he'd obviously decided ahead of time that he would be honest with her. His sigh was colored with shame. "Yes. Sentient androids like yourself are freely bought and sold for many things, especially given your legal status. Hence why I wanted to take you in."

Pine didn't reply. She continued to stare out the window, watching the dark shapes of the plants swaying under the soft yard lights and waiting for Joseph to disappear.

"My wife Mara and I were responsible for much of your category's design. Did you know that?" He waited then continued into the silence. "That's why they let me have you. A token gesture of respect. I've never exploited my standing in our rather exclusive community before, but when I heard that your type was being…relieved of duty, I threw my hat into the ring and called in a few favors and fond memories. I never could've afforded you otherwise."

Afforded me. It was galling. Pine gazed pointedly away.

Joseph took the hint and stood, his joints mimicking his groan. "Sounds like I need a bit of oil in my gears," he joked.

Pine pressed her forehead to the cool glass.

"Look, it's going to be fine. Like I said before, just give it a couple of months, and you'll be old news. And the people who get to know you *will* like you—you just have to give them the chance." He crossed the room and stood in the doorway.

"There are some clothes in the dresser—pajamas, shirts, pants, and skirts, that sort of thing. They used to belong to Mara, but I figured they'd do until we could get you your own. Goodnight." He stepped into the hall. "There's a charging port in the nightstand, if you need it, though I know Mara designed your battery to last for months." He smiled to himself as he left, and she heard him moving around the kitchen, singing under his breath. How could he be so happy about all of this? Was he that oblivious to her feelings? Or was it something more? Like hope that she would come around? Either way, it left a hollow feeling in her chest.

But, finally, she was alone.

Pine lifted her head from the pane. She opened the dresser drawers carefully and rifled through the layers before pulling out a cotton pajama set tied with a pearl-white ribbon. As she shook out the clothes, a pattern of birds in tiny cages mocked her, trapped forever in the navy fabric.

Taking off the smothering jeans was one of the most exquisite sensations of her life. How did human women stand it? She rubbed the backs of her knees, feeling the puckers and creases the denim had left behind. Had they needed to give her so many touch sensors? At the moment, it all seemed a bit unkind.

Now for the shirt. She didn't even bother to undo it. Just as she'd fantasized in the car, she simply hooked her fingers into the gaps between the buttons and yanked. The blouse tore, the buttons clattering gratifyingly on the floor.

Free at last.

Pine crossed the room to stand before the window again. She unlocked the latch and pushed it open, reveling in the fresh air that filled the room.

Backing away from the window, she closed her eyes and lifted her arms. If she ignored the smooth floor beneath her feet and the rhythm of the rain outside, with the cool air washing over her body, she could almost pretend she was back underwater. She turned slowly in place, her head tilted back, and wished.

But when she opened her eyes again, she was still in an unfamiliar bedroom in a strange city, small and naked and alone.

Not for the first time, Pine wished she could cry. It seemed such a cruel thing to give synadroids all the emotion with none of the release. For a moment, she tried, scrunching up her face and letting everything that had happened to her in the last few days carry her away. Maybe this time would be different and the tears would finally come…but as always, her eyes stayed dry.

Pine pulled on Mara's pajamas—which were surprisingly soft against her skin—and climbed into the yielding bed. She didn't need to sleep, but if she had to live as a human, she should try to act like one, at least while she was here. The better she fit in, the more likely they would be to take their eyes off her. She lay in the darkness, soothed by the lulling patter of the rain. Finally, she could think.

It hadn't been as bad as she'd feared. Yes, James had looked at her like she'd swum out from under a rock, but Joseph had shown her so much kindness, as had Antonio. Maybe waiting for her chance to escape wouldn't be *that* unbearable, if it was only for a short time. Besides, she had to figure out how best to make her move. She would probably only get one attempt, so she needed to do it properly.

And then she would go as far away from here as possible. From Portfade, from a human life, and most of all, from *him*.

FOUR

Two weeks later, Pine sat in an overstuffed armchair in the living room as the news scrolled across the wallscreen. She hadn't left the house other than to wander aimlessly around the overgrown backyard. Each day that she watched the outside world through that flat screen, her restlessness increased. Who would've thought living as a human would be so *boring?*

The news anchor had just finished an interview with a woman who'd recently woken up after being in a fifty-year coma. She'd been living in a constructed reality in the Portfade Hospital and was describing what it was like to finally live in the real world after all that time. An elderly man stood next to her, periodically raising her hand to his lips as she spoke. The naked adoration in his eyes impossible to miss.

No one's ever looked at me like that.

And probably no one ever would, seeing as she seemed destined to spend the rest of her life in that armchair.

Now the anchor read from a report detailing the status of the Perimeter bordering Foxwept Province. Apparently, the mutated wildlife encroaching there showed no signs of slowing down, and more recruitment drives for men and women to fight it were in effect across the country.

I think I'd almost prefer fighting monster plants to just sitting here. At least I'd get to see something new.

Joseph came into the room carrying his breakfast. "Looks like they're still having a hard time getting that mess under control. Even with the new androids." The replacements for Pine's generation. On the screen, they stood stoically in the face of the nightmare on the border, their non-sentience probably their greatest weapon.

"Will it ever stop?" Pine asked.

"I hope so," replied Joseph. "Otherwise, they might have to send you back to making the sea habitable."

Pine looked at him sharply. "Do you think so?" Maybe wishes *did* come true after all. James would be thrilled.

Joseph set his plate down and rubbed the back of his neck. "Oh, Pine, I'm sorry. I was making a joke. That was insensitive of me. I know you're probably a bit homesick."

Pine nodded, crestfallen. The confines of the house suddenly seemed very small. She turned her attention back to the screen, now showing an aerial view of a sharp division of land. Beyond the normally bucolic terrain of Foxwept, the earth had been strategically salted. Devoid of plant life, the barren, brown soil stretched for half a mile before ending abruptly in burning, blackened earth. Between the two stood a line of men and women in the red and black military uniforms of Foxwept Province, large cannisters strapped to their backs. The hoses attached to the cylinders spewed a sticky fire, which the soldiers aimed at the wild tangle of foliage on the other side.

The Perimeter. It was the reason Pine existed *and* how Foxwept had finally gained its independence.

"Did you know about all of this? I mean, did they explain to you why you were created?" Joseph asked, waving his fork in the air.

"Yes. We were supposed to be soldiers in the war. Then the Goldhare Horizon disaster happened, and we were sent to the ocean instead." Pine had been several months into her military training when she was told that, instead, she was going to be a farmer. She was taken to have her capabilities altered the very next day.

The disaster had been the fallout of genetically engineered crops intended to increase yield and bolster the self-sufficiency of the Blackmoth Republic. And they had, but unfortunately, they'd also caused mutations in the weeds sharing the same soil, and in the insects and animals feeding on them. The result had been catastrophic: an impenetrable jungle of monster plants and strange creatures that spread swiftly across the center of the country, leaving only small pockets of civilization as the citizens of Blackmoth were pushed into the outlying provinces to survive.

Joseph shook his head. "We thought the whole country was going to starve."

But despite the looming threat of food shortages, it had been an unexpected coup for Foxwept. For years the governors of the bioregions that would eventually become Foxwept Province had wished to unite their assets into a new territory within the Blackmoth Republic. But since the regions were so rich in resources, the provinces that held them were loath to let them go and a civil war, the war that

Pine was created for, had nearly broken out to stop this separation.

But to prevent countrywide famine, the government had hastily agreed to the reformation, diverting the war and allowing each bioregion to increase productivity. Foxwept had responded promptly and sent workers—human and synadroid—into the ocean to farm the abundant sea life there. Then, when it had looked like the new wilderness would take over and push humankind into the ocean itself, the same workforce began constructing habitats in preparation for a new era for humanity.

"Good thing they figured out how to fight it," Joseph remarked as the relay drone focused on the gouts of incendiary gel, known as Foxwept Tar, streaming into the seething vegetation.

"Why weren't they able to stop it?" asked Pine. "It's just plants and animals, right?"

Joseph wiped his mouth with a napkin, seemingly pleased that Pine was making conversation even though she had the information in her database. "It is, but the mutations make them grow incredibly fast, and reproduce even faster. They tried pesticides and herbicides, and initially they worked, but then the wildlife adjusted and became resistant—and even more vigorous." He pointed at the screen, where another drone transmitted a vast stretch of stories-high buildings blanketed by twisting vines. "At first people thought the cold winter would kill them off, so they waited. But it didn't. And by the time we realized that nature wasn't going to help, it was too late."

"Why not just burn them all down at once? If burning works—" Humans seemed very adept at destroying things. Why was this any different?

"The area under siege is too large. If we burned it all at once, or even large parts of it, the ash and smoke would cover the sun and the temperature would plummet...and then who knows what would happen? It's not a risk the government's willing to take." Joseph appeared to be enjoying himself. His voice had the same enthusiastic tone Pine heard whenever he explained some obscure technical concept to James.

James.

"And this...this is what James used to do?" She tried to look nonchalant, as though she was still simply making conversation.

She hadn't seen much of him in the two weeks since her arrival. He was formal and painfully polite, greeting her stiffly then retreating straight to the workshop. A few times, he'd lingered in the doorway, his eyes burning into her, as though he'd wanted to say something, and she'd waited for him to confront her, to say what was on his mind. Maybe then she could stop straining to hear his voice. *Why are you punishing yourself?* The hostility practically radiated off him, and yet she burned with a perverse need for him to declare his loathing out loud.

"It was. Until— Oh my goodness, will you look at the time!" Joseph gaped at the screen. "Sorry, Pine, I have to get going. We can talk more later."

Don't go! her mind screamed at him. *Please don't leave me alone here. I'll suffocate inside these walls. Stay here and tell me more about James.* Calmly, she asked, "Can I please come with you?"

Joseph frowned, his expression sincerely apologetic. "Pine, I wish you could. But I think you should get settled here first."

Settled? It's been two weeks and I'm still sitting

in the same damn chair. How much more settled can I get? "I thought we were going to buy clothes?" Pine couldn't have cared less about the clothes. She just needed to get out of this house.

Joseph grimaced. "We are. But the errands I need to do this morning can't wait, and I won't be able to keep an eye on you while I'm doing them. Where I'm going is…well, remember what I told you a couple of weeks ago? About your value?"

Pine gave a curt nod and looked away. It was the same answer every time she asked.

"But," Joseph said hurriedly, "when I get back, we can go out for a meal and—"

"I don't eat," Pine pointed out.

"Of course." Joseph colored. "I'm sorry. It's so easy to forget. Well, we can do whatever you like then—take a walk, go get you some new outfits. Is there anything you'd like to see or do?"

Go home. She shook her head.

Joseph stood awkwardly by the door. "Are you sure you'll be okay?"

What would he do if she said no? She was tempted to make a fuss, to ask him to stay, but she *had* promised herself she would play along. Still, she watched carefully as Joseph typed the exit code into the keypad by the door. He'd programmed it the day after she'd gotten there.

67B44N388. Just in case.

With a last clumsy wave, Joseph closed the door behind him.

An hour later, Pine had had enough. On the wallscreen, the roving reporter stood with his microphone in hand, speaking to a large group about the Synadroid Emancipation Project. The crowd beamed at the camera, patting each other on the back as the reporter congratulated them on their victory. "I hope the synadroids know how lucky they are, and how grateful they should be to you," the reporter said to the woman next to him.

She didn't even bother to demur. "Yes, but all life is precious. It was only right we rescued them from servitude."

Yeah, so precious and right you didn't even bother to include any actual synadroids in your celebration. A figure weaving through the crowd caught Pine's eye. *Oh. Except for the one at the back, serving the drinks.*

Hypocrites.

The walls pressed in on her again. She had to get out, despite Joseph's warnings.

Now.

In her bedroom, Pine hastily checked her reflection in the mirror. Her hair was an odd shape, but she had no idea whether that was part of the style or not. Biting her lip, she deliberated for a few moments before smoothing it down a bit with her hands. Hopefully, that was better.

There was nothing, however, she could do about the clothes. Although they were much more comfortable than the ones she'd arrived in, they didn't suit her any better. Folded in the drawer, they were charming, the large-patterned flowers vibrant colors that emulated the coral reefs of the Ghostlight. But on Pine, the dresses hung awkwardly, the mid-calf hem of the skirt obviously cut for a much taller woman.

It will have to do. Pine checked her reflection once more, wincing, then closed the bedroom door behind her.

At the front door, Pine hesitated, her fingers hovering over the keypad. Her courage quailed, more from what Joseph would think than the unknown dangers outside.

But that was exactly what Joseph wanted her to feel. Afraid. Afraid of the outside and his reaction. Then she would sit quietly and do as she was told. Well, that didn't seem to be how humans acted. And she was trying to be human, wasn't she?

You can't have it both ways, Joseph.

She hadn't chosen to be here. She hadn't chosen Joseph or his fears. Going outside on her own might be foolish, but was it more foolish than blindly following the orders of someone who could sell or even destroy her on a whim?

An unpleasant heat seared through Pine. Her senses were ready to overload and burn her out. If she stayed here one second more, she would start glitching.

Is this what it feels like to be human?

She punched in the code, stepped out into the fresh air, and didn't look back.

FIVE

James sat in his car across the street from Joseph's house, composing himself to go in. Joseph's car was gone, which meant Pine would be in there alone. He'd had another sleepless night, tossing and turning for hours. He couldn't stop thinking about her, and it was as maddening as hell. He stood by everything he'd said, no matter how benign she seemed, sitting there quietly at Joseph's, day after day. It was even more alarming than if she'd been overtly hostile. Of course, Joseph wasn't going to believe him, the way she behaved. But time would tell, he was sure of it. She wouldn't be able to keep up her façade forever.

He and Joseph hadn't really talked about Pine since that first day, and though things between them had gone on as normal, it felt *different*. Strained, somehow.

And it was all down to her.

He just couldn't understand Joseph's instant and inexplicably strong attachment to her, and even Antonio's seeming lack of concern. Was *he*, James, the problem? Like Joseph seemed to think? He frowned at the waiting house.

I wish I felt differently about it. But I just can't.

What had happened to him wasn't Pine's fault, but he couldn't separate her from the rest of her kind. Pine, as harmless as she seemed, as fascinating as she might be, was still one of *them*. Sometimes, her proximity tightened his stomach with anticipation, while at other times it closed off his throat and opened his ears to the screams of his dying comrades, filling his head with a face at once dispassionate and crazed, a god-in-the-moment exacting his revenge.

Even now, James's chest tightened, and his vision narrowed. He lowered the car window and drew in deep breaths of the crisp air.

Pine was a ticking time bomb. But arguing with Joseph wouldn't help the situation. He would have to play along, protecting Joseph while he waited for a chance to…what? Expose her? Get rid of her? *Kill* her?

He'd have to worry about that later. But one thing he knew for certain—what had happened out on the Perimeter would not happen here, not with Joseph, not with Pine. He would make sure of that.

Time to quit stalling. He glanced in the rearview mirror, groaning at the dark circles under his eyes. He looked like hell, and Joseph, in his fatherly way, was sure to comment on it. Well, it couldn't be helped.

Movement from Joseph's front door caught his eye. Pine was on her own, turning her head as she peered up and down the street.

She's sneaking out.

James *should've* jumped out of the car and demanded she return to the house. Joseph didn't want her out and about just yet. Sentient androids like Pine were valuable and desirable, often for less than savory—and legal—purposes. And since the idealism of emancipation had outpaced the legislation, she was at risk alone.

And she knew that. Joseph had told her more than once. So what was she doing? Yes, being cooped up all day was probably unpleasant, but was putting herself in danger worth the risk? She should've been grateful Joseph wanted to keep her safe. It seemed a fair trade. Well, maybe now Joseph would start to understand how untrustworthy she was.

At the end of the walkway, Pine opened the gate and stepped into the street. She watched several women walking on the other side for a few minutes then straightened and headed down her side of the pavement in the same direction. She mimicked their casual stride, the carefree toss of their hair.

She was trying to fit in.

Good luck with that.

Even if she *had* been human, the way she was dressed made her stick out in the fashionable downtown. The ridiculous hair they'd given her had lost its carefully constructed style and become flat in places and spiky in others, and the flowery dress was obviously for a taller, more matronly woman. And peering out from underneath it all was her small, pale face, so incongruous with the sunny sky.

If Joseph had been here, James would've grabbed his arm, thrust him in front of Pine and said, "You see? She can never be human."

So what should he do? He pulled out his transcomm and tapped the screen, intending to call Joseph, tell him she'd escaped. But he didn't.

I'll follow her. Maybe if I'm lucky and she truly is trying to escape, she'll actually manage it. Problem solved.

And if anything bad happens to her...

He pushed that last thought away, but he'd already decided. If anyone tried to hurt her, he would step in and protect her. He might be happy to let her escape, but he wasn't a monster. Besides, Joseph would never forgive him.

Better get a move on then.

She was at the top of the street now, just turning the corner onto the main downtown street.

James walked quickly, afraid he would lose her in the crowds.

He needn't have worried. Unused to such a cosmopolis, Pine had stopped only a block away and was staring into one of the large bay windows, captivated. Her gaze moved slowly down the length of whatever she was looking at, and her hand unconsciously reached up to stroke her awful wig then dropped to her shoulder where she rubbed the fabric of her sleeve between her fingers.

James stepped back around the corner, so she wouldn't catch him. What was she looking at that had her so enthralled? What would pique a synadroid's interest?

When he stepped out from around the corner, hoping she'd moved on to the next set of stores, she'd disappeared. *Damn.* He sped up, craning to catch sight of her, then slowed as he came to the store window where she'd paused, curious to see what had been so appealing. It wasn't what he'd expected.

It was a clothing and beauty store catering to young women. Not the carefully composed, glossy urbane styles that seemed so popular these days, but simple, unassuming clothing that made the mannequin in the display appear effortless and graceful, as though she were standing in a field of wildflowers on a bright spring day.

The hair that had captured Pine's interest was long and straight, the dark sable unadorned by highlights or accessories. Blunt bangs had been cut into the hair at the front, falling just above the model's eyebrows. Her black sleeveless jumpsuit was made of a thin, soft-looking fabric that was cuffed at just the right length on the mannequin's ankles.

Pine must've been programmed with good taste. *Speaking of Pine, where the hell is she?*

He couldn't see her, even with his considerable height. *Damn.* Maybe it was time to call Joseph.

As James flicked through his contacts, a commotion further down the street caught his attention. A crowd was gathering on a corner just a few blocks away. James closed his eyes and said a quick prayer. *Please don't let it be Pine.* Out of the house less than thirty minutes and already she was causing trouble.

But she wasn't, not exactly. Much of the street was alive with buskers, and this particular corner housed a magician—the focus of the crowd. His sign boasted that he, The Amazing Julian Saturna, was a craftsman, using no technology in his magic tricks. Despite Foxwept's reputation, there had been a resurgence of anti-tech sentiment lately, and this young man seemed happy to capitalize on it.

Pine was watching from the crowd, her back to James. He blended with the throng as well as he could and waited to see what the peddler had to offer.

The magician, a young man with sparse facial hair that James had no doubt was his most prized possession, held a crystal-clear bottle of water up to the crowd. He circled slowly on his heel, making sure everyone assembled saw the bottle from all sides.

"I need a volunteer."

The crowd laughed self-consciously, shrinking in on itself. James hunched his shoulders. A public spectacle like this was one of his worst nightmares.

"Anyone? No? How about you, miss? You look like a discerning young woman." He winked charmingly at Pine.

James groaned inwardly. Out of all the women in the crowd, the magician had to choose her. Probably because she looked like an ignorant tourist, fresh from the countryside, which wasn't too far from the truth.

"Hold out your hand, miss, and take the bottle," the young man instructed.

Pine did as she was told, wrapping her fingers around the plastic.

"Now, please, inspect this bottle as much as you like." He flashed a confident smile at the crowd. "Am I correct when I say it's just a plain, plastic bottle filled with nothing but water?"

Pine examined the container with a slight frown.

"Well?"

"Yes, but—"

"You heard her, folks—an ordinary bottle of water. But watch!" He placed a sparkly black cloth over the top of the cap. "Now," he said, gesturing to another young woman standing next to Pine, "tap the top of the bottle. When I pull off this cloth, there will be a live goldfish swimming inside."

The young woman giggled as he winked again, and murmurs of disbelief and excitement rippled through the crowd. She tapped the bottle with a perfectly manicured fingernail then glanced up at the magician from under her eyelashes. "Like that?"

"Exactly like that! Now, behold—" As he pulled the cloth away with a flourish, the crowd gave a collective gasp. Inside the bottle circled a tiny orange goldfish, its wide eyes unconcerned by the chaos outside.

The audience applauded and shoved coins into the collection box at The Amazing Julian's feet. He bowed deeply, his hair flopping over his forehead and into his eyes. "Thank you! Thank you so much for your time and generosity. I have a show later this—"

"It's magic!" a young boy exclaimed to his mother.

"It's a trick." Pine's face was troubled. No one heard her except James, Julian, and the enchanted boy. The magician scowled at Pine then turned his attention back to the young woman with the silvery laugh.

The little boy glared up at Pine. "It's not a trick. It's magic."

"It's a trick," Pine repeated. This time, those of the crowd who'd loitered heard her, and all eyes turned to the magician, who was tracing the young woman's palm with his finger and telling her all about the love of her life and how it was someone she'd very recently met.

"Yeah? Well, how's it done then?" the boy demanded.

The crowd fell silent, waiting.

"Pine—"

But if she heard James, she took no notice. "There's a plastic tab underneath the bottle cap. The goldfish is in the cap, on top of the tab. When he pulls off the cloth, he pulls out the tab, the fish falls into the bottle and—"

"Stop!" The young magician had forgotten his paramour's hand and was pushing his way through the crowd toward Pine. "What are you doing? It took me months to learn that trick. Do you know what you've done?"

Angry mutters swept through the throng.

James winced at the crowd's discontent. They all *knew* it was a trick, of course, but they'd been happy to give their money for the illusion—as long as everyone else believed. Pine's exposure had broken an implicit rule.

For a moment, they didn't know what to do. Some shrugged, while others elbowed each other and exclaimed that that was how they *thought* it must've been done, because wasn't it so obvious now? The magician's chuckle had an edge, and he began gathering the tools of his trade.

James breathed a sigh of relief. Now to collar Pine and return her before Joseph got back.

Then a voice piped up from the middle of the crowd. "I want my money back. This show's damaged goods now."

James closed his eyes and swore. He *knew* she was going to be trouble.

"If he's getting his money back, I want mine back too." Another voice joined the first, then another, then a chorus. They converged on the young man, their hands outstretched.

"No refunds." His voice had climbed in pitch and he skimmed over the crowd, searching for the most likely escape route. He clutched his metal box to his chest.

"Oh no?" the initial requestor asked. "What if we just *take* it then?"

"You can't. Only I know the combination— you'd never get in." The young magician cleared his throat. "So piss off."

"Are you *sure* you wouldn't tell us? Even with a bit of...encouragement?" There was a flash of silver, and James pushed through the crowd. He'd seen people stabbed for less than a soured magic trick.

Someone else in the crowd caught the glint of metal and screamed. Like a skipping stone, panic flew through the horde and bedlam ensued, people tussling with each other as they scrambled out of arm's reach. Only Pine stood still, not realizing what she'd just done.

"Pine!" Before James could reach her, three police officers swarmed the crowd, administering mild shocks left and right, leaving recipients on their knees as they lost all sensation in their legs.

When they reached Pine, James held his breath. Did they know what she was?

One of the officers laid his baton on her calf. Her skin twitched slightly, but she barely seemed to notice. The officers gaped, and the man looked at his rod with a bewildered frown. The rest of the crowd took advantage of the officer's astonishment and fled—including the thug who'd started it all.

At the second shock, Pine turned around. "What are you doing?" she asked the officer. "Please, stop."

James grimaced. Did she not know who the police were?

"Stay still," the officer demanded.

James stepped over the legs of a woman lying on the sidewalk who was whispering furiously into her transcomm. "Can you effin' believe it? Now I'm going to be late for my— Hey, watch it, you—"

He extended a hand to the officer closest to him. He was going to have to handle this carefully.

"Officers. Hi... This is just a misunderstanding."

"Oh?" asked the policewoman. "And what exactly does that mean?" The insignia on her shoulder indicated she was the chief officer.

"My friend here," James slapped Pine playfully on the shoulder, "spoiled the magician's trick." He leaned forward conspiratorially. "She's smart enough to figure out the dupe, but not smart enough to keep her mouth shut." He flashed Pine a grin of faux exasperation. *Play along, damn you.*

"That might be, son, but I'm more interested in *who* she is than whatever ridiculous transgression she may have committed." The officer's voice was dry; she hadn't taken her eyes off Pine.

Should he play dumb and pretend not to know what they were talking about? *Whatever do you mean, Officer? There's something odd about her?*

No. No point in making this situation any worse. Pine's tattoo was evident, uncovered by the short-sleeved dress. He'd have loved nothing more than to leave her to the mercy of the police, but there was no way he'd be able to justify that to Joseph.

"She belongs to Joseph Polendina. The robotics designer. Perhaps you know of him?" They probably didn't, but maybe it would give him an air of authority.

Or maybe not.

"Never heard of him. But you're not him, right?" The officer stared at him, her expression bland.

"Right, but—"

"Then why are *you* in possession of the synadroid?"

"Oh. We were just out for a walk, when—" James glanced around for the magician, but the young man had bolted.

"Just out for a walk? Is that true?" The officer addressed Pine.

She stared back, mute.

James could practically see the gears turning in her head as she decided what to do. He tensed. Would she get violent? What would he do if she did? Finally, she looked at him then the police then crossed her arms over her chest and nodded curtly.

The officer waited for a few seconds then raised her eyebrows and turned back to James. "I'm going to need to see her license. We've had reports of synadroids such as these being trafficked. Registration number?" She initiated her commscreen as she looked at James expectantly.

"I, uh...I don't have the registration number. If—"

"So you're not Joseph Polendina, and you don't have a registration number for this synadroid? Is that correct?"

The officers behind her adjusted their grips on their batons.

"Yes, but—"

"We're going to have to take you both into custody then."

"No, please. Look, Mr. Polendina lives just a few blocks around the corner. If we go there, I'm sure he'll have all the right documentation." James pointed in the direction of the house.

The officer eyed James and Pine suspiciously. "Just around the corner?"

James nodded.

"What do you think?" She turned to her colleagues.

The other woman shrugged. "It would save a lot of paperwork if we just checked her number."

Right," the lead officer said. "Take us to the house. But if you're messing with us—"

"I'm not, I promise." James held up his hands.

"And don't try to run," the officer warned, opening her coat. Strapped around her torso was a lethal-looking weapon.

James had never seen a barrel that big on a handgun before. He grabbed Pine's arm and began propelling her down the street. "We won't." Throughout the exchange, Pine had remained quiet. Now, however, she spoke up.

"Let go of my arm."

James loosened his grip slightly and whispered furiously to her under his breath. "Pine, listen to me. This is very serious—"

She went taut, as though she were about to jerk her arm away from his grip.

The policewoman narrowed her eyes.

"Just keep walking. Not for me, for Joseph, and yourself. I don't know what will happen if they take you, but I do know he'll feel responsible."

"Is there a problem?" The lead officer's hand wrapped and unwrapped around the hilt of her baton.

For a moment, Pine looked like she was going to keep arguing then she leaned into James's arm and flashed the officer a baleful look. "No, ma'am." She had to trot to keep up with his long legs, but at least she was cooperating. For now.

James kept his gaze straight ahead. *Just get her home.* Because Pine was a synadroid, if they shot her, they'd get barely a slap on the wrist. James, however, would lose Joseph's trust.

As they opened the gate to the front yard, Joseph was just closing the door behind him. His face was flushed, and his hands shook as he tried to engage the lock. When he caught sight of Pine, he stumbled over the last step and James rushed forward, afraid the older man was going to fall.

"Pine! Where have you been? I came home to get you and—" He caught sight of the officers and paled. "What's happened? Is something wrong?"

"Are you Joseph Polendina?" the officer asked, hooking her thumbs into her belt loops and rocking back on her heels. Her colleagues remained stiff and alert, carefully watching Pine for any sudden movement.

"I am. What's this about?"

"I need the registration number for this synadroid."

Joseph lost even more color. "I'm afraid I don't have it yet. The license is coming any minute now."

James silently cursed Antonio. That man procrastinated about *everything*.

"So, you acknowledge that you are Joseph Polendina, and also that you claim ownership of this synadroid?"

"Yes." Joseph proffered his thumb and pressed it onto the screen of the policewoman's transcomm. A few seconds later, confirmation of his identity scrolled across the screen.

"But you have no proof that you legally own this synadroid, as you claim, Mr. Polendina?"

"Well, I—"

"You're going to have to come with me, then, sir, down to the station until we can get some substantiation that you actually are the owner. You understand the penalties for illegally possessing a sentient android, right?"

"I do, but—"

"Let's go." The officer reached for Joseph's arm.

Pine came to life. "Don't touch him!" She tried

to force her way between Joseph and the officer.

"Pine, no! Stop. Please, Pine, it'll be fine." He shook his head then, as she persisted, shouted, "*Pearlvitae!*"

Pine froze, her eyes wide. Every single part of her stopped moving.

"I'm sorry, Pine." Joseph's face pinched with remorse.

James stepped forward. Joseph shouldn't feel guilty. The safe words had been installed into the synadroids for situations just like this, when they were out of control. Pine should've known better.

She was just trying to help Joseph.

Annoyed, James pushed the voice away; empathy for her was dangerous. "Surely this is enough proof of ownership?" He gestured toward the suspended synadroid. "Only her owner would know the word."

"Sorry, but it's not enough. Please, sir." The officer put her hand on Joseph's arm again.

"What about the synadroid?" the young male officer asked. "Shouldn't we take her in too? I mean, we *were* going to, weren't we?"

The lead officer glared at him as she remembered. "We *were*."

The third officer cringed. "Oh god, Shaz, do you remember what happened the last time? Stevens only just got his desk replaced."

Shaz chewed on her lip, considering. "I'll tell you what, Aldicott," she addressed the young man. "*You* stay here outside the house and wait for us to contact you. You two," she pointed to James and Pine, "go into the house and stay put. You are officially under house arrest until I say otherwise. Is that clear?"

"Yes," James replied. "But—" Surely they

weren't going to *arrest* Joseph?

"*Is that clear?*"

"James, it'll be fine. Don't worry. Call Antonio and tell him to get down to the station." Joseph nearly dragged the officer down the walkway just as something else occurred to James.

"Wait, Joseph!" he shouted as the two officers, Joseph between them, filed through the gate. "How do I...turn her back on?" Pine's fury was palpable, burning into his back.

"It's Mara's favorite flower—" Joseph called over his shoulder as he disappeared from view.

Well, that's just great. I don't know what Mara's favorite flower is. To the waiting officer, he asked, "Can you please help me carry her inside?"

"No way. I don't get paid enough for that kind of hazard." The officer turned away and took up his post, slouching outside the front door.

James swore. He was going to have to try to move Pine himself.

His stomach twisted as he approached her. The look in her eyes was murder. What if the failsafe didn't hold? It had happened before. If she got emotional enough... Flames licked at the edges of his vision, and his hands clenched compulsively at his sides.

This isn't the same. You're in control here. Both of you need to stay calm. He took a deep breath and waited until the flames receded.

He should just leave her as she was. What had possessed him to ask Joseph how to reanimate her? He could've simply kept an eye on her until Joseph got back. Maybe some time as a statue would get through to her what Joseph obviously couldn't.

But Joseph would expect him to at least try. If James was lucky, he wouldn't be able to figure out what Mara's favorite flower was. Hopefully, it was something esoteric or scientific.

"Pine—"

She glowered up at him, unforgiving. Her body was stiff, her joints unbending. Her back was slightly arched, her arms stretched down and out from her sides, slightly behind her as she'd stepped in front of Joseph to shield him with her body.

There was no way for James to move her without seriously invading her personal space. "Let's just get this over with." He stood in front of her and, bracing himself, wrapped his arms around her, pulling her body to his chest and lifting her off her feet.

She wasn't as heavy as he'd expected her to be, but James was still breathless by the time he'd carried her over the threshold. He tried to ignore the peaks of her breasts pressing into his chest and the solid smoothness of her abdomen against his. The officer watched him with mild amusement then found something more interesting on his transcomm.

With a final grunt, James deposited Pine in the living room and returned to the door, sticking his head out. "You know there's a back door, right?" he asked the officer.

He shrugged. "Don't worry about it. If you run, I have permission to shoot you." He returned to his screen.

"Great," muttered James, and shut the door. He hadn't actually been thinking of running, but the officer's nonchalance after the way they'd treated Joseph irritated him. *Ass.*

Back in the living room, he considered Pine. How best to go about this? "I just have to make a quick call then we're going to figure this out.

47

Okay?"

Her expression told him clearly that no, it was *not* okay. Although her face was immobile, her eyes flashed with anger...and something else. *Fear.* She was terrified. Of *him.*

She knows damn well how you feel about her—it's not like you've tried that hard to hide it. And right now, she's helpless. So why wasn't he happy about it?

Like it or not, she was here to stay—for the time being, at least. And if Joseph thought she was afraid of James... *You really don't want to force him to make a choice, do you?*

He relented, just a little. "Look, Pine, I'll figure it out." His hand rose unthinkingly to smooth a few strands of ridiculous hair sticking out over her ear, and he snatched it back just before his fingertips touched her.

What are you doing? He dropped his hand to his side.

Now what?

Just leave her. She brought this on herself.

But one look at Pine's eyes told him that the longer he postponed, the worse the situation would become. With a sigh of surrender, he hurried away to his mentor's office to find the answer. He just hoped he wouldn't regret it.

SIX

Pine stared straight ahead, her eyes fixed in place as James left the room. She desperately wanted to believe he would help her, but how could she trust him? He held all the power here. She'd thought she'd been helpless here since the beginning, but this—This was her lowest point yet.

The feeling of his hands on her...she'd wanted to scream, to lash out at him. Why couldn't he have just left her alone to her humiliation? And now what? If he wanted to abandon her, or worse, hurt her, she wouldn't be able to stop him.

I can't stand him. Even now, he was probably laughing at her.

James's low voice murmured for a few minutes in the other room, too soft for her to make out what he was saying. The next ten minutes were filled with the sounds of him going from room to room, rifling through papers, muttering and swearing under his breath. Either he really *was* trying to help her, or he was putting on a good show of it. She suspected the latter.

If Pine could've spoken, she'd have told him the answer: tiger lilies. James had dumped her facing the portrait of Mara. In the background, on the far side of her workbench, was a vase stuffed full of them, a riot of color amid the metal components on her desk. She smiled at Pine, then bent back to her work, unmoved by Pine's predicament. As she turned her head, a tiny mark behind her ear, near her hairline, was revealed.

James returned, his face tense. "I can't find anything. I'm just going to list every single flower I can think of, and if none of those work, I'll look up some more. We'll keep at it until we figure it out."

We. Like they were in this together. He was mocking her.

She stared hard at the picture, willing him to turn his damn head and look at it. *Tiger lily. Tiger lily. TIGER LILY.*

James was reeling off an impressive list of flowers—all wrong. "...hibiscus?" He waited. "No. Sunflower? No. Cherry blossom?"

Pine's eyes were ready to burst from her head. *Probably no less than he'd expect from a crazy synadroid.*

"Tulip? No. Queen Anne's Lace?" He walked over to the window and peered out, as though looking for inspiration. Finding none, he turned back to Pine, and the picture of Mara caught his eye. He stood before it, rubbing his hands over his face. "Come on, Mara, talk to me. What was your favorite flower?" Mara ignored him, too intent on her work.

Never mind my eyes. Her *head* was about to explode.

James started to turn away from the portrait when something grabbed his attention. Whether it was Pine screaming in her head or the incongruous flash of color in the picture, James froze and leaned forward, the start of a smile curving his lips.

"I think I've got it," he said to Pine, the smugness in his voice almost infuriating enough to override her programming. He wiggled his fingers in front of her face, mimicking The Amazing Julian. "Tiger lily!"

Pine was free. Ironically, though, now that she *could* move, she didn't know what to do with herself. Should she would make a run for it, despite James and the policeman? Or maybe she should just collapse. Scream? Something, *anything* to release the tempest swirling inside her.

James also seemed to be struggling with her freedom. He stood tautly, as though anticipating an attack. What did he think she would do?

"Thank you." Petulance was the best she could manage right then. Too bad for him if he'd expected anything more.

James seemed to accept it, though, giving her a curt nod. The tension in his shoulders dissipated, and he leaned against the wall next to Mara.

He *had* helped her. It would've been so easy for him to let the police take her away or leave her outside like a glorified lawn ornament. But he hadn't, even though it had meant not only touching her, but touching her *closely*.

And she hadn't hated it, though she'd wanted to. The yielding firmness of his body was so different to an android's. Her skin was supposed to emulate his, but it wasn't even close. His—

It doesn't matter how his skin feels. He's still horrible.

But he *had* felt just like she'd thought he would, the lines of his muscles cording smoothly just underneath the disfigured skin.

He was looking at her. Not just looking, *staring*. As though he'd read her mind and for a time saw her as something more than an unwelcome machine.

James cleared his throat. "Thank you for defending Joseph."

"I—"

"You're not regretting it now, are you?"

Was she? She hadn't stopped to think about it; she'd seen the officer raising a hand to Joseph and she'd simply reacted. Was it because he was kind to her? Or was it because, on some deep level, she knew she was lucky to have him as her owner?

Then she caught herself, disgusted by her disloyalty. *Am I so cheaply bought?* Yes, Joseph wasn't a monster, far from it, but he still *owned* her.

And James? Was he simply patting her, the way he would an obedient dog? *Good girl, defending Master. Who's a good girl? Pine's a good girl!* It rankled.

She gazed at James, at his sunlight-through-the-water eyes and the dark hair falling over them. He *seemed* genuinely thankful. It was so frustrating, not being able to read him. They had the same emotions, but humans seemed privy to nuances that she, having spent most of her time with other synadroids, had yet to fully grasp.

But it was obvious James cared about the older man. And he *had* remobilized her. *And* thought enough of her to thank her. For now, she would give him the benefit of the doubt. Maybe it would preserve this fragile new beginning between them. "No, of course I'm not."

"You know, if you *really* want to help Joseph, next time, do what you're told." He crossed his arms over his chest.

The delicate connection smashed like a wave

against rock, obliterated. "Be a good little robot, is that what you mean?" she flared. She'd been an idiot to think his opinion of her might have changed.

"Look, you're very lucky—" he began, echoing her earlier thoughts.

"Lucky? *Lucky?* We were created to clean up *your* mess. To do whatever you told us—fight, farm, die. Then we were given the sentience to understand our situation but denied the right to do anything about it." How could he not see what a sick, cruel joke it was?

"And you think I should feel *lucky?*" Pine couldn't stop; everything that had built inside her over the last few weeks rushed out in a torrent. "Why? Because we're free? We're not *free*, James. We're just in a different prison."

She advanced on him. A tiny thrill of pleasure shot through her at his shocked expression. He'd probably never had a synadroid shout at him before. "How can you be so blind? So *arrogant?* The only difference between us, James, is that my flesh is synthetic—that, and the fact I have to submit to things that would be considered illegal and inhuman for you."

James stepped back, putting a chair between them. "But, Pine, you've got to understand *our* position. Without humans, you wouldn't exist. And I agree, they shouldn't have given you human emotions, that it is problematic—"

"It wasn't the *giving* that was problematic. It's *your* reaction. Once we started *acting* human, the emotions you gave us on a whim became inconvenient."

He gave a brittle laugh. "It's not about inconvenience. It's about them being *dangerous.*"

"Dangerous? Did you not see what happened earlier? A single word and I was paralyzed. Does that seem dangerous to you?"

"Safe words don't always work." His fingers dug into the back of the chair.

"You mean the master can't always make his puppet dance to his tune? How devastating to your human ego."

"Stop." The chair began to warp under his hands as his voice rose. "You have no idea what you're talking about. I—"

"Of course not. How could I? I couldn't possibly fathom—" Her voice rang in her ears, her frustration reaching boiling point. She didn't need to keep hearing about what she didn't understand, especially from this man.

"*Sentient androids kill people*, Pine. They're unstable and dangerous, and they never should've been created!" The top rail snapped, splintering in his fists. He looked down at the wood in his hands with an expression akin to surprise. The color rose in his cheeks and he dropped the fragments on the table.

It was like he'd thrown a bucket of ice water over her. Was that what he really thought? That synadroids were *murderers*? It couldn't be true. But the expression on his face was controlled, not vindictive. "I've never—"

"Did Joseph tell you I used to be a soldier, out on the Perimeter?" James sank into the ruined chair and laid his hands on the table. Blood spotted his palms, but he didn't seem to notice.

From what she knew, human and synadroids had worked together, fighting the mutated wildlife, not each other. "Yes, but—"

"I was a lieutenant, head of one of the teams in

charge of beating back the...the monstrosities out there." He shuddered. "This was before they invented the Tar. All we had then were flamethrowers and strategy...and it just wasn't enough. It was like trying to dam a flood with a feather. They just kept coming."

He closed his eyes and leaned back, seemingly oblivious to the jagged timber at his back. "I had a mixed team of humans and synadroids. We would send the synadroids in first to clear out the worst of it then the rest of us would go in and clean up what we could. Everything was all right at first, but soon, some of the synadroids began...going berserk. It started with convulsions, their heads twisting to the side, their jaws biting." He touched his own neck as he remembered. "At first, they only hurt themselves, but then one of them turned on us." He opened his eyes and gazed at her.

"I was the only one who survived. I don't blame you, Pine, for what you are, but after what happened, I just can't *trust* you."

What you are...can't trust you. The words echoed painfully somehow, though she harbored the same doubts about him. "Was it only the synadroids who...lost control?" Pine asked quietly.

James seemed confused. "No, but—"

"Why send only the synadroids ahead, and not the humans? You threw them into the worst of it then wondered why they broke?" She bit her lip in irritation. Why couldn't *he* understand? "They saw everything you saw, felt everything you did...why did you expect them to react differently?"

He didn't answer, but she appeared to have his attention.

"When humans suffer emotional trauma that causes them to lash out, they get treatment, counseling. Synadroids get destroyed. How would you feel if your superiors killed another human for being traumatized? Especially during service for everyone in this damned province? Synadroids fight and serve just as you do, only they don't get medals, or recognition, or even respect. They get *terminated*. And you say you can't trust *us*?" The furious tide within her rose again.

"The country was nearly destroyed because all you saw was the end result. You created us to resolve it, but that wasn't enough. You had to make us just like you. Then when we *acted* like you, you treated us like you do everything else—as a commodity."

Fury shook her body, as much as any human's. "You create life but have no concern for it. Can't you see how heartless it is? And you want us to be *grateful*. I just—" Rage snatched the words from her mouth. "You'll never understand."

"You're right, I won't. Pine, *you* must understand. You might have human emotions, but you're not alive. *And you'll never be human.* That's why we don't treat you like one." He pushed back from the table, his chair overturning and crashing to the floor.

"We don't *want* to be human, only to control our own destinies. Would *you* want to live like *this*?"

The pressure overwhelmed her. She had to do something to vent or she would drown, and she was damned if she would give him the satisfaction. She stared calmly into his face and reached up with both hands, knotting her fists in her hair. With a sickening rip, she tore it off her head, and handed it to him, just like she'd daydreamed about doing her first day here.

"Is that better? Does that make you more comfortable, for me to look less like you? To know my place?" She was no longer herself, but there was nothing she could do to stop it. And truth be told, she didn't want to. Maybe now she would finally get through to him, to show him how his disdain for her *life* was one cut too many.

James stood dumbstruck, holding her hair in his hands. Patches of synthetic scalp clung to it, and Pine ran her hands over her head, touching the exposed metal.

"Pine—"

"Not enough for you? I mean, we can't have people mistaking me for *human*, can we?" She snatched a cut-crystal bowl off the coffee table and smashed it against the antique wood, gouging the surface as the bowl came apart. She gripped the largest shard and held it to her wrist.

"Pine, *don't*." James stayed where he was, but his face had drained of color, and Pine nearly dropped the glass. Maybe she *had* lost control and was behaving the very way he'd predicted, but she no longer cared. He had to understand how wretched she felt, how desperate.

She cut a ring into the skin around her wrist then peeled it back, up over her arm, baring her intricate synthetic flesh. "Is *this* better? I—" She took a step toward him, her teeth bared.

"*Pearlvitae*."

Pine froze. The glass shard stopped, its cutting edge just biting into the skin of her other arm.

She'd thought she couldn't feel any worse, but she was wrong. After everything she'd told him, how hard she'd tried to make him appreciate her situation, he'd betrayed her in the worst possible way.

It *hurt*. Much more than it should have. Why had she gotten so upset, needed him to understand so badly? How had she ever thought he would?

Because of Joseph. It had to be. There could be no other reason than because Joseph *loved* this man, and that made him part of her life for as long as she was here. And if a man as kind as Joseph could care about James, there must be some compassion there, some redeemable quality.

But there wasn't. Shame flooded her. She'd known James for a couple of weeks...but she'd known his thoughts about her kind within the first hour. And still, she'd taken the bait, had let him turn her into a spectacle, all in the hopes he would just *hear* her. She was a fool.

But she'd never trust him again. What was more, the coward couldn't even look at her. He was now on the couch, his head bowed. Probably laughing at her, enjoying his power over her, or at the very least, feeling smug that she'd proven him right.

She wanted to hate him. She *did* hate him.

Then why do I still care what he thinks?

The front door opened, and Joseph came through it with a smile, his voice cheerful. "Hey, James, did you make a call to The Blue Fairy, by any chance? Because as soon as they pulled up my information, the license was there. You should've seen the look on that police officer's face—"

He saw Pine first, frozen, the flesh of her skull and arms in tatters. Then James, perched on the couch, his head in his hands, Pine's hair on his lap.

"What the hell is going on here?" His voice broke. "James, *what have you done?* Tiger lily!"

Released, Pine sank to her knees, done. She crawled over to the damaged coffee table and leaned her back against it, too wrung out to do anything else.

Joseph eased himself down beside her. "Pine, are you okay?"

She wouldn't look at him. Couldn't bear to see herself reflected in his eyes. "Yes."

When Joseph next spoke to James, his voice was flat and cold, every word loaded. "I'll ask you once more, James, what did you do?"

"I didn't do anything but try to stop her. She did *that* to herself. *This* is the sort of thing I was worried about. She's not—"

"Is that true, Pine?" He took her hair from James, rubbing a piece of her scalp between his fingers.

Pine raised her head and looked at James, taking in the strain on his face. If this had been a victory for him, he didn't show it. He didn't seem to be taking any pleasure in her misery. Instead, he looked as distressed as she felt. Pine waited for the flush of *her* victory to come, but all that followed was a dull ache in her chest.

"It's true," she whispered.

James closed his eyes and dropped his chin to his chest.

"James, I think you need to go." Joseph laid Pine's hair on the coffee table.

"But, Joseph— I didn't—"

"I know. But I still want you to go. Please. I'll speak to you tomorrow." He walked with James to the door.

"I'm sorry, Joseph. I never wanted—"

"It'll be okay." Joseph patted him kindly on the shoulder. "Just give us some time."

Only when the door had closed behind him did Pine allow herself to lie on her side, her knees curled up to her chest and her shoulders shaking with tears that would never come.

SEVEN

James walked the short path to the gate in a daze. He was still shaken by what had happened. Hell, he wasn't even sure what *had* happened. He'd never been so confused about anything in his entire life.

He kept replaying the exchange in his head. How had it gone so wrong, so quickly? Was life for the synadroids really as dire as she claimed? Did they really feel the limitations of their existence so keenly? It was an uncomfortable revelation. James had always thought of himself as empathetic, as understanding his world. Could he really be as blind as she claimed?

She'd said the only difference between them was their physical bodies. But was it true? Were her feelings, programmed as they were, as real as his? If so, there was far more truth in what she'd said than he'd like to admit. He *knew* that the sentient androids had the full range of human emotion, but he'd never truly *believed*. He'd never actually thought of them *feeling* their feelings, as stupid as that sounded.

Confusion made him lightheaded as he tried to reconcile what he knew with what Pine had told him. If she'd behaved that way—mutilating herself—before their fight, it would've been a grim confirmation of everything he'd warned Joseph about. But after what she'd said… Her anguish had been so real, so *human,* it had been painful to watch. At least, until she'd exposed the raw metal of her skull—an appalling reminder of what she was. A machine.

He'd almost been taken in. He was going to have to be careful, or he would become as duped as Joseph, fooled by the alluring tragedy of her.

But he couldn't avoid her. Joseph was too important in James's life for him to abandon his mentor. And despite what she'd said, he still wasn't ready to trust her. If anything, now that he knew how she felt about her life, he trusted her even less.

Nothing James said would sway Joseph, but if he wanted to stay where he could protect the older man, he would have to make amends, or at least *pretend* he was. But how?

By playing nice.

Which meant apologizing to *her.*

Could he do it? As far as he was concerned, he hadn't done anything wrong. How could he make his contrition sincere? He was an awkward liar.

He sighed and glanced around him. His feet had taken him up the main street where the magician plied his trade. Today, in his place, a young woman played a violin, the haunting melody creating a cascade of colors over her head that fell like the northern lights. Her long hair was knotted on her head, streaked with the same fashionable cerise that had been applied to Pine's.

That gave James an idea. It would be a small token, but at least it was a start.

* * *

James rang the doorbell at Joseph's early the next day, before Joseph was likely to leave the house. A pang of anxiety almost made him turn around. What if Joseph didn't answer the door? What if he was still angry? What had Pine told him about yesterday?

He set the bags he was carrying down on the step and wiped his hands on his trousers. Why was he so nervous? He hadn't slept well last night, even once he'd planned his atonement. He'd tossed and turned, reliving what Pine had told him and struggling to refute it. He'd thought the time away from her and some sleep would've made things clearer. But instead, his mind was even more disordered. He wasn't used to feeling that unsure of himself, and he didn't like it. *Damn her.*

Why is Joseph taking so long? Should he just leave? Joseph would contact him when he was ready. He picked up his bags again, just as the door opened.

Joseph stood in the doorway, looking as exhausted as James felt, dark circles under his eyes and his hair even more unkempt than usual. He said nothing, but stood aside to let James in.

The living room was empty, granting James a reprieve.

"She's upstairs," Joseph said.

"I'm sorry about what happened yesterday, Joseph. I'm still not entirely sure *what* happened." Why wouldn't his hands stop sweating?

Joseph smiled at him, his expression kinder than James had dared hope. "I think both of you finally let out things that have been building inside for a long time. It's a difficult situation." He gestured for James to sit down. "With the way you feel about synadroids and how Pine feels about us... Throw

in a spark of attraction, and things got...heated."
Joseph raised an eyebrow.

"We're not attracted to each other," James
protested. How could Joseph even think that?
Especially after what had happened the day before?
Attraction was the last word James would use to
describe how he and Pine felt about each other.

Joseph laughed. "That's what Pine said too."

She did? "Joseph, she's a *machine*. Sentient or
not, I could never—"

Joseph cleared his throat. Pine stood stiffly in the
doorway.

"Pine, I—" James flushed. Insulting her was *not*
going to help him. He cast about for something to
say. "You're looking better."

That, at least, was the truth. The reason for
Joseph's insomnia was obvious. Pine's skull was
again covered by smooth skin, her arms those of a
young woman. They must've spent the entire night
in the basement workshop.

She looked small and fragile, and even more out
of place than she had with that outlandish hairstyle.
"Yes, well, that's what so great about being a
machine—all it takes is a bit of glue and it's like it
never happened. I mean, it's not like we have
feelings or anything."

Of course she isn't going to make this easy.
James proffered her the bags, his token of
surrender. "I...uh...brought you something."

Pine didn't move. "What is it?"

"Open them." He set the bags down in front of
her. What would he do if she refused?

She looked at Joseph, who smiled at her and
dipped his head. She picked the bags up and carried
them over to the other couch. "Which one should I
open first?"

Maybe this was a bad idea. Was it too late to grab the bags and run? "The purple one."

Pine pulled out the tissue paper and reached inside. She kept her hand in the bag, and an odd expression crossed her face.

"Well, what is it?" Joseph's eyes were sparkling—he seemed more excited about the contents than Pine. What if he thought it meant more than it did? *Especially* after his comment about a spark...

Pine withdrew her hand. She held a shining mass of hair.

"Hold it up." Joseph nearly snatched the hair from Pine's grasp. James had never seen the older man so giddy.

Pine obeyed, putting the cap of the hair over one hand and shaking it out. She pressed her lips together as she combed her fingers through it. It was the hair she'd admired the day before.

She stared at James with suspicion. "You were following me."

He rubbed the back of his neck. "Yeah, well. I was trying to make sure you didn't get into trouble."

Pine snorted. "You did a great job."

At least she wasn't being hostile. "Just open the other one." He needed this to be over.

From the second bag, she pulled out the black jumpsuit. She smoothed the fabric over her lap and ran her fingers across it. This time she didn't look at James. "Thank you."

Is that good or bad?

"Shall we see how they look?" Joseph bounded off the couch with an alacrity that amazed James. "Come on, Pine, it won't take more than ten minutes to set your hair."

Pine closed her eyes, and James's temper flared. Was she going to insist on being stubborn?

And so what if she is? The point was that *Joseph* was pleased.

Wasn't it?

A few seconds later, she put him out of his misery by following Joseph down the stairs.

While James waited anxiously in the living room, he studied the picture of Mara. He'd only met her a few times before her death, and then, briefly. In fact, one of the reasons Joseph had hired him was because he was so lonely after she died. "It's too quiet around here," he'd said, which was funny since neither Joseph nor James spoke very much.

"What do you think?" a voice behind him asked.

James turned.

Joseph stood beaming, Pine at his side.

Heat rose in James's face, burning with now-familiar warmth. She was radiant, like the dawn rising over the ocean. Although she stood self-consciously beside Joseph, trying her best to shrink, James couldn't take his eyes off her. Her hair looked as though she'd been born with it. Its deep color made her remarkable eyes even more arresting, and the silky length framed her delicate face and cascaded over her narrow shoulders. The jumpsuit fit her perfectly, her lithe frame making the 'v' in front look elegant rather than daring. The rest of the fabric flowed over her body and legs, loose and graceful.

What had he done? He'd warned Joseph how dangerous she was, and yet he'd just made her even more disarming. Again, he cursed her.

"How did you know my size?" She spoke gruffly. How could he answer that? He couldn't very well say, "I looked up your model number," after what had happened yesterday and what she'd overheard this morning. That would just set them back to square one.

"I...uh, well, you know, when I carried you into the house yesterday, I—" Great. Now instead of being insensitive, he sounded like a pervert. "I just made a lucky guess." *Change the subject.* "Do you like them?"

Pine pursed her lips then gave him a small smile. "I do. They're...perfect. Thank you."

Perfect. That was more than James had hoped for; he'd take it, and gladly. Things between him and Joseph should be back to normal now, and that had been the point. Nothing more.

He awkwardly bobbed his head. Standing in front of him now, smiling, she almost obliterated the sight of her yesterday, in this room, peeling off her own skin, the wires and shining metal inside her exposed.

"Can I get you a drink of anything, James? I'm going to have coffee." Joseph bustled off into the kitchen, humming under his breath as he left the two of them alone.

"No, thank you, Joseph. I—" *I should leave while I'm ahead.* But still he stayed.

"Pine, why don't you show James what you've been up to?" Joseph called from the kitchen, where he was squinting at the brewing machine. "Now, how the hell do I—"

Pine hesitated then gestured for James to follow her. She led him past Joseph, and James paused to punch a few buttons over the older man's shoulder—James was normally the one to make the brews—then into the small backyard.

James's curiosity was piqued. Joseph had never

shown an interest in doing anything with the yard. When Mara was alive, she'd had her beloved flower garden and a fish pond, surrounded on three sides by a flowering-vine-covered fence, carefully tended so that she could relax outdoors on her chaise and pretend she wasn't in the heart of the city.

The yard was still an overgrown mess, but Pine had clearly been busy. The tiny pond had been meticulously cleaned, scrubbed of slimy algae and tidied of fallen leaves. The water inside was now pure and clear, and swimming in circles was a familiar miniature goldfish.

It couldn't be. "That's not—"'

"Amazing Julian's fish? It is."

"But how?"

Pine grinned, clearly pleased with herself. "My mouth."

Had he misheard her? "Pardon?"

"My mouth," Pine repeated with a sly smile. "During the...distraction, I rescued her. It didn't seem right to put her in my pocket."

James laughed. It was a surprising side of her. "But how?"

Pine gazed down at the tiny fish, her smile gone. "Magic."

"And you had her in your mouth all that time? Even when—" James faltered. Were they ever going to get past that?

"Yes, I did. It was easy, being a *machine* and all."

They couldn't go on like this, no matter what they both felt. "Pine, I'm sorry. It's not easy for me—"

"Having to consort with a synadroid?" She lifted her chin as she glowered at him.

He glared at her, his regret dissipating. "Yes.

Just like it's going to be hard for you to not always be the martyr."

"Didn't Pine do a fantastic job, James? She's going to do the whole garden." If Joseph noticed the tension between them as he came into the yard, he gave no indication. "In fact, she's going to go out tomorrow and shop for whatever tools and seeds she needs to replant the entire thing."

"Really?" James didn't care about the garden, but Joseph wasn't seriously considering letting her out unsupervised, was he?

"Yes. She's been here long enough now. I think she's ready."

Was he joking? After what happened the other day? "You think she's ready to go out on her *own*?"

Pine glared at him, but he refused to wilt in the face of her anger. Her feelings about it were the least of his concerns.

"Of course not," Joseph said, as though it were a ridiculous idea, which it was. "*You're* going with her."

"*What?*" they said in unison.

It was obviously news to Pine as well. *I'm not surprised Joseph didn't tell her beforehand.* She probably would've refused to go outright.

"Pine, I know it's unfair of me to expect you to sit inside all day. But I'm still not convinced it's safe for you to be out on your own yet. Until it is, I figured James should act as your protection."

"But I—"

"Pine, we made a deal," Joseph reminded her.

What? What kind of deal did he make with her? James didn't like the sound of that.

"Yes, but I thought *you*—" A quirk of Joseph's eyebrows changed her mind. "Fine."

But James wasn't going to give up so easily. "But what about all our work, Joseph? Blue's got a lead on those—"

"That's the beauty of it, James. Pine's also going to work for me. So with the two of you, we'll get the same amount of work done in half the time." Joseph folded his arms over his chest, pleased, and waited.

How could he show Joseph this was a bad idea? He couldn't come up with anything plausible. *Damn.* "Okay. When do you start?"

"Tomorrow. Today, Joseph and I are going shopping." The expression on her face was unreadable.

"Which means, James, my dear boy, that you get the day off."

A day off. What would he do with himself? He usually filled his life with as much work as possible. Unless... *Maybe Blue can spare some time for a chat today.* If anyone had the insider knowledge on synadroids, it would be the Blue Fairy. "Thanks, Joseph. Okay, Pine, I guess I'll see you tomorrow." A flash of gold caught his eye and he peered into the pond again. "What did you name it?"

"Her. Cleo," Pine replied. "By the way, Joseph disabled my safe word. You have no power over me anymore."

James bit the inside of his cheek and walked through the kitchen door. Was that the deal they'd made? How could he deactivate his best guarantee for safety? James sighed. He would just have to trust that Joseph knew what he was doing.

Perhaps Blue will put my mind at ease. His pace quickened as his brain raced through all the questions he wanted to ask her, although he wasn't yet sure what he would do with the information, especially if it wasn't good news.

Ugh. When did life get so complicated?

Despite himself, he glanced up at the house as his car pulled away, almost hoping to catch a last glimpse of Pine. She'd followed him to the doorway, and stood watching him, her haunting eyes filling him with unease. That, and something far more disturbing.

Doubt.

EIGHT

Pine trailed behind James on the way to the botanical center. She was being petty, but James being there solely to keep an eye on her riled her. Was it actually about her safety? Or was it more about Joseph keeping track of his property? And why James, of all people? Joseph knew how they felt about each other.

He has a perverse sense of humor if he thinks this is a good idea.

James clearly wasn't thrilled either. He'd stalked ahead after picking her up, knowing damn well she couldn't keep pace with his long stride. At first, she'd trotted beside him, but when it became clear he was doing it on purpose, she dropped back, intentionally slowing *her* gait so that he had to constantly stop and wait for her to catch up.

All in all, Pine was *not* in a charitable mood. So what if he'd gotten her the hair and clothes she'd coveted? Did he think that would erase what had happened? She still knew how he felt about synadroids, even if, for a moment, his thoughtfulness had suggested otherwise.

Don't kid yourself, Pine. He didn't do it for you. He did it for Joseph, just like you're doing now.

Maybe she could lose him among the plants and

wheelbarrows, even if it was just for a few minutes. Maybe he would trip over a rake. She slowed even more, pleased by his huff of exasperation.

A group of men and women was gathered on the pavement ahead. One of them turned in Pine's direction and— *Is that— It can't be. Daisy?*

Pine sped up, her pace taking James by surprise. "Pine? Pine!"

She took off at a jog toward the imposing theatre at the end of the block, a regal gray-stone façade with roundly suggestive cornices. The large gilt name over the door proclaimed it *The Red Dove.*

James hurried after her, catching up just as she reached the small group milling around outside.

"Pine, what are you doing?"

She ignored him and the annoyance in his voice.

It *was* Daisy, just not quite as Pine remembered her. Her hair was still a startling shade of platinum silver, her eyes the same rich blue and white of a sunny day, but one side of her face was covered by a lacy half-mask and she wore an expensive-looking brocade mini-dress in a rich, jewel-colored diamond pattern. She'd bent at the waist to hug Pine, her movements oddly puppet-like.

"Pine?" James stood right behind her, casting a shadow over her shoulder.

Does he have to get involved in everything? Well, let's see how he feels being surrounded by synadroids. "James, this is Daisy. She was in my sector of the algae farm." She lifted her chin in challenge. If he was rude to her old friend...

Daisy put her hand to her cheek and flashed James a coquettish look. "It's Harlequin now," she said, extending her hand to him. Inclining her head toward Pine, she whispered, "It's more suitable for the customers."

"When did you get here? What are you doing? What kind of place is this?"

"Come inside and I'll tell you all about it. I'm not technically on shift for another hour. We can catch up." Harlequin's smile was dazzling as she clapped her hands in excitement.

Daisy was the first synadroid Pine had seen since she'd gotten to Portfade. What were the chances? If she was here, maybe the city wouldn't be so unbearable after all. "Of course. James, I—"

"Absolutely not. We're leaving, Pine. Say goodbye to your friend." His expression was unyielding, his mind already made up.

Pine's smile fell. "But Joseph would—"

"Joseph put *me* in charge. Pine, this place—" He glanced at the entrance and grimaced.

What did that have to do with anything? Nothing. Of course. He just wanted to be an ass. "You can't tell me what to do."

"I can. And I just did. Joseph would be—"

"To hell with Joseph," Pine burst out. "I've done everything he—"

"Now, Pine," Harlequin's sugary voice cut through Pine's strident one. "Perhaps James is jealous." She tucked her arm through his, and as she smiled up at him, she winked at her companions.

Three of them smiled and joined her in surrounding James. They were all as elaborately dressed as Harlequin, one dripping with precious stones, one shining with iridescent scales, and one cloaked in soft fur that looked suspiciously like cat. They ran their hands over James's arms, his back, his chest. One slid her hand up the back of his neck and into his hair, teasing his scalp. Their laughter tinkled like warning bells.

"What the— No, stop that—" James twisted, trying to push their exploring hands away.

Harlequin caught Pine's eye and nodded toward the door, where another synadroid beckoned. Pine took the hint and slipped through, leaving James to the mercy of his enemies.

* * *

The door slammed behind Pine, plunging her into darkness. Almost as quickly, her eyes compensated for the dim lighting, and she found herself in a foyer of sorts. An empty ticket booth sat on one side, across from a line of chairs and a low coffee table. At the far end stood a set of grand double doors.

The synadroid who'd opened the door bowed and ran her finger down Pine's cheek. She was dressed in artfully placed feathers and, from what Pine could see, a lot of sheer, pointless fabric. "Welcome," she whispered, and sashayed into the booth, where she perched on a red-velvet-topped stool.

A sliver of light crossed the floor as Harlequin stole through the door behind Pine.

"Come on," she said, grabbing Pine's hand and pulling her away. "They won't keep him busy for long."

Pine didn't like the idea of the exotic creatures keeping James busy for *any* length of time. "I can't just leave him." Besides, though it had felt rather delicious to sneak away right under James's nose after he'd forbidden her, she'd had her fun now. Antagonizing him even more wasn't going to help the situation between them, especially after Joseph had trusted her.

"Of course you can. He can wait, or you can find your own way to…wherever it is you are now. You can tell me all about it, but let's grab a table first." She pushed one of the double doors open just wide enough for her and Pine to slip through. Inside was a vast room that mimicked an old-fashioned speakeasy, dripping with more red velvet and crowned by an ostentatious crystal chandelier. Dozens of small round tables and matching chairs crowded into the considerable space, all positioned with an ample view of the curtained-off stage.

No wonder James hadn't wanted her to come in here. It looked *fun*. Daisy was right. He could wait. He could've just given in to her on this, rather than spoil everything. He'd made his choice; now she was making hers.

Harlequin pulled Pine into a banquette along the back wall. Taking a seat across from her, she dropped her chin into her ornately manicured hand and looked at Pine expectantly. "Well? The last time I saw you was off the coast of Fanglass Island. What's happened to you since then? Tell me everything!"

So Pine did.

"I can't believe you've been here only weeks. It's been nearly three months for me. What were you *doing* all that time?"

Daisy had been here for months? Pine had been moved only a few weeks after the emancipation. Why had Daisy gone so early? "The usual, plus some training on how to fit in up here. Why—"

"Well, now that you're here, it's not so bad, is it? It seems like you've landed on your feet, anyway," Harlequin interrupted. She was so different than Pine remembered, all glitter and drama. Daisy had possessed the same calm serenity as all the synadroids in their sector.

"Are you serious? You mean, you're actually *okay* with all of this?" Pine glanced around. "What *is* all of this, anyway?" She never seen so much red.

Harlequin laughed. "God, Pine, you still seem so...*green.*"

Pine's confusion must've been evident.

Harlequin sighed. "Not all of us are owned by kindly old men, Pine. Although, I suspect he's probably not as benign as you think." She gave Pine a sly look that quickly turned into exasperation. "Oh, for goodness' sake. This is a burlesque hall, Pine. And a brothel. For men and women who want to have company and sex with sentient androids."

Pine's stomach turned. Although Joseph had told her places like this existed, she'd thought he was just trying to scare her into obedience; no sentient android she knew would submit willingly to such a life. Would they?

"Don't look at me like that. It's not that bad."

"How can you say that? I mean...you—" Pine didn't want to insult her, but...

"Grow up, Pine," Harlequin said, her voice harsh. "What did you expect? Few of us get lucky."

"But how can you let them... I mean, why don't you—"

"What? Fight? Run away? That's not really a luxury we can afford, Pine. I mean, why are you still with your old man? Although," her eyes glittered in a way Pine didn't like, "that one you left outside looks like he might be worth staying around for. Is that it?" When Pine didn't reply, Harlequin's mouth dropped open. "That's it!" she crowed.

"No! It's not," Pine insisted. "I just— I'm working on it. I don't plan to be here any longer than I need to be." It sounded unconvincing, even to her. But that *was* still her intention. She just hadn't figured out the details yet.

"I thought like that once," Harlequin said dreamily then her gaze hardened. "But it's a fantasy, Pine. And honestly, it's not so terrible. Hell, I could be fighting giant monsters at the Perimeter. Here, I have a roof over my head, beautiful clothes, and when my work is done, my time is my own. All The Showman requires is loyalty and a convincing smile." She flicked an invisible speck off one of her nails. "It's a fair price, if you ask me."

"But your freedom— Why shouldn't we have the same freedom as biological humans? I mean, we have the same emotions they do, the same hopes—"

"Oh my god, just listen to yourself. They're not any freer than we are, Pine. Their freedom is an illusion. Everyone is owned by someone else. The sooner you figure that out, the better off you'll be."

"But—" *Is it true?*

"Tell me, Pine, what would you do, if you were 'free?' How would you support yourself? House yourself? Fix yourself? *That's* what it means to be human. Be grateful for what you have."

"Excellent advice," a deep voice rumbled next to Pine.

She started; she hadn't heard the man approach. He was huge, both in height and breadth. He wore trousers of the same red velvet as the room, his substantial torso encased in the palest green overlaid with an emerald brocade vest. He hurt Pine's eyes.

"Pine, this is The Showman."

"A pleasure," he said, holding out a meaty hand.

He waited for a few seconds while she stared at him then withdrew his hand and gave a hearty laugh.

"What remarkable eyes you have. Tell me, my dear, are you looking for work? Perhaps a new living arrangement?" He stroked the curve of his full mustache.

"No," Pine said hastily. "I'm not. I'm very happy where—"

"Really? Because that's not what it sounded like."

"No, I—"

"Who's your owner, then?"

"Joseph Polendina. But—" The Showman rattled her, making her feel as though she were walking across hot sand.

"Ah, yes, the robotics designer. I know of him." The Showman gazed at Pine with new interest. "You're from the same place as dear Harlequin here?"

That, at least, she could answer. "I am."

"It just so happens that I have an idea for a mermaid show. Perhaps I shall buy you off Polendina."

Panic swelled in Pine, the same kind of icy fear that had washed over when she'd been told she'd been sold the first time. "Joseph would never sell me." *Would he?*

"Oh, I don't know about that. If the price was right—"

He'd found her tender spot—she *did* have a price. "I won't do it. Even if Joseph sold me, I would never do...what Harlequin does," she finished lamely. She grimaced at her friend. "I'm sorry, Daisy, I just... I'm sorry."

An expression Pine couldn't read crossed The Showman's face before he cocked his head. "Well,

Harlequin, I guess you'll have to do it. You're the only other water synadroid here." He gave an exaggerated sigh and waited to see how his news would be received.

Pine turned to Harlequin to decipher the strange undercurrent between them and got another shock.

Her former friend sat stricken, her hand covering her open mouth, as though The Showman had idly suggested she was to be destroyed.

"No. Please." Harlequin's fingers dug into the polished surface of the table, scarring the varnish.

The Showman *tsk*ed as he eyed the scratches.

"Daisy? What's wrong?" Daisy was obviously resigned to the aspects of her job that would've troubled Pine, so her terror must be with the tank of water. But why would Daisy be afraid of that? Until a few months ago, she'd lived in water her whole life.

"It seems that since finding her legs, so to speak, dear Harlequin here has developed a pathological fear of the water. Isn't that right, love?"

"Dai— Harlequin, is that true? You're afraid of the *water*?"

"I'll never go back there. You promised. You *promised*." Daisy's polished façade had cracked.

Is this like Finch? During their service, both she and Daisy had known a synadroid who, one day, for no reason they could fathom, became hysterical, screaming that the water was crushing him. He'd ranted and raved as he'd tried to get to the surface. Then one of the handlers had spoken Finch's safe word, and he'd been taken away. They'd never seen him again. Was that why Daisy had left so much earlier than Pine? Had The Showman *saved* her?

"Now, Harlequin, I promised I would never

send you back to the *ocean*. This is just a tank of water, no more than a few hundred pounds. Or is it thousand? Never mind. You'll crush it!"

"I won't do it. I *won't*." She stood then sat down again.

"Ah, that's a shame. I guess I have no choice but to sell you on then. Can't have a member of staff unwilling to do their job. Now where—" He tapped his beard in mock deliberation. "Where could I send you? I know." He leaned forward and placed his thick hands on the table. "Deserter's Island, yes? They always have a use for synadroids...or their parts, at least. I'll go make the arrangements." He stood and walked away from the table, humming as he went.

"*No! Please!*" Harlequin stumbled and fell to her knees in her haste to follow him.

He turned as she grabbed his ankle. "I'm afraid you've given me no choice," he said. "Either you get in the tank, or you go."

"I can't— I—" Harlequin's head jerked to the side. Pine remembered what James had told her, about the synadroids on the Perimeter. The ones who'd gone mad. Who'd hurt themselves and then—

"I'll do it." Pine stepped out from the banquette. Neither The Showman nor Harlequin seemed to hear her. She spoke louder. "I said, *I'll do it.*"

That time, they did hear.

"Oh, Pine, thank you. Thank you, I—"

"Shush, dear." The Showman put a gentle hand on Harlequin's head. He gazed at Pine with renewed interest. "You would do that, for your friend? Leave what I know to be a safe place with Polendina to come here and take up a position you find repugnant, that goes against your values, to spare her?"

"I will," said Pine. And she would. She would be strong and do this for Daisy. But what were James and Joseph going to think? Was James still out there, pacing back and forth and thinking of new ways to lecture her? Well, this time, she wouldn't blame him. She'd have given anything to be outside, listening to him tell her off.

"Very well," The Showman said. "Wait there. I will return shortly." He peered down at his feet. "Harlequin, please get up. Our guests will be here soon." He gripped her chin. "Remember, smile."

Harlequin gave him a weak grin and tottered to her feet. She returned to the banquette and sat heavily back down in her chair. "Pine, I—"

Pine shook her head. "Let me think." What was she going to do? Would Joseph really sell her? Probably, if he thought she'd rather work in a brothel than be with him. She was running out of time. People had begun filing into the room and The Showman once again materialized by the table.

"Come with me." He offered Pine his hand again.

She stood and accepted her fate.

As she walked away, Harlequin grabbed her arm. "Thank you," she whispered. "I'll find a way to make it up to you."

Pine barely heard her. Her mind raced, weighing her options and finding none.

The room The Showman led Pine to was small, its modern aesthetic clashing with the flamboyant bordello on the other side of the door. On the neat chrome-and-glass desk sat several pieces of what looked like tech, although Pine couldn't begin to identify them.

What were those? Were they for her act? Had he

called Joseph and already done the deal? Again, Pine wished she could cry. Maybe she would've been less scared if she could. Daisy's head twitching on her elegant neck flashed through her mind.

Stay calm, Pine. You'll get through this.

"You see these items here?" The Showman asked her.

"Yes."

"I want you to take them to Polendina. He can either use or sell them, whichever will benefit his— him more." He collected the items and placed them carefully in an oxblood satchel.

"I don't understand. You're sending me home? I thought—" That James was right—her life could be a lot worse. *Damn him.* That wasn't the point, but it was impossible to argue with even the specter of him right now.

"I've always been curious whether you synadroids would risk yourselves for each other, the way few humans will, and now I know. Could be good for the people fighting for your freedom to know. Now, please. I'm a busy man." He looped the bag over her shoulder. "Go straight home."

"What about Harlequin? You're not going to make her go in the tank, are you?" Pine asked as he prodded her toward the door.

"No, of course not. Not if she doesn't want to. Besides, do you know how expensive those tanks are?" He shut the door behind him, leaving Pine in the dark in more ways than one.

She found she was not-so-surprisingly eager to get home, longing for the relative safety of Joseph's house. And if she was honest, the comfort of Joseph himself. She'd even be glad to see James. They were both going to be so angry with her.

I didn't do anything wrong. Mutiny flared in her

again, but she quickly tamped it down. *Just get out of here. Don't make it worse.*

Harlequin was nowhere to be seen. *I'll come back and find her another time.* Pine headed for the exit on the far side of room, winding her way between customers taking their seats in front of the stage. The air buzzed with a distracting anticipation. Her attention snapped back, however, when the bag was bumped off her shoulder, spilling its contents on the dubious-smelling carpet.

"Oh my goodness, I'm sorry," a voice above Pine exclaimed as she bent to retrieve the items, stuffing them back into the bag.

As Pine straightened, she came face-to-face with a man and woman. They were both older, the man sporting an antiquated prosthetic arm and the woman a visor to help her see.

"It's okay," Pine assured them. She just wanted to get out of there, go home and make amends with Joseph and James.

"Are you all right?" The woman pawed at Pine's arm; her fingernails had been filed to points.

Pine drew away. "I'm fine, thank you." She tried to push past them. She didn't have time to make small talk.

"Are you sure?" the man asked. His face was triangular, accentuated by high cheekbones and a pointed red beard shot through with white.

"You need to be careful, dear." The woman purred. "Especially considering what you're carrying."

"Wait. You know what these are?" Pine patted the bag.

"We do. And we also know where you can get an exorbitant price for them."

Why would that matter to Pine? "No, thanks.

Look, I have to get home, my…father is waiting for me."

"Your *father*? I didn't realize synadroids *had* fathers." The man chortled. "Did you hear that, Tabby? This synadroid has a *father*."

"Shut up, Todd." The woman bared her teeth at him. "I'm sorry. Todd is an idiot. What's your father's name, dear?"

"Joseph Polendina. He's—"

"Joseph!" The woman clapped as though delighted. "Joseph is a very good friend of ours. My name is Tabby—and you've already met Todd. Hasn't Joseph told you about us?"

He hadn't. But then, Pine hadn't shown much interest in his personal life. "No, but—"

"Are you thinking what I'm thinking, Tabby?" Todd stroked his beard as he considered Pine.

"I am." The couple pulled her to the side, away from the crush of other patrons. Tabby lowered her voice, her face serious. "Those items you have there? They're very valuable—to the right people. But we could help you make them even *more* valuable. Perhaps we could—"

"No. Tabby, I've changed my mind. She won't be interested. We should just let her go. She needs to get home to her father. He'll be happy with what she has, just as it is." Todd turned to go, tugging gently on Tabby's arm.

Tabby gave an exaggerated sigh and agreed. "Perhaps you're right. It just would've been so lovely to help our dear friend Joseph out." She shook her head sadly. "I'm sorry we wasted your time, dear." She turned to walk away.

"Wait." Pine grabbed Tabby's arm. If they really were friends of Joseph's, maybe they *could* help her. She was going to need a good apology after she'd skipped out on James, and *he* definitely wasn't going to help her now. Where better to start than with Joseph's friends? "What did you have in mind?"

The companions glanced at each other and grinned.

"What did you say your name was, dear?"

# NINE

As the light rail pulled out of the station, Pine's stomach clenched. Maybe this wasn't such a good idea, after all. It was growing late, and whatever grace she'd gain by bringing home a prize for Joseph was fading as the sky grew darker. "Is it much farther?"

"No, no. We're almost there. Just a little farther," Todd promised.

Pine would just have to trust them. They were on their way to the sprawling market sector of the city, nicknamed The Field of Miracles. It was famous, the couple had explained to her, for the buying and selling of unique and hard-to-find cutting-edge technology, among other things. They'd guaranteed Pine that, with their help, she could get a fortune for the equipment The Showman had given her, or, if she preferred, could exchange the three pieces for one or two that would be of even *more* use to Joseph.

But the farther away from Joseph's they got, the more Pine began to doubt their story. Their answers to her questions about their relationship with her owner had been vague enough to be truthful, but still oddly dissatisfying. And before she knew it, she had no idea where she was. Should she ask someone for help? Or keep trusting the two were who they claimed? As she agonized over the right choice, Tabby announced brightly, "This is our stop. Come on, love, this way."

Swept away, Pine disembarked with them. What else could she do? She had no money and no way to get back, even if she could figure out how. Tabby had paid her train fare, had guided her in the right direction. As though she saw Pine's misgiving, Tabby batted it away. "Don't worry, Pine dear. We'll have you back at Joseph's before your bedtime."

Todd laughed at that, a callous sound Pine detested.

"Right." Todd rubbed his hands together. "Let's stop here for a quick refreshment then carry on." He indicated a shabby-looking tavern. Just beyond it, a pair of ornate gates soared, heralding the entrance to the market.

"I don't need any refreshments," Pine said. "I just want to get this over with."

"Perhaps you don't, but *we* do," Todd said, his expression sharp.

Pine had no choice but to acquiesce.

"Don't worry, we won't be long," Tabby comforted her. "One drink then we go."

They sat in a booth near the front door. A waiter in a blue-checked shirt came over to take their order. He seemed to know Todd and Tabby but gave a Pine an appraising look.

"The usual?" he asked with a smirk. After they agreed, he turned to Pine. "And you?"

Had he not seen the tattoo on her wrist? Or was he just mocking her? Synadroids didn't eat or drink—all the nourishment they needed to keep their copycat bodies functioning was injected every few months. *Everyone* knew that. She glared at him until he chuckled and walked away.

See, James? No respect for life that isn't their own.

After they'd finished their drinks, Todd stood and stretched, grimacing as he did so. Without a word, he headed toward the back of the bar, where the waiter lounged against the grimy wall.

"Where is he going?" Every minute that passed was a torment.

"To the bathroom. Something you lucky synadroids don't need to deal with." Tabby strolled off toward the pay point of the bar, leaving Pine to follow.

To Pine's relief, they left as soon as Tabby paid, Todd joining them outside. She blinked in the relative brightness and swarm of people, jostling against them as she struggled to keep up with the pair as they dodged expertly through the throng. The anxiety that had been swirling inside Pine bobbed and eddied, threatening to rise to a flood.

Pine clutched The Showman's bag close to her chest. She'd never seen so many different people as were in the Field of Miracles, nor so many intriguing, exotic items. Spices, fabrics, clothing, ceramics, food, technology... *Everything in the world must be here.* It was like the shallows of her beloved ocean—the colors, the shine, the mysterious and glamorous creatures mingling in an enchanted landscape. She could barely tear herself away.

The district they were headed to was at the far end of the market. They made their way through the warren of vendors, but the deeper they went, the seedier the merchants became. It wasn't what

Pine had expected of the elite purveyors the couple had described.

And speaking of Todd and Tabby, where had they gone? She must've lost them in the crowd.

Just keep walking. You'll find them...or they'll find you.

The canopies of the stalls grew closer and closer together, blocking out the natural light. Customers became increasingly scarce, and those who remained kept their faces hidden, their movements through the arcade furtive.

I should turn back. Tell them I've changed my mind—

Strong hands reached out of the gloom, grabbed Pine's arms, and wrenched them behind her back, trying to pin them together while a third scrabbled at the satchel on her shoulder.

"Stop!" Pine squirmed in her assailant's grasp. "Let me go." Anxiety morphed into a rush of adrenaline, and she managed to yank one arm free and strike the hooded aggressor hauling on her bag across the side of the head. The person stumbled, and a feminine voice let out a string of curses. Emboldened, Pine grabbed the hand holding her arm and twisted it. To the surprise of both Pine and her would-be captor, the hand was no match for Pine's synadroid strength, and it rotated grotesquely on its wrist with a screech as she made the metal warp and buckle.

Pine had a moment of savage victory before her legs were kicked out from under her. She hit the ground hard, narrowly missing landing on her precious cargo. Two figures cast their shadows over her, their breaths coming in ragged gasps. Pine dug her fingers into the asphalt and hauled herself forward as she tried to get clear of the attackers and scramble to her feet. She had little experience with fighting, but she knew she had to keep moving.

A heavy foot slammed into the small of her back, pinning her to the ground, while another kicked the bag away from her grasp. "Grab it," the owner of the foot hissed, and the other blocked Pine's view of the bag as they stooped to pick it up.

"No!" Pine yelled again, and the boot lifted from her back and connected with her skull. The blow dazed her, but not enough to stop her from using her sudden freedom to lunge after the other attacker, who'd thrown the bag over their shoulder and was already a dozen steps away down the narrow corridor.

Pine tackled the fleeing thief, and they fell in a tangle onto the ground. Disorientated, Pine fumbled through layers of fabric, searching for her satchel. Both her and the prostrate attacker saw the bag at the same time, just a few feet away.

"Todd, the bag," screamed the cloaked thief.

Todd? Pine's surprise lasted only a second before her rage kicked in. She should've known. She was so stupid. Why else would two humans be so kind to a naïve synadroid they'd just met? They had no intention of helping her; they never had. They'd probably never even heard of Joseph. All they'd wanted to do was get her alone and rob her. And they'd picked their location perfectly—an unfamiliar place where everyone looked the other way and their prize could be sold to the highest bidder immediately. Well, they weren't going to get away with it.

As Pine crawled toward the bag, trying to reach it before Todd did, Tabby's hand closed around her ankle. The older woman was surprisingly strong, and Pine's chin smashed into the concrete as she slipped. Screaming in frustration, she kicked her leg, trying to break free of the other woman's grasp.

Todd pushed his hood back and grinned at Pine as he bent and retrieved the now-scuffed bag from the ground with his human hand. His archaic cyborg hand was twisted at the wrist, the fingers brushing uselessly against his forearm. His grin turned into a snarl, and he came and stood over Pine, brandishing his damaged limb in her face. "You'll pay for this."

The sliver of sky still visible over Pine's head went dark. Todd's face contorted first in confusion then fear as a much larger figure straddled Pine and grasped him around the throat.

James. He had come for her.

"Pine, run." His voice was deadly calm, his face impassive; he didn't even glance at her. Tabby lay on the ground behind him, out cold.

Pine scrambled to her feet and lurched away then spun and snatched the bag out of Todd's frozen fingers. "James, I don't— Where do I—"

"Forward, out the back of the market. Don't stop, don't look back. There's a massive oak tree in an abandoned lot a mile beyond." The muscle in his jaw jumped. "Wait for me there."

With that, he drew his fist back and blocked out the sun.

TEN

When James saw Pine on the ground, the broken fingernails on her outstretched hand, his anger at her duplicity evaporated and a tsunami of wrath unlike anything he'd ever known surged inside him.

How dare they lay hands on her?

He'd been searching for her for hours. After she'd escaped into the theater, James had tried to follow her, but his way had been blocked by the sudden materialization of a colossal bouncer, who'd ignored his explanations and entreaties with a bored stare. Harlequin's coworkers, their mission accomplished, had wandered off, the lure of paying customers much more interesting.

James had paced outside, seething, lecturing Pine in his head and trying to think of some way, *any* way, to get it through her metal skull that his refusal hadn't been about controlling her, but about *protecting* her. She didn't know what kind of establishment this was. After half an hour passed, his frustration turned to concern. *I knew this place was trouble.*

But when patrons began to arrive for the early performance, James saw his chance.

"Excuse me, ma'am, have you seen a synadroid?

She's got black hair…" He described Pine to a woman wrapped from head to toe in luxurious white furs. When she shook her head, he moved on to the next. "How about you, sir? Have you—"

"Please stop bothering the customers." The bouncer smiled at him through gritted teeth.

"Get me Harlequin and I will." James raised himself to his full height, nearly a foot more than that of the hard man.

"I've already told you, I'm not—"

A man in an elegant brocade smoking jacket attempted to sidle through the doors behind them. "Sir, what about you? She'd be your type—"

The man tried to step past James, while surreptitiously glancing around him. The Red Dove had a reputation for being discreet and selective about its patrons. The Showman didn't even advertise—visiting a synadroid bordello was still a gray area, and not one that most clients wanted to draw attention to.

Two guests approaching saw the disturbance and turned on their heels and walked away, exactly like James had hoped; his plan was working. Their retreat didn't go unnoticed by the bouncer.

"Look—"

"Get. Me. Harlequin. Now. Unless you want me to take this from awkward to spectacle?" James raised an eyebrow. "I was a lieutenant. I've got a very good set of lungs." It was a bluff. His lungs had been irreparably damaged by toxic smoke and ash, but the thug didn't need to know that.

The doorman's face twitched as he weighed his options. His head tilted as though a disembodied voice had whispered in his ear. "No, sir— Yes, but— Yes, sir." He glared at James then lifted the lapel of his blazer to his mouth and spoke furiously into it.

Two minutes later, Harlequin came through the doors. She smiled sheepishly when she saw James.

"Harlequin, is there someone named Pine with you? This young man here is looking for her. And he won't leave until he finds her." His face was stony.

"No. I saw her come out of The Showman's office then she was talking to a couple. After that, I'm not sure. Fantasia needed my help, and—"

"What did this couple look like?" If she wasn't still in The Red Dove, the situation was far worse than he'd thought.

"Like a couple. They were older…the woman wore a sight-visor and the man had a metal arm. At least I *think* it was an arm. I've never seen one without skin on it." She shuddered delicately.

"Damn," James swore and glared at doorman. "You let *them* in here?" He knew the pair she was talking about all too well. They were notorious swindlers and cheats, and yet always seemed to be one step ahead of the law. But what interest could they possibly have in Pine? Synadroid-trafficking was too big a fish for them. "Do you have any idea what they wanted with her?"

"It's not my habit to interrogate our customers," the doorman said stiffly.

James ignored him. "If she's with them, she's in trouble." They might not hurt her, but they'd happily turn a blind eye for the right price. He paused before the door, his mind in turmoil.

Why in the world would she have gone with them? She couldn't stand humans at the best of times, and to go off with two strangers, knowing he was waiting outside? *She's willful and angry with me, but she's not stupid.* They must've offered her something important. *But what could be that important to her?*

Then it hit him. Was she trying to escape? He wouldn't put it past her.

"The Showman gave her something." A frown creased Harlequin's painted face.

"What? What did he give her?"

"I don't know. Some kind of equipment. I saw it when she dropped it and—

James was already half a block away. He knew exactly where she was. Where else would someone go if they were dodgy as hell and had a bagful of expensive tech?

Unease broiled in the pit of his stomach. The Field was definitely not a safe place for Pine. If she thought going there would help her escape, she was mistaken. He had to find her, before the wrong person did.

I'm coming, Pine. I'm coming for you. He didn't dare think about what might happen if he didn't make it in time.

* * *

But he had. Barely.

As Pine took off running, the bag of precious components flying behind her, James tightened his grip around Todd's throat. This man had hurt Pine. Now James was going to hurt him.

"What are you doing?" the captive man clawed at James's hands as he tried to break free. "This has nothing to do with you."

"Oh, but it does," James replied coldly. "That synadroid you were beating? She belongs to Joseph Polendina." When the man didn't react, James squeezed harder. "But you knew that, didn't you?"

Why bring her here? What had they planned to do with her once they'd stolen her goods? Ransom her? Joseph wasn't rich. So it had to be something worse. His hand continued to close like a vise.

Todd gasped, a wet rattle in his chest. *Careful, James. Don't go too far. Or you'll be no help to Pine.* James shook him once then threw him to the ground. A consummate coward, Todd stayed down.

James glared over his shoulder at Tabby's prone body. "This isn't the end. For either of you." He stalked away in the direction he'd told Pine to run, determined to find her and get her to safety.

His world went dark.

* * *

James woke up on the outskirts of the market. His head throbbed, and when he raised his fingers to the back of it, they came away slippery with blood. More was caked on the side of his face, and one of his molars was loose.

He sat up and groaned as the world swam before his eyes. What the hell happened? He'd been tracking Pine when something had rushed at him. A person. A man wearing a blue-checked shirt.

Pine. No. No. No. I have to find her.

How much time had passed? Judging by the lengthening shadows, he'd been out for nearly an hour. James needed to find her before it got dark. He staggered as he climbed to his feet, his head pulsing violently.

He could only hope they hadn't caught up to her. And that she'd listened to him for once and gone to the tree like she was supposed to. He'd start there. After that, well—

She'll be there. Don't think about it, just go.

It took him less than ten minutes to skirt the market at a full run and find the empty lot he'd directed her to. He was almost afraid to look. What would he do if she wasn't there?

But she was.

Hanging by a noose from the lowest branch of the tree, her body twisting slowly in the air.

No, no, no.

Her head was bowed, her eyes closed. She'd been badly beaten, large scraps of skin torn from her face and limbs. Ugly horseflies landed on her exposed flesh before flying away, disinterested in her bloodless offering.

James nearly vomited.

No human could've survived what they'd done to her.

But Pine's not human.

She might still be alive. She had to be. He sprinted to her and wrapped his arms around her body, trying to lift her and slacken the noose.

What are you doing? It's not like she needs to breathe. The damage is done.

But still he held on. Maybe she could feel him, would know she was safe now.

"Pine?"

She didn't answer. *That doesn't mean anything.* She may have shut herself down. James swore. There was no way to tell if she was alive. They'd given synadroids emotions, so why couldn't they have gone the whole mile and made them breathe as well?

I'll be having a word with Joseph about that oversight.

The thought was giddy, wild. He needed to calm down and focus. It wasn't like him to be so frenetic;

his years of training had made sure of that.

Breathe and focus. You're not going to help her this way.

He took a shuddering breath and examined the rope they'd used to lynch her. It was made of thick fiber—there was no way he'd be able to untie her.

I've got nothing on me. He'd rushed after her without a second thought, totally unprepared. A laugh that was more of a yell burst from his lips. He'd been in such a hurry that he hadn't even called Joseph.

Joseph.

The thought of Joseph was like a steadying hand. *One foot in front of the other.* He had to be going out of his mind by now. What was this going to do to the old man? Keeping one arm around her, James yanked his transcomm from his pocket, willing the dark screen to give him the answer. When it lit up, nearly a dozen missed alerts from Joseph scrolled across the display. James was about to hit reply when he had a better idea.

He tightened his arm around Pine's waist. *Please let her feel it. Let her know I'm here, that I've come for her.*

He lifted his transcomm to his mouth and spoke into it.

"Private line, 1883. Blue Fairy."

ELEVEN

Pine floated, her arms adrift, her body weightless. Hair caressed her face as she spun slowly in place, cocooned in the weight of her beloved water.

Home at last.

A shadow passed over her head, plunging her into a murky gloom.

It must be a boat. Maybe a cruise ship.

Something dark coiled around her legs and began to pull her down. She tried to draw her legs to her chest, but whatever held her fast tightened its grip.

Is this what Daisy was afraid of?

Pine sank rapidly, bubbles rushing from her nose and mouth. *Bubbles? That's not possible; I don't breathe.* But her body rebelled, struggling to draw a breath. Water rushed into her mouth, choking her as she tried to scream.

Above her, stark in the darkening water, a corpse-pale face appeared. Long blue hair swirled around it, seamless with the sea. She'd seen faces like this before in humans who'd drowned, with bone-white skin, blue lips, and milky eyes.

The corpse smiled and stretched out her hand, beckoning to Pine. *Come to me.*

Pine reached, trying to seize the outstretched fingers.

She breathed her last.

Slowly, the darkness receded. Whatever had caught her in its grasp released her and recoiled into the gloom. Free, she propelled herself toward the surface and the promise of salvation.

Pine opened her eyes.

Four faces hovered over her: James, whose eyes were oddly red, his face misshapen, a man with hair as black as sea glass and even darker eyes, another man whose hair and face were as white as the crest of waves, his eyes the violet of a mauve stinger. And a woman, her cheeks round and studded with obsidian, her hair the blue of the deep ocean. Her smile revealed small, pearly teeth and her eyes, so cold in the water, were bright coral-blue.

She was the most dazzling thing Pine had ever seen. "We'll give you a minute," she said, and the three strange faces withdrew.

"Oh, Pine, thank god." James pressed his forehead to her shoulder. His hand held hers, the palm clammy and fingers not quite steady. When she tried to squeeze them, she found she couldn't move.

James tried to reassure her. "You're okay, Pine. Blue had to immobilize you from the neck down. But you're okay." He took a deep breath and leaned forward, as though he was about to say more. But the words didn't come and after a few seconds he pulled away, shaking slightly.

He wasn't angry? She'd expected him to be livid. She'd done everything he and Joseph had told her not to do, had put herself in mortal danger, and yet, here he was, her nemesis, clutching her hand like he would never let it go.

"James, I'm sorry. I—"

Bright white tape covered a grisly split in his eyebrow.

"You're hurt."

"It's nothing." He dismissed it with a wave.

"How did I get here? What happened in the market?"

James came, and I ran away. She'd made it to the lot. She'd seen them coming; they'd somehow escaped James. And then, pain. Dizzying pain. Pain so bad her mind stopped making sense of it. *All for the bag.* The bag. She'd hidden it. And then— Pine snatched her hand away from James, her fingers flying to her throat. "They hung me. *Hung* me. They tried to *kill* me."

"Yes." James winced and pulled his hand from hers. "After you ran away, someone attacked me from behind. Took me by surprise." His hands knotted into fists.

"But then—?"

"When I came to, they'd dumped me outside the market. I *hoped* that for once you'd done what I'd asked, and I went to the tree where I'd told you to go. And you were there. They'd—" He pressed his lips together at the memory. "And so I called the Blue Fairy."

I hoped that for once you done what I'd asked. There had been no malice in James's voice, but it still washed over Pine like water, bitter cold. She opened her mouth to apologize, but he wasn't done.

"I just— I just don't understand, Pine. Why did you sneak off like that? Going into the theater was bad enough, but then to go off with two strangers to an unfamiliar part of the city— What were you *thinking?*"

"I'm sorry—"

"How can I protect you when you won't even listen to your own common sense, Pine? You rant and rave about being treated like a mindless object, then you try to prove us wrong by acting like one." He scrubbed his hand down his face. "Over the last couple of weeks, I thought you would finally see that Joseph only wants the best for you, yet you insist on throwing it back in his face every single time. I just…I just don't know what to do with you, Pine. We can't go on like this."

Whether James had intended the latter as a threat or not, Pine didn't know.

And she didn't care.

Her remorse evaporated under the sudden heat of her anger.

"*I'm* not the problem, James, *humans* are. Why kind of species are you that I have to constantly be on my guard? That you'll be kind to my face one moment and string me up from a tree the next? You shouldn't *have* to protect me, James." She wished she could wrap her arms around herself, create some kind of barrier between them. "And what are you saying? That if I'm not good, you'll get rid of me? I'm still nothing but a pile of metal to you, aren't I?"

And so what if you are? After everything humans have done to you, to sentient androids, why do you care what James thinks?

"Just tell me why you did it, Pine. I'm trying to understand." His voice was weary.

"When I found my friend, finally something from home, you dismissed it and treated me like a child. It…" It pained her to admit it. "You hurt my feelings."

"I hurt your feelings? You put your life at risk

because I *hurt your feelings?*" James was incredulous.

It *had* sounded ridiculous when she'd said it out loud. No wonder he treated her like an idiot.

Pine was tired of feeling stupid. "I wish I'd never met you. I wish they'd taken me away for parts." She didn't mean it—the thought filled her with horror—but she just didn't know what else to say.

James stood abruptly, overturning his chair.

"James?" The woman from Pine's dream spoke from somewhere out of sight. "Can we come back in?" Her voice was bland, as though she hadn't just overheard their fight.

"Yes, of course." James turned his chair upright and sat down again, looking everywhere but at Pine.

Movement behind Pine's head startled her. What was that woman doing?

"James?"

"It's okay, Pine. She's almost finished." He still wouldn't look at her.

"He's right...I've just about got it." The blue woman disappeared from Pine's view, and there was a slight pressure behind her ear. "That should do it. Try to sit up."

Pine complied, James relenting and steadying her from behind. Even though she could now move, everything in the room kept shifting, and she sat dumbly while the two strange men buzzed around her.

"I wonder how extensive the damage is. Do you think she still works?"

"If not, do you think she's salvageable? I know a buyer who—"

"We could always just replace some of the more expensive parts with—"

What were they talking about? Salvageable? A buyer? The unnamed shape in the dark water rose up to coil around her.

"Enough!" James roared, and the two fell back, stunned. "She's not a piece of— She's— Just, that's *enough*." He stood and leaned protectively over Pine, his heart pounding audibly against his chest. She reached up and splayed her fingers over it. Slowly, the darkness retreated.

The blue-haired woman seemed amused by James's outburst. "Ignore them, Cricket. They mean no harm."

"I don't care," James flared. "They can't speak about her like she's not here. Like she's a—"

"Machine?" the white-haired man asked helpfully. He shrank under James's returning glower.

"James?" Pine was afraid. Despite everything he'd just said, he *had* promised Joseph he'd protect her.

"I think you two need to go take a walk. Please."

They took the hint and withdrew, skirting carefully around James as they did.

"When did The Cricket get so sensitive?" one man muttered to the other as they left.

"Who were those men?" Pine asked. Her hand was still pressed to James's chest and, self-consciously, she withdrew it. With his heart no longer beating under her palm, Pine wished for the hundredth time that she could burst into tears.

James sat heavily back in his chair beside her and grabbed her hand. "The white-haired man is The Owl, the dark-haired one The Crow. Don't let their talk bother you. They're completely out of touch with reality and see everything in binary." He glanced up at the woman. "I don't want to hear them talking about Pine like that ever again." He seemed to have forgotten that, not so long ago, he'd been quick to do the same, but Pine held her tongue.

The woman smiled dryly at James's warning, unintimidated. "I'll tell them. Especially since it seems so *important* to you." Her gaze flicked from James to Pine and back again with a keen interest. "It's nice to meet you, Pine."

"Pine, this is The Blue Fairy—" James began.

"But you can call me Blue," she interrupted. "No need to be formal." She went to the other side of the room and fiddled with some equipment on a long counter covered with various bits and pieces.

The Cricket. The Blue Fairy, The Owl, and The Crow. Did all humans have these other names?

"Blue's been putting you back together." James glanced down at Pine's hand in his but didn't pull away.

"Thank you." It sounded so inadequate.

Blue dismissed her with a smile. "Not a problem. Joseph, James, and I go way back. They'd do the same for me." She pushed the hair back from her face. "Besides, it's mostly just cosmetic work now, after I reattached your spine to your head. When Joseph sees you, you'll be good as new."

James squeezed her hand then let go. "Which reminds me, I've got a phone call to make. Pine, will you be okay?" He stood and stretched.

She nodded, too proud to beg him to stay.

"You've made quite an impression on him," Blue remarked after James had shut the door behind him.

"What do you mean?"

"Well, after what happened to him...to see him so protective of one of your kind..."

The other woman's candidness was disconcerting. "He's just making sure Joseph's property gets back to him in one piece."

"I don't think you're giving The Crick—sorry, James enough credit." Blue turned back to her, a mammoth syringe in her hand.

"I— What is *that?*" The bore of the needle was so big, Pine could actually see inside it. She wasn't going to use that on Pine, was she?

Blue glanced down at the syringe in her hand. "What, this? Pine, do you have any idea what you look like right now? I didn't patch you up while you were unconscious just in case—"

"I was ready for the scrap heap?"

"Well, yes. But since you're alive and all...we'd better get you fixed up."

For the first time, Pine became aware she wasn't wearing the clothes she'd left Joseph's in. She was clad from neck to feet in a gown made of a material that felt like paper; even her arms were covered, all the way to her hands. Only her back was bare, and she couldn't *see* that.

"I've turned your pain sensors off, so you shouldn't feel anything. But—"

"*Feel* anything? What would I feel?" The same, sickening panic swelled in Pine again. She was so, *so* tired of its familiarity. She'd felt it more since she'd come to Portfade than the entire rest of her life.

Blue studied her then made a face. "Maybe I *should* put you out for this. What do you think? Just put you to sleep. Then you won't—"

"No! No. You *can't*." Despite how kind Blue had been, how much she'd already helped, she couldn't let Blue put her to sleep; she just couldn't. Look what had happened the last time she'd trusted one of them. *If she does, you'll never wake up again*. They would disassemble her, picking over her remains like vultures. She scrambled off the table and backed toward the door, keeping her eyes on Blue. She wasn't going to be so gullible this time.

Blue held up her hands. "Pine, you can trust me—"

"I'm sorry, I can't...I just can't." The room grew smaller, forcing her closer to Blue's wicked needle. The door behind Pine opened, and she stumbled back against the solid weight of James.

"Pine? What's going on?" He caught sight of the tools Blue had been gathering. "What the hell are you doing?" He pushed Pine behind his back, his arm around her. With him between her and Blue's instruments, the room expanded again. James was here.

You're safe.

"I'm *trying* to fix her." The Blue Fairy was clearly becoming exasperated. "Isn't that why you called me?"

James tightened his arm around Pine. "Yes, but—"

"But what? If you don't let me fix her, what are you going to do? Let Joseph see her like this? Take her to the maintenance shop? How would you explain her injuries? The authorities would snatch her away from Joseph in an instant, and you'd never see her again. You *know* that."

James stiffened, and Pine knew Blue spoke the truth. She buried her face in his back, though trying to delay was pointless. "James, please."

"I'm sorry, Pine, but she's right." His voice was gentle. "You have to let her do this, or I don't know what will happen. You can't—you can't leave here looking the way you do."

"How *do* I look, James? What did they do to me?" The paper gown gave away none of its secrets.

"Pine, you don't—you don't need to see it. Just let Blue fix you up, and I'll take you home."

"No! If she puts me to sleep, I won't wake up. What if she takes me apart?"

"She won't, I promise. I'll be here with you the entire time. You—" His voice grew hesitant, as though he already knew the answer and it wasn't the one he wanted to hear. "You trust me, don't you?"

Did she? Her first instinct was no, of course not. But he *had* come to find her, not once but twice. He'd been beaten, and yet he came for her, she who represented some of his worst nightmares. He'd stayed with her, gotten help for her. And he was still here, protecting her. So did she trust him?

"Yes. I trust you." Maybe it was crazy, and she was making a mistake, but there it was.

The stiffness melted from him and his back shuddered as he drew a ragged breath. "Thank you, Pine. I promise, I won't move from your side." He helped her back onto the table and glanced up at The Blue Fairy. "Let's get this over with as quickly as possible."

"We can do it quick, or we can do it well. And since I'm in charge, it might take some time. But," she added, with a strangely comforting smile, "you'll never be able to tell what happened. You'll look as good as new." She peered into Pine's eyes. "Pine, can I please help you?"

"Yes." Pine wasn't afraid anymore. "Thank you."

"It's my honor," Blue replied, and she began cutting the paper away.

TWELVE

The damage was even worse than James had feared. Her synthetic skin hung off her body in ribbons. Wherever it was intact, there were gouges and dirty, bloody footprints. If she'd been human... *She's not, so don't think about it.* He just hoped she didn't look down.

But she did.

Her gaze traveled the length of her body slowly, her face expressionless. Once finished, her only reaction was to rub some of the tattered skin wistfully between her fingers.

Could synadroids be in shock? "It's going to be okay, Pine. I know it looks bad, but—" But what? *Don't make her any promises you can't keep.*

"It's fine," she said. "It's not the worst I've seen."

His mouth dropped open. "*Not the worst you've seen?* Are you joking?" She had to be.

"No," she said, obviously amused by his reaction. "I lived in the *ocean*, James. Do you know how big some of the sharks are there? Not to mention the other beasts. Although," she mused, "I never did understand why they couldn't tell the difference between us and the humans."

Horrified, James could only shake his head. She'd just touched on something he feared even more than rogue synadroids.

Pine smiled, her lips curved in an expression he couldn't quite interpret. "James, it's *fine.*"

But it wasn't, and that made it so much worse. They'd done this to her, *knowing* she wasn't likely to die. Knowing she could feel the damage they were inflicting on her, that she had no choice but to endure it. The next time she raged about how awful humans were, he wasn't going to argue.

As Blue worked, James fretted. He'd never felt as useless as he did right now. She looked so fragile and vulnerable, his hands ached to gather her up in his arms and protect her. He regretted saying what he had earlier, scolding her like a child. He'd been unable to do anything else, desperate to have her understand. It was so unlike him. He'd never been this volatile on the battlefield.

"Are you sure she can't feel anything?" he burst out when Pine winced as Blue melded together a particularly large patch of skin. "Because—"

"She can't, I promise you. I turned off her sensors the moment we got her here. It might feel a bit strange, but it won't *hurt.*" She paused. "May I continue?"

"Yes," he said, his throat tight. Her reassurance wasn't much comfort.

"I wasn't asking *you,*" Blue said sardonically. "Pine?"

"Yes, please." Pine's voice was steady, and James's heart squeezed. She was such a strong woman. Why hadn't he seen it before? *Because it was her strength you were afraid of.*

"James, are you okay? I mean, you were hurt too." Pine peered into his face.

In truth, he was feeling a bit woozy. Despite being treated by Blue, every bruise, every split in his own skin throbbed. But it was superficial, and he'd had far worse. "I'm fine. Blue fixed me up as much as she could."

Pine nodded, although she didn't look reassured.

He ran a thumb over her knuckles and smiled. "I used to be a soldier, Pine. I never stopped in the middle of a battle to put a bandage on."

"Why don't you distract yourself by telling us what happened?" Blue asked Pine. "James gave me his version, but tell me yours." She pressed the edges of a tear together and passed a device over the line, fusing the seams with a faint scent of burning rubber. "It'll make the time pass faster, if nothing else."

She spoke casually, but something more than simple curiosity bubbled below the surface. James's mind raced ahead. What could she be fishing for?

"What do you mean?" Pine asked, and James was sadly proud of the suspicion in it. She was learning. "James probably told you everything."

"He told me that a couple—well-known to us, I might add—convinced you to go to the Field of Miracles with them. And then they beat you."

"That's pretty much it. What else would there be?" Her expression was impassive.

"Well, for starters, what did they want from you? It wasn't you, because they wouldn't have dared to...damage you." She fused another seam and nodded approvingly as she checked it under the light. "Which leads me to think you had something they wanted. And that they didn't get it. So what was it?"

Pine glanced at James, and he groaned inwardly. Knowing Blue and trusting her were two different things, and although she'd never given him reason to doubt her, she always seemed to know more about things than she should. Still, she *was* doing them a favor. A big one. If Pine had ended up in the hands of the authorities...who knew what would've happened? Joseph would never willingly let them take her away, but he may not have had the choice. "It's okay, Pine. We can trust her." He made sure to catch Blue's eye as he said this, and her mouth twisted in knowing amusement.

"I got some...some components from The Showman. I was supposed to give—"

"The Showman?" Blue asked, her voice sharp. "Who's The Showman?"

"The Fire-eater," James clarified. *That* name she would recognize. They'd both known him by his other name for years.

Blue gaped at James. "The *Fire-eater* got involved? Oh, this is good. Sorry for interrupting you, Pine. Please, keep going."

James pressed Pine's fingers in encouragement.

"I was supposed to give the parts to Joseph. But as I was leaving, I ran into a man and woman—"

"The Fox and The Cat?" Blue interrupted before she caught herself.

Pine looked askance at James. "Does *everyone* have one of these nicknames? How does anyone know who anyone is?"

James snorted. She was right. From the inside, it didn't seem strange to him, but to her... "No, but it does seem that way, doesn't it?" No wonder Pine thought humans were all duplicitous.

"Does Joseph have one?"

Now *that* was an interesting story. "Yes. We call him The Wood Carver, because he makes—"

"Can we please get back to the story?" Blue

shifted from one foot to the other, impatient.

Pine acquiesced. "I bumped into Ta— The Cat and The Fox in The Red Dove, and I dropped my bag. They saw what was inside. They said they were friends of Joseph's and offered to help me." She hesitated. "I feel so stupid, now."

"Don't worry about that," Blue said. "They've hoodwinked all of *us* once or twice. Right, Cricket?" She looked pointedly at James and prodded Pine's shoulder. "Sit up."

"It's true." Even though it wasn't, he appreciated Blue's kindness.

Pine continued. "They said...they said that if I went with them to the Field of Miracles, they'd be able to get even better components or more money than I could've gotten otherwise. And since The Showman said that Joseph could use or sell them as he liked—"

"Ah, yes. I know how that one goes." Blue shook her head. "One day, they'll get what's coming to them."

"I-I thought that if I could get something better, or more money for the ones I had, I could give it to Joseph, and...maybe he would forgive me for being so difficult and wouldn't send me away." She dropped her head to her chest. "It sounds so ridiculous."

"Pine, listen to me." James seized her other hand. "Joseph would never do that to you. Ever. No matter what you did. He loves you, Pine."

"He doesn't really know me," Pine said, looking away.

"He doesn't need to. He loved you before he even met you. And he'll do so forever." He treaded carefully over the next part. "I don't know if synadroids have families." If he was honest, he'd never cared enough to learn. "But Joseph truly sees himself as your father. And for a man like Joseph, that won't change. Unlike most people, his love for you is unconditional."

"You mean he won't be upset?" Her hope was almost childlike.

"Oh, he'll be upset. But not at you." James glanced down at Pine's partially reformed skin. "He's going to be all kinds of upset."

"What did you do with the components?" The Blue Fairy looked straight at Pine.

Pine avoided her gaze. "They must've gotten them." She'd barely spoken when her body went as rigid as a piece of oak.

"Still don't trust me, I see." Blue's disappointment was clear.

"Pine! What's happening, Blue? What have you done?" James was halfway out of his seat. "Whatever you're doing, stop it right now."

"*I'm* not doing anything," The Blue Fairy said. "*She's* lying."

"What?" James peered down at Pine, but her expression was fixed, doll-like. Only her mouth and eyes could move, and they were wide open in surprise.

"She's lying. It's a mechanism they put in the synadroids to better control them. Like those ridiculous safe words." Her face darkened. "Bloody hypocrites."

The force of her anger was a surprise. He'd never really known how Blue felt about sentient androids. He'd always assumed she did what she did only for the profit. Well, shame on him.

"Can you...fix her?" James hated using that word. Pine wasn't *broken*, just...well, James didn't know how to describe it.

"If by 'fix' you mean mobilize her, then no. She must tell the truth to do that. But I *can* tweak that part of her programming afterward."

It wasn't legal, but for the first time, James didn't care. Everybody had secrets.

"Pine, please. You have to tell her what happened to the bag."

It took some effort, but Pine was able to close her mouth and speak between gritted teeth. "I hid it. While I was running away." Her body relaxed, her fingers once again pliable in James's hand.

James didn't know whether to laugh or grab her shoulders and shake her. Even as she was being chased by the same people who'd just beaten her, she'd still thought to hide the bag. But she'd also put herself in even *more* danger by risking it. If she hadn't, would she have managed to get away? He opened his mouth then shut it.

It's done, James. Saying that now isn't going to help the situation.

"*Where* did you hide the bag?" Blue asked. She put down her tools and gripped the sides of the table.

James narrowed his eyes. Why was she so interested in that bag?

Blue caught his look and laughed. "Oh, for goodness sake, Cricket, use your common sense. If I wanted that bag for myself, I'd simply hack one of the city drones to find it for me. Not to mention I'm sure it doesn't hold anything I couldn't readily get my hands on." She shook her fingers at him. "I just figured it might be safer to send Owl or Crow to retrieve it. Since Pine didn't give them what they wanted, I'm sure they'll be scouting the area, waiting for one or both of you to come back."

Of course. "Sorry, Blue. I know better than to

doubt you." And he meant it. "I'm not sure why I'm so out of sorts these days."

"Hm, yes, I wonder." Blue turned away, but not before James saw the tickled look on her face.

"There was a hole in the trunk, very high up," Pine said. "A rat came out of it as I ran up. I slipped the bag in there when I saw them coming. They didn't notice—they thought I'd dropped it and was in the tree trying to hide from them." She pulled a face as she remembered.

"Why didn't you just stay in the tree, then?" He doubted the two old crooks would've dared to climb the tree after her.

"While one of them went off to find the bag, the others threatened to burn the tree down to get me." She shrugged. "It didn't seem fair—to the tree, I mean."

James burst out laughing, startling Pine. He didn't blame her—he wasn't sure why he was laughing himself. "You were worried about the *tree?*"

"It's alive, isn't it?"

James sobered and squeezed Pine's hand. She was unlike anyone he'd ever known, and not because she was a synadroid.

"Pine, I— Well, I don't know what to say, to be honest. I think *I'm* the one in shock." Giddiness rushed through him and he chuckled against the smooth skin of her hand. When he glanced up at her, she was gazing at him with a half-smile, and a look that was... Was it warm?

"I think that should just about do it," Blue said, and she packed her devices away.

"Already? That was so quick." Pine dropped James's hand and stretched her arms out in front of her, turning them over as she examined the reconstructed skin.

His fingers felt strangely empty without hers.

"I did the metalwork while you were still out of it," Blue replied.

"How long have I been here?"

"Almost a day and a half."

No wonder James was so tired. Blue, Owl, and Crow had taken turns working on Pine, but James hadn't slept; he'd refused to leave her side while she was out, afraid she would disappear again.

"What's Joseph going to say?" Pine asked, her expression apprehensive.

"We'll find out soon enough," James said. "He's on his way here now."

When he'd slipped out earlier, James had finally called him. He'd kept Joseph in the loop, but he'd refused to give him their location until Pine was in reasonable shape. Joseph had been incensed, but James insisted. He knew how badly it would've shaken the older man to see Pine in such a state.

"Really? Can I go and meet him?" Pine swung her legs over the edge of the table and stood.

"Pine—" James was in a bind. He didn't want to crush her enthusiasm, but after what had just happened to her...

That decided it for him. *No way am I letting her out of my sight.* "Okay, but I'll come with you." He waited for her to protest.

"It never occurred to me that you wouldn't," she replied. "Now let's go see my father."

THIRTEEN

Pine could hardly wait to see Joseph. She had so much she wanted to say to him. Although she had no idea where she was going, she darted ahead into a narrow corridor. At the end of the hallway, a set of stairs led up out of view. Sunlight fell down the steps, swirling with tiny motes.

She ran up them two at a time then stopped dead.

They were in a large cemetery. Rows of sculpted tombstones fanned out from where they stood, lining the stone path and cresting gently undulating green hills. Several hundred meters away, a timeworn bell tower soared into the sky.

Turning back, Pine gazed up at the building they'd just left. Constructed from large rough-hewn blocks of stone, it sat back from the rest of the cemetery, discreetly screened by a copse of leafy trees. A bas-relief angel had been carved into the stone above the doorway, her wings outstretched, and her eyes raised imploringly to the heavens. A mausoleum. Blue lived in a *graveyard*?

The landscaping across the cemetery was meticulous and eerily enchanting, verdant with bright flowers and fruit trees, and thick close-leafed hedges fashioned into animals and people that, rather than feeling incongruous, gave the cemetery a peaceful, gently cheerful air. Someone obviously cared a lot about this place and its inhabitants. Were all graveyards like this?

"James—"

A large black shape dove from the top of the mausoleum, narrowly missing Pine's face. Caught off guard, she stumbled backward and would've tumbled back down into the maw of the crypt had James not wrenched her back and crushed her to his chest.

"Pine? Are you all right?" His chest rose and fell in rapid succession, his heart thudding deafeningly against her ear. He dragged her away from the sepulcher entrance and onto the grassy lawn. "What happened?"

"That enormous black bird almost took my head off. Didn't you see it?" She craned her neck to peer at him.

James frowned. "No. I didn't see anything. Are you sure?"

"Of course I'm sure. It was huge. I—" *I'm still standing here in James's arms.*

He noticed at the same moment she did, and they broke apart self-consciously.

"Are you...are you okay now?"

"I'm fine. Let's just go find Joseph." She waited for him to take the lead, and when he didn't move, she stepped forward.

At the same times as James.

"Sorry. You first."

"No, you go."

They both stepped forward again. Why was it so uncomfortable?

After all, he just spent nearly two days holding my hand.

He must be exhausted, and *she* must still be recovering. Why else were they bumbling around like a pair of idiots?

"Okay, *I'll* go." She marched back onto the nearest path. "Which way is out?"

As they followed the widest stone-lined path toward the exit, they passed a couple kneeling beside one of the headstones, heads bowed and lips moving.

"What are they doing?"

"They're speaking to their loved one."

"*Speaking* to them? Why talk to someone who isn't there?"

James's brow creased as he tried to explain. "It makes people feel...closer to those they've lost. Like they still have a connection with them."

"That's very sentimental." And surprising, considering how many humans tended to treat other beings, including their own kind, so badly when they were alive. To be so emotional about people that no longer existed...it was a strange paradox.

"We humans are a sentimental bunch," James said. "It's one of the reasons sentient androids were created." He winced. "Sorry, I didn't mean—"

"It's fine." He hadn't meant anything by it. *Besides, when did we get so polite?*

It was odd walking amongst the human remains. If one of the synadroids Pine worked with broke—physically or emotionally—they were perfunctorily carted away. Sometimes they came back. Sometimes they didn't.

Lost in thought, Pine brushed her hand against James's, and discomfited, jerked it back. *What's wrong with me? Did he notice?* "Do you...do you know anyone buried here?"

"No. My parents were cremated, like everyone nowadays. I have their ashes at home." He gestured to the rows of headstones. "There simply isn't space to dig anymore. Older cemeteries like these are only kept for their historical value." His mouth twisted. "Mind you, if the Perimeter keeps shrinking, this one may go as well."

Fascinated, Pine read the different inscriptions to herself as they passed by. "You said people cremate their loved ones? And you keep the ashes at home?"

James nodded. "That's right. Why?"

"Why doesn't Joseph have Mara's ashes? He's got everything that belonged to her, there are pictures of her everywhere...but I don't remember ever seeing any ashes. I thought she died only a few years ago." Mara's ashes should've had a place of honor in his house. Maybe he kept them in his bedroom.

James stopped so suddenly Pine ran into the back of him. "You're right. I've never noticed that before."

"Did you know her well?" Pine had long been curious about Joseph's deceased wife, but too shy to ask him, although he lit up whenever he talked about her.

"No. I only met her a couple of times," he mused. "But she was always friendly. She seemed like a very kind woman. Her death hit him hard."

"What happened?" Why did she want to know? Was such morbid curiosity part of her programming?

"That part I'm not really sure about. Joseph's happy to talk about her life, but... I think it was some kind of illness. It happened very quickly, but there was no mention of an accident or anything. Whatever it was, it must've been very advanced if the doctors weren't able to treat her." He continued walking.

It had to have been very difficult for Joseph, to lose someone he'd been so close to. Pine had lost synadroids she knew, but they'd been moved in rotations so that the same synadroids were never together for longer than a few weeks at a time, though they might see familiar faces year-to-year. Romantic relationships were severely discouraged, and Pine had known of only one couple to spurn the rules. She'd never seen either of them again.

Imagine waking up one day to find your life partner gone. Was that why Joseph wanted a synadroid daughter? Because they were more resilient than humans?

They continued in silence. Outside the front gates of the old graveyard, they turned onto the sidewalk and Pine spotted a familiar figure in the distance. *Joseph.*

"Pine, before we... I just wanted to—"

But Pine couldn't wait. She pushed past James and started to run. What was Joseph feeling? Was he angry? Would he send her away? She wouldn't be surprised if he did.

But I don't want him to.

When he was close enough to see her, he didn't react other than to raise a hand in acknowledgment.

Pine slowed. He *was* angry. Well, she deserved that and would face it head on.

As she drew closer, however, he broke into a grin. Warmth flowed over her like the gentle south-Ghostlight current. Joseph barely had time to raise his arms before Pine threw herself into them, slamming so hard against his chest that he staggered.

"Joseph, I am so, so sorry. I didn't mean for any of this to happen."

Joseph patted her back and pressed her to him. "Pine, James explained everything. Please, don't let it trouble you. I'm just so thankful you're all right."

His kindness tore at Pine. His anger would've been easier to bear than this unconditional, undeserved compassion. "I'm so sorry," she said again.

His shaking arms rocked her gently, and he murmured in her ear. "Pine, you don't have to be sorry. I knew things would be a bit difficult for you at first—" His arms stiffened.

She pulled back. He was glaring over her shoulder, and as James came to stand beside them, an unwelcome sight sauntered into view.

Todd and Tabby, the former with the stump of his arm in a sling and the latter with her eyes under cover and a long sensor-stick in front of her, approached them, three policemen and a heavy force-droid in their wake.

The warmth Pine had been feeling condensed and froze. What was happening? Was this a good thing? Had they been arrested for what they'd done to her?

James swore. "Now what? I hoped we'd seen the last of those two."

So, no, not a good thing, then.

Joseph frowned. "Let me handle this." He stepped in front of James and Pine, his small figure stiff with dignity. "Can we help you?" he asked when the entourage was within earshot.

"That's her." Todd pointed, his crooked finger trembling. "That's the woman who stole our property."

James's face paled, and when he grabbed Pine's fingers, his grip was too tight. Why was he acting like that? Surely they didn't believe the old crook?

"Her?" the lead officer asked, his dubious gaze taking Pine in.

Or maybe they did.

She dipped her head, trying to look as harmless as possible.

"Yes," Tabby said, her voice quivering. "It was awful. She snatched it right from my shoulder. I begged her to stop, but she—"

"Yes, she brutally forced it from you. You've said. Several times," the officer replied.

"Then poor Todd tried to retrieve it for me and, she—she broke his arm." She wiped her nose with her sleeve. "These synadroids, Officer, they're out of control."

"That's not what happened!" Pine forgot to be diffident, stepping toward the officer before James yanked her back. "They're lying! I—"

"Pine. I'll *handle* this." Joseph's voice could've shifted the tectonic plates. "Officers, I think there's been a misunderstanding. I believe these two are well-known to you and—"

"Yes, they are. Unfortunately, they seem to be on the side of the law this time."

"What? How is that possible?" Joseph was palpably surprised. So was Pine. They had blatantly tried to rob her; nothing could prove otherwise.

"Show them the video," Tabby all but shrieked, triumph in her shrill voice.

"Video?" Joseph asked. "I don't know—"

The officer held up his transcomm. "This was captured at the Portfade Central Market a couple of days ago."

Joseph, Pine, and James crowded around the tiny screen. On it, a miniature Pine could be seen tackling a twisted-limbed Todd, knocking him to the ground and grabbing the oxblood satchel.

"That's not what happened." The indignation bit deep. How could they possibly think she was the attacker, despite what was on the video? Surely their common sense told them this wasn't the full truth?

"Oh no?" The officer was amused. "People always say that."

"No, I mean, it *did* happen, but—" How could she explain?

"So you admit to assaulting this man and woman?"

"Pine, don't say another word," James whispered furiously.

Joseph spoke again, his voice calm. "That bag held some equipment of mine. Pine was merely bringing it to me as I'd asked."

"And what was this equipment?" The officer glanced at Joseph, his finger hovering over a new screen.

"Ah, not much really," Joseph explained, his voice casual. "Just some replacement parts for Pine, in case she breaks down. I'm sure they'll be deservedly disappointed with it." He smiled at the other officers. "You know how frail these older versions can be." Joseph's nonchalance was impressive. Pine never would've guessed he was such a consummate fibber. She could learn a thing or two from him.

"That's not true!" Tabby exclaimed. "It was—" She stopped and pressed her lips together.

That sparked Pine's curiosity. What *were* the components?

"My eyes. It was a visor," the woman finished lamely.

"Mm." The officer didn't look fooled. "And where is this tech now?" He arched an eyebrow at Pine.

Joseph radiated tension. Whatever had been in that bag had been important. Pine gazed directly into the officer's face, her eyes wide and guileless. "They took it from me." She pointed at the mangy pair. "They must have it."

"That's what I thought. I told you, Barbara," he said over one shoulder. "Drinks are on you tonight."

"She's lying!" Tabby's snatched the cover off her eyes and lunged at Pine, her hands raised in claws as though she would scratch her eyes out.

"Synadroids *can't* lie," the officer said, bored now. He gestured in turn to Todd and Tabby. "Now get out of here. If you come to us with this nonsense again, I'll arrest *you*."

"You stupid little—" Tabby's teeth pierced her tongue as Todd snatched her by the arm and hauled her away. She threw her sensor stick over his shoulder at Pine, but it fell far short of its mark. Her curses carried back on the air even after they disappeared from sight.

"Right, let's go," the officer said to Pine. "I'm not going to have to cuff you, am I?"

Shock crackled up her spine. They were *arresting* her? For what?

James seemed as surprised as she was. As the officer put his hand on Pine's shoulder, James tried to push between them. "What are you doing? She didn't do anything wrong. Joseph's already told you—"

"Oh, we believe Mr. Polendina. Those two are

very familiar to us. And," he lowered his voice and gave Pine a crooked smile, "well done on wrecking that parasite's filching hand. But," he raised his voice for the benefit of his colleagues, "you *did* assault two members of the public. Two *human* members. And that, I'm afraid, is a punishable offense."

James was relentless. "But they attacked *her*. She was trying to get away from them and keep Joseph's property. That video you showed us is only part of what happened."

"Please calm down, sir," one of the other officers said. "Or we'll arrest you too."

"Relax, Jensen. He's not going to do anything. Are you?" The officer gave James a pointed look. "We know what happened. We saw the entire video—including *you* getting a few good hits in before you were blindsided. *But*, at the end of the day, *she* is a synadroid. As gross as it may be, she's not protected by the law—and those two pieces of trash are. As such, I have no choice but to arrest her."

Joseph raised his hands in supplication. "I understand, but—"

"I'm sure I don't have to remind you that if you object, your rights to ownership can be reviewed."

Fear curled around her ribcage at the officer's threat, a dread that chilled her heart. Even when she'd ridden in the car with Antonio on the day he'd brought her to Joseph, her fear had been tempered by other emotions—anger, resentment. This fright was pure and glacial, like one of the ice floes that moved like heavy ships across the northernmost reaches of the Ghostlight.

There was nothing they could do to stop this. Joseph had put his faith in her and now she was going to jail. And it was all her fault. Regret burned in her throat like a mouthful of swallowed seawater.

Joseph swayed where he stood and nearly fell, his legs unsteady. "Father!" Forgetting her fear, the officers and their threats, Pine rushed to his side, slipping his arm over her shoulder.

He let her support him as he implored the policemen. "But what will happen to her? She—"

"She'll be jailed. Probably as soon as tonight."

"What? No trial?" He seemed shocked. Human likely *always* got a trial.

The officer shrugged. "What for? We have her on video. We *know* she committed the crime."

"How long will she be in for?" It was Joseph's turn to support Pine.

This is actually happening. They're going to take me away.

The officer tapped his chin as he mulled it over. "Well, it's her second run-in with the law—yes, that incident with the magician was logged—and the people she 'assaulted' *were* injured, although we know they were lying about the property...so, she's probably looking at about...oh, four months hard labor."

"Four *months*?" James was incredulous. Was that good or bad?

"That's the minimum sentence required by law. She's lucky the arm she broke was metal and so counted as property. We're also aware of the extenuating circumstances." That decided, the officer turned to Joseph. "Do you want to make a claim on the property they stole? I mean, you'll probably never get it back, but it's up to you."

His arm tightened around Pine's shoulder "No, I don't care about those damned components, I just want—"

"Fine. Okay...Pine, was it? Let's go. I'm assuming you'll come willingly? Otherwise," he pointed to Joseph, "we'll have to take him in as well."

What choice did she have? She could run. But where would she go? Besides, she'd already given James and Joseph enough grief. No. This wasn't Joseph's responsibility. She would do this, and then, when she returned to them, things would be different. *She* would be different. "I'll come."

The officer seemed relieved. "Good. Bones here will escort you." He rapped on the metal chest of the police droid. Its armored head turned toward Pine, and she gazed into its shielded eyes, trying to find a sympathetic sentience. There was none.

She stared over her shoulder at James and Joseph as Bones led her away, burning the sight of them into her memory to keep herself company over the next four months. She'd been so desperate to leave them and now...now that it was happening, all she wanted to do was get back to them.

Both of them.

She was still astonished at herself when the door of her cell locked behind her.

PART TWO

FOURTEEN

James paced outside the Portfade Central Police Station at nearly the very spot he'd left her. He'd received word late last night that this was where she'd be released, and he'd arrived early, determined not to miss her. He checked the time again. Any minute now, she would be a free woman. Well, as free as she could be.

He replayed the last hours between them, over and over, just as he'd done for the past four months. The softness of her hand in his, her concern for him even as she lay there at the mercy of strangers, her own body broken.

You trust me, don't you?

Yes, I do.

But where the hell was she? Had there been a mistake? It was bad enough that Joseph—

The front door of the police station slid open, and there she was. She looked exactly the same as the last time he'd seen her, her long hair tied neatly back, her loose linen jumpsuit the one she'd been wearing.

And why would she look different? He caught himself with a chuckle.

The sun was behind James, and at first, she

didn't see him, giving him time to wipe his clammy palms on his jeans. Now that the moment had come, he didn't know what to do. Did she regret coming home? Would she be angry with him? At Joseph, because they hadn't been able to help her? All he'd thought about for the last four months was the unexpected hollowness she left behind.

"You're here." She stood in front of him, and every conscious thought was swept away by the sight of her strange eyes, gazing at him with—

"Of course I am. I—"

"Move along, you two." An officer stood in the entrance, hands on his hips. "This isn't a café."

James sighed. "Let's go."

They walked side-by-side down the sidewalk, separated by an unfamiliar shyness as their feet carried them toward the cemetery.

"How are—"

"How is—"

James chuckled. Why were they so clumsy? Was it just the time apart? "You first." He could compose himself while she talked.

"Thank you, James, for coming to get me." She paused. "I don't mean to sound ungrateful, but where's Joseph? I thought— I thought he would be here to meet me as well. Is he...is he okay?"

The unspoken questions in her voice were loud and clear. *Did he give up on me? Is he getting rid of me after all?*

"He wanted to Pine, truly," James assured her, "but there were some complications with your release." That was putting it mildly. Poor Joseph might never forgive himself.

"Complications?"

"Yesterday, we were told that you would be released out on Bowglass Island, where you'd done your time, so Joseph left me to hold down the fort and rushed out five minutes later, determined to be there the minute you were free. He even forgot his transcomm." James's mouth quirked. Joseph had been so flustered in his excitement, tripping over his own feet as he'd darted about, getting together any paperwork he might need. "But about four hours after he left, I got the call that you were, in fact, being released here." They turned up the paved stone path into the secluded graveyard. "I haven't been able to get in touch with him."

"Bowglass? I wasn't there. I went straight back to the algae farm I used to work at off the coast. Except they consider it 'hard labor' now." She scoffed.

"I know. He's going to be so disappointed." James paused by a headstone near the path to replace a fallen bouquet. "But at least you're here with me now, and Joseph will be home soon. Wait until you see all the gifts he bought you. He's single-handedly supporting the downtown boutiques—and that's *almost* as good, right?"

Pines gazed up at him, her expression uncertain. "James, about—" Then her eyes widened and she gasped. James twisted around. What now? He didn't want anything to interrupt their reunion.

A tall, brand-new hematite tombstone had been placed back from the path, in line with the others. The inscription which had caught Pine's attention read:

Here Lies
The Blue-Haired Child
Who Died of Sorrow
On Being Deserted by Her
Little Sister

Pine

Pine pressed the back of her hand to her mouth in horror. "James! It...it can't be true, can it? She's dead?"

James frowned at the tombstone, trying to see through the riddle. The last time he'd seen The Blue Fairy was the day after Pine was arrested. She'd shown up at Joseph's door, the scuffed oxblood satchel in her hands. After thanking her yet again for everything she'd done, James, despondent, had bent back over his work and hadn't bothered to listen to the hushed conversation—Blue and Joseph often huddled together like that, Blue playing white noise on a nanocomm to cover their voices as they discussed barely legal technological developments, exchanged orders, and pondered the slowly moving personhood machine for sentient robots.

Had there been any urgency in her demeanor? If so, James hadn't noticed.

But then, he hadn't really noticed anything since they took Pine away except the ripples of her absence. So often he'd caught himself thinking of her, of things she'd said, or the ways she'd looked at him.

Or the ways you looked at her.

It was more bitter than sweet, much more, but he forced himself to dwell on every painstaking detail, promising himself it would be different when he saw her again. That *he* would be different. The sight of her hanging from that tree, and then the aftermath, had brought home what he'd suspected deep down, the source of his uneasiness ever since he'd met her: that despite everything he'd believed to the contrary, she wasn't the enemy.

And *he* wasn't hers.

Although, that left the question of what exactly they *were.*

He shook himself and dragged his attention back to the question at hand—where the hell was Blue?

"I don't think so, Pine. I think it's a message, although what it means, I'm not sure. Blue's imagination was always more complex than mine." He rubbed the bridge of his nose as he considered Blue's motives. The tombstone was supposed to mean *something*, but what? "I wonder if she's disappeared again. She has to, every so often, to keep one step ahead of the authorities." He laid his hand on the hematite. "She was very entertained by having her newest headquarters right next to a police station." He shrugged. "But maybe you getting arrested here was too close to home." It was the most plausible reason he could think of.

Pine sank to her knees in front of the tombstone and traced the inscription with her fingers. "I've caused everyone so much trouble. First you and Joseph, and now Blue."

He put his hand on her shoulder. "Pine, it's okay. She likely wouldn't have been here for much longer anyway."

"I wanted to thank her." Pine's time away seemed to have softened her. James couldn't imagine the old Pine worrying about such a thing.

"Both Joseph and I thanked her. Repeatedly. And Pine, she helped you because she *wanted* to. She's very interested in your...freedom. I don't think you've seen the last of her." In fact, he *knew* it; he'd never seen the enigmatic woman so invested in anything that didn't directly affect her. He helped Pine to her feet. "Come on, let's go home."

* * *

Once they were in James's car, he waited before giving the vehicle its instructions. She'd been away for a long time, longer than she'd lived at Joseph's. He wanted her to be ready.

"Do you want to talk about it?"

"Not yet." She leaned back in her seat and turned to look out the window. That wasn't the reaction he'd been hoping for.

But then, what *had* he been expecting? For her to chatter excitedly away? To gush about how much she'd missed them?

Well, yes. A little.

He instructed the car to take them back to Joseph's house. As it pulled away from the curb, Pine pressed her forehead to the window. But still she didn't speak. What had happened to her during those four months? Did she regret waving goodbye to the place she'd spent most of her life for a second time? Was she dreading returning to the house she'd once been so eager to leave?

They pulled up to Joseph's house less than half an hour later. She stood with one hand on the car, gazing up at the tall house. Made from bricks of rich, gray marine clay, its classic, weathered façade reminded James of the older man.

Maybe it was still just another sentence to Pine. Something to be endured without choice.

"Are you glad to be home?" He held his breath.

"I am, you know. It truly feels like home to me now."

It feels like home to me now. Relief, and something else, swept through him. *She's glad to be back. She's standing here, with me, and it feels like home.* "Yeah?"

"Yes. I can belong, I think, if I can avoid getting arrested again."

James held up his hands. "Don't look at me—I did my best to keep you out of trouble."

"Well, you did a great job."

Their awkward laughter trailed off, leaving James self-conscious. She'd been gone for four months, but for all the damn tension, it could've been four years. "Shall we go in?"

He followed her up the path. Inside, she wandered around the house, trailing her fingers over the familiar surfaces as though making sure they were real. She stopped in front of Mara's portrait and smiled then leaned over and whispered something too quiet for James to hear.

James didn't know what to do with himself. He still hadn't been able to get hold of Joseph and being here alone with Pine was...discomfiting. Unexpectedly so. He'd been waiting for this day for months, had thought through all the things he'd like to say to her.

But now...those thoughts seemed so inadequate, the apologies self-serving.

I wish I'd never met you.

Did she still want nothing to do with him? Was any friendliness she showed him only for Joseph's sake?

"James? I'm going to go upstairs and have a shower. They seemed to think synadroids are self-cleaning."

A few minutes later, the sound of running water filtered down to James in the living room. He paced, sat, then paced again. What was wrong with him?

An exclamation of shock came from Pine's room, and James didn't think twice, sprinting up the stairs two at a time. "Pine, are you—"

She stood gaping in her doorway, wrapped in a

towel with her old clothes in her hands.

Her bed was obscured by parcels and bags of every size and color.

James laughed. "I told you Joseph's been propping up the local economy."

"This is all for me?" She walked over to the bed and picked up a parcel wrapped in shiny pink foil.

"Who else? I wasn't joking when I said he missed you."

She turned to him, her face serious. "Did *you* miss me?"

"I—" Why was his mouth so dry? He couldn't look away from the water that dripped from her hair and beaded on the curve of her shoulder. "I did. I—"

She tossed the present back on the bed and crossed the space between them.

"Did you miss *me*?" He gazed down at her, his throat tight around his voice. Damn it, why couldn't he swallow?

"Yes." There was a vulnerability in her expression, so different to when he'd first met her. Not self-conscious and defensive, but open. Her face was so close to his, tilted toward him, her mouth only inches from his own. If he just leaned down a little further...

The alert from James's transcomm cut through the air between them.

Relief mingled with disappointment washed over him as she pulled back. Her expression was unreadable.

"I, uh...damn. Where is it?" He cast about for his comm. Had he left it downstairs? No there it was, peeking out from under one of the gift bags. Reluctantly, he picked it up and turned on the screen.

No. Horror seeped from the device and into his body. He sat slowly on the bed.

"Pine—" He swallowed, hard. "It's Joseph."

She dropped the bag she'd been holding. "What's wrong? *James?*"

Her expression was so vulnerable, he almost couldn't speak. "He's...Pine, he's—"

"No. No, no, no. He can't be. I'm back now. I'm here, and we're all going to be happy, and I'm his daughter so he can't be—" She wrapped her arms around herself. As though she could hold Joseph there.

The shrillness of her voice cut through his shock. "Pine, I'm sorry. I— He's not dead. Well, they don't know if he's dead. The boat he was taking to meet you has disappeared."

"Disappeared? How is it possible for an entire boat to disappear?" She rushed over to him, peering at the screen. "I mean, they knew if even a single one of us stepped ten feet out of our designated zone."

"It shouldn't *be* possible. It's not even like he's out in the middle of the ocean. He was just going from the mainland to Bowglass. People do it in sailboats, for god's sake. They said there was some kind of freak storm. It lasted less than twenty minutes, and he was gone." He shoved his fingers through his hair. "It's not possible," he repeated.

She straightened, her voice calm. "James, we've got to go." She turned away and yanked open her dresser drawers.

James stared up at her, uncomprehending. "Go where? The authorities have dispatched search crews."

"*Human* crews. James, up until five months ago, that part of the ocean was my home. If Joseph's there, I'll be able to find him." She twirled her finger at him. "Turn around."

He obeyed.

A few moments later, Pine dressed, they thundered down the stairs.

"Pine, this is—" What did she think she was going to do?

"I don't care. We just have to get down there and see what's going on."

That much he could agree with. Maybe there would be more news by the time they arrived.

They were at the door when Pine spun around and ran back to the living room and up to Mara's portrait.

"We'll be back soon," she promised it.

Mara smiled up her then returned to her work, her hands deftly manipulating the tiny tools.

FIFTEEN

They arrived at the harbor shortly before dark. At this time of night, the dock would've normally been quiet, but tonight, it teemed with activity. Boats were being moored in rapid succession, their captains rushing to secure their vessels. Massive spotlights illuminated the dock, so bright James had to shield his eyes.

What was going on? Was this all for Joseph? Somehow, he doubted it. "Is this normal?"

"No." She bit her lip. "They only do this when there's a large storm approaching. They're trying to make sure the boats are all safe."

So not for Joseph, then. James's stomach twisted. Would they call off the search? A man in fluorescent-lit gear approached them. "If you're looking to get out to one of the islands, I'm afraid you're out of luck."

"What going on?" James flipped up his collar against the cutting salt wind. "Is a storm coming?"

"A hell of a big one, unless I was born yesterday." He squinted at James. "And I wasn't."

"What about the search and rescue? For Joseph Polendina's missing boat?" James tried to keep his voice steady.

142

"Oh, there'll be no searching tonight, my boy. We'd just be sending them out one after the other." He scratched his chin with a grimy thumb. "That was an odd one, all right. Storm was over before it started... Guess it was just a prelude to this monster, though."

James was at a loss. What would they do now?

"But he's my *father*." To James's surprise, Pine pushed past him and grabbed the front of the man's jacket.

He stared down at her impassively, her clutching fingers doing nothing to move him. "Oh? Well, I'm sorry, my dear, but we can't risk many lives for one. If your father hunkers down in his life-pod, he's bound to ride the storm out. If he's lucky, he'll wash up on one of the islands. The coast is riddled with 'em, you know."

"But if he's safe in his pod, why won't the rescue crews be?" Pine demanded.

James was impressed. Gone were her reservations, her uncertainty of her place. Synadroid or not, she was a daughter wanting her father to be safe. What had changed over those four months to give her such confidence?

"It's not the *storm* that's the problem for the rescue crews, see? But what the storm *brings*." The man shivered. "You wouldn't catch me out there, no sir." He gently pried Pine's fingers from his coat. "Now, miss, best to go home and wait. Harbormaster Paloma won't be letting anyone out of the dock tonight."

"Paloma?" Pine's eyes shone with sudden interest.

But the man was already out of earshot.

"Pine, what does he mean, what the storm brings?" James didn't like the sound of that. He'd always been uncomfortable being too close to the ocean. As a child, he'd imagined the jaws of some great beast lurking just below the surface, waiting to gobble him up.

Pine pressed her lips together. Even though she could now lie, a lifetime of truth-telling had left its mark.

"*Pine?*" She was obviously keeping something from him. Something important.

She scrunched up her face as though she could stop the truth from escaping. "When a storm this large happens...there are things that live in the ocean. Big things. It attracts them."

Oh my god. His darkest nightmares were about to come true. It was as though he was already out in a boat, the world shifting and rolling beneath his feet. "What kind of *things?*"

Pine gazed out over the water. "Creatures. I don't really know for sure. I've only ever seen...shadows, shapes bigger than freighters moving through the water."

James shuddered. The horror he'd seen at the Perimeter paled in comparison to the unknown of his childhood fears.

"It's odd, though," Pine continued calmly, as though enormous sea monsters were a normal thing—which, for her, they might've been. "I think it's the other way around, that the creatures, whatever they are, *bring* the storms with *them.*"

This was getting better and better. Storm-*bringing* sea monsters. He swore. "That's going to make our rescue mission impossible, isn't it?" *Damnit, Joseph. Where are you?* He looked out over the dark water beyond the undulating boats. Even from this distance, the inky water filled him with foreboding. "I think we're going to have to go home and wait, like that gentleman said."

"It'll make it more difficult, but not impossible." Pine smoothed her hair back from her face.

"What do you mean? We can't go out there if—" Dread filled James. He was *not* going to like whatever she had planned.

But she was already gone, striding with confidence toward the harbormaster's office. A woman, presumably Paloma, stood on the other side of the glass walls, barking orders as she delegated duties down the ranks.

James jogged after Pine, trying to catch her before she went in. He was too late.

He cracked his knuckles as Pine walked straight up the harbormaster, her back to James. The master herself was a tall woman, her swarthy complexion well-suited to her profession. Her features were heavily creased, her brows mirroring the gathering storm outside. A long gray braid lay over one shoulder, and James winced when she flicked it back, nearly taking out the eye of the sailor next to her.

She towered over Pine with a stern expression that made James's heart quail.

Well, at least until she swept Pine up in a crushing embrace. Pine spoke, turning her head and gesturing out to the roughening sea.

What was she doing? She wasn't actually trying to convince her to let them go out in the storm, was she?

Of course she is.
The harbormaster crossed her arms over her chest and shook her head. Thank goodness—no one could leave the harbor without her permission, and Pine couldn't risk being arrested again for the infinitesimal chance that they might find Joseph.

The old man wouldn't have wanted that, and neither did James.

Pine hung her head and turned around, pushing her way back through the crowd gathering to vie for the harbormaster's attention. Out on the dock, a fine rain was falling.

"I'm sorry, Pine." He put his arm around her and guided her back toward the parking lot. "Look, we don't have to go home. There a hotel right next to the docks." It wasn't much, but at least it was something. He typed a few instructions into his transcomm as he spoke. "I can book us a room, and we can stay as long as we need to, until the storm clears. Then we can help look—"

He stared at a small code stick dangling from a chain between Pine's fingers. *Oh no.* "Pine, what is that?"

She flashed him a wicked grin. "The code for Paloma's personal cruiser."

"A *cruiser?* But—" He didn't know much about boats, but he was pretty sure a cruiser wasn't the type you wanted to take out into the middle of a squall.

"She can't *let* us go out in the storm, but she *can* look the other way. Come on." Pine led him down a flight of stairs leading off the central pier. "Just act like we're supposed to be here."

"How did you—" He'd been impressed by her new confidence at first, but this, this was alarming.

"I'll tell you when we're out on the water. But don't worry, it's not illegal—Paloma's a friend."

"Look at you, four months inside and you've got connections." James had hoped the joke would ease some of his anxiety. *No such luck.*

"I did meet some interesting people. I was going to tell you all about it, but then— Joseph." The beginnings of her smile fell.

"Pine, this is insane. Even if you technically have the harbormaster's permission—which you know damn well she'll deny if we get caught—we still shouldn't be going out into this storm." He grasped her hands as she frowned. "We don't know how to find Joseph. If they can't find him, why would we be able to? Plus, what about those...creatures?"

"James, he wouldn't be out there now if it wasn't for me—" She pressed her fingers to his mouth. "Before you say it, I don't feel *guilty*. That's not what I mean. I did a lot of thinking when I was away. Joseph is my family now. He's out there in that storm looking for me. Now I'm going to look for him."

"But, Pine, he wouldn't *want* you to. He'd want you to be safe. Besides, Pine," *I feel like such a coward for saying this,* "I'm *not* a synadroid. If we capsize, *you* can survive underwater. *I* can't."

Pine's driven expression fell. "I hadn't thought of that. You're right—it *is* too dangerous for you. Those storms—"

"Will be over soon, and we'll be right here, ready to start searching for Joseph." He stroked his hand over her hair, relieved. He would be useless to her in the water, would probably even put them in danger. Here on land, at least, they could take care of each other. "Let's go get that room."

"James...I'm still going. Like you said, *I* can survive underwater. You get the room and wait for the storm to pass. With any luck, I'll be back with Joseph before then."

"No way, Pine. You can't go out there on your own. What if—" *No, she can't by herself. It's too dangerous.* But the determination in her eyes told him anything he said was useless. Pine was going, no matter what.

Visions swam before his eyes of massive shapes gliding silently through the water, above and under him, their jaws— "I'm coming with you." As terrifying as those images might be, the thought of Pine out there alone was worse.

She drew back. "No, James, you were right before. You can't survive under the water like I can. If something were to happen to you... I can't lose both you and Joseph."

James pulled her close. "I couldn't do it, Pine. Wait in a hotel room knowing that you and Joseph were out there in the storm somewhere." His mind was made up. "I'm coming. There'll be protective gear on the harbormaster's boat. After all, she's human too."

Pine stared up at him as though trying to divine his motives. "Are you sure? I'll do everything I can to help keep you safe, but I can't promise you that. I've never had to save anyone before."

"Well, today's as good a day as any." James tried to smile. "Looks like we're going fishing." *Maybe I'll catch some courage.*

The harbormaster's cruiser was sleek, top-of-the-line. James took in the dashboard controls with dismay. "Um, Pine? Do you have any idea how to drive this thing? Because I don't." James's time in the military had kept him firmly inland. Sure, he'd been *on* a boat more than once, but he'd never been in control of one.

Pine nodded as she leaned over, checking a few of the gauges before engaging the engine. "It's not nearly as complicated as it looks. The boat does most of the work." She leaned back, satisfied, as the vessel slowly pulled away from its mooring. "We'll have to keep our power to a minimum, but hopefully the storm has picked up enough to cover us." She stared hard at the dashboard again, her tongue pressed against her bottom lip.

It was too late to turn back. *We're doing this.* But at least they were together. *That* was the most important thing. If James was going to be swallowed by a sea monster, there was no one he would rather do it with.

The storm was gathering force now, rough wind whipping the heavy drops of rain across the boat's windows. Darkness shrouded the sky, and the cruiser plunged into blackness as soon as they cleared the harbor. In the distance, the faint beam of the lighthouse glowed on the Point and James breathed a sigh of relief. As long as they could still see the land, he was— The lighthouse disappeared, swallowed by the gloom.

James took a deep breath.

They traveled in tense silence, Pine navigating manually away from the shoreline. Outside, the storm lashed the boat, attacking then withdrawing into eerie quiet before assaulting them again.

Just as James couldn't bear the unnerving rhythm any longer, Pine stepped back and flooded the cabin with light. She turned to smile at him. "There, I think we're far enough— James? Are you all right?" She grabbed his arm and steered him toward the captain's chair. "Here, sit down."

James sank into the seat, his muscles crying out in relief. Nausea roiled inside him, and he leaned forward, dropping his head between his knees. "Now what?"

"I've set the radar to scan for Joseph's pod. If we get within fifteen miles of him, we'll know."

"It's sounds a bit like searching for the old needle in a haystack to me." It can out harsher than he'd intended.

"I know." Pine's shoulders slumped. "But at least we're doing something." She wandered over to a closet tucked in the back and retrieved a strange-looking apparatus. After checking it over, she handed it to James. "Here. Put this around your neck. If something starts to go wrong, press it up to your face. It'll filter oxygen out of the water for you."

Skeptical, James held up the device and peered at it. "Really? It's so...small." James had been expecting some kind of suit and helmet. Something more substantial between him and...whatever was out there.

"Really. It's not good for any long-term use, but if something happens, it'll give you enough air for me to get you to safety. It's mostly a last resort. If we get tossed around too much, we can always get into the life-pod."

She'd lived in the ocean for much of her life, but still, how could she be so relaxed? They were going out into a storm in little more than a glorified canoe. James shook his head. When he'd gotten up that morning, he'd been filled with anticipation. *Thank god I didn't see this coming.*

But *she'd* trusted *him* when he'd asked, though she'd had every reason not to. "Okay, I trust you." James looped the device over his head and settled it snugly against his throat. The boat lurched to the left, and James clutched the sides of his chair. "So, you seem pretty comfortable in the harbormaster's ship," he said, trying to distract himself from the maelstrom in his stomach.

"I had to report to Paloma when I first got here. For whatever reason, she took a liking to me. Sometimes she would request that, instead of farming, I came back to the port and did my time with her." Pine took the seat opposite James and spun it idly.

"You mean you were *here* for part of your sentence?" *I can't believe she was barely a few miles away.* He'd imagined her on a far-off island, toiling away in misery.

"Yes. But I was under strict instructions to stay away from the shore. I mean, I *was* technically imprisoned."

So this Paloma would turn a blind eye to Pine breaking harbor law, but not to a secret quick hello to the people who were virtually her family?

Tiny minnows of doubt darted around James's heart. She'd seemed so glad to be home. to be with Joseph. To be with *him*. She'd nearly kissed him, hadn't she? In that moment, he'd thought...it had seemed like the start of something. Could he have got it wrong?

Stop it. You're just disconcerted by this damned ocean. Why would Pine risk her life for Joseph if she didn't love him? He leaned back, trying to be satisfied with this proof. And he was. Almost. But the nagging voice wouldn't stay silent.

She isn't risking anything, though, is she? If the boat went down, she'd be fine. It would be James who'd—

The minnows bit.

She hadn't even considered his safety until he'd mentioned it. Then she was perfectly happy to go on her own. He reached up to touch the device at his throat. It could be anything, something to suction barnacles off the side of the boat for all he knew. He glanced up at her.

Pine caught his eye and smiled. "Are you feeling a bit better?"

His misgivings eased. He was just being stupid. Pine was who he thought she was. "I guess synadroids don't get seasick either."

"No. But we didn't spend much time on top of the water. We worked much closer to the bottom."

"It was a huge relief for Foxwept when your kind was brought into the Ghostlight Rehabitation Project." James stood and walked over to the cabin window on unsteady legs.

"Yes. We were so much more efficient because we didn't need to rest for more than a few hours and didn't need special equipment to breathe. I think we ended up saving them millions of dollars."

"Not to mentioned thousands of lives."

"What do you mean?"

"Oh, I just remember the news reports from before the synadroids joined the Project. They used to lose so many workers to accidents. Before they were replaced with synadroids, people were being crushed, swept out to the deep ocean, killed by the marine life. The deaths nearly stopped once the synadroids were employed."

"The *human* deaths stopped, James." Pine's voice was soft even in the relative quiet of the cabin. "But those accidents still happened. More, even, because the people running the project didn't have to take as much care when it wasn't humans."

Distracted, he missed the warning in her tone. "Well, yeah, but I mean, that was the point, right? Why synadroids were created in the first place?" James said it carelessly because it *was* the truth, not his opinion, but the moment he saw Pine's face, he wished he could take it back. "Pine— I'm sorry. I didn't mean it like that."

She bent over the dash and fiddled with the dials. "I know. It's fine."

But her brusqueness told James it was anything *but* fine. "I'm sorry." How could he still be so thoughtless after everything she'd told him? He must be more affected by the water than he'd thought.

Just stop talking, James, and you'll be fine.

She twisted around. "What you said was true. It just hurts—"

Something slammed into the side of the cruiser, sending shockwaves through the cabin. James and Pine staggered against each other, trying to find purchase on the heaving floor.

"Pine? What's happen—" His stomach tried to claw its way up his throat.

"I don't know! There's nothing on the radar." James hadn't been afraid until he heard her panic, sharp and crystalline. Pine was scared. And if *Pine* was scared—

The boat turned inside out. James grabbed the gadget around his neck and crushed it to his face, inhaling deeply. Nothing. *No.* He tried again but tasted only the salt of the water as it engulfed him.

SIXTEEN

What happened next was a blur, even to Pine's synadroid mind. The boat rose out of the water, hurtling upward into the darkness of the open sky. It rolled violently then plummeted downward with sickening force, breaking through the surface of the water with a bone-jarring smack.

Thick, dark seawater poured in through the smashed windows, filling the cabin. Pine could no longer tell which way was up, or if she was even still inside the boat.

James! Where was James? She groped about her in the dark, desperately wishing for a light.

Pine, stop. Calm down. You have a light. You are the light.

She stopped thrashing about, and instead tore at her clothes, stripping them off as quickly as she could. Naked, she spread her arms wide and tilted her head back.

Better.

Indigo light glowed from every inch of Pine's skin, illuminating the shapes in the murk around her. Gradually, things came into focus—the pale hull of the boat, descending leisurely into the shadows, and another form, limp, sinking more slowly.

James.

She kicked toward him, catching him just as his feet entered the darker water. His face was pallid, his eyes closed. He hadn't been able to get the breather on in time; it covered only half his mouth—useless.

James!

Anguish screamed inside her head. She shook him, checking for signs of life, but no bubbles escaped his nose or mouth, and his eyes stayed shut. She jammed the breather against his mouth and secured it. Then she pinched him, trying to startle him into taking a breath, but his lungs were stubborn.

No. This was all her fault. But she could still save him. She had to.

Thanks to her light, their path to the surface was clear. Hooking James under the arms, she kicked hard.

And went nowhere.

She let out a string of expletives she'd learned from Paloma. Pine hadn't been designed to haul heavy things through the water—her model tended toward litheness and flexibility instead. If she was going to save him, she would have to do it with sheer will.

Focus.

She rearranged her grip on James, and as she pressed her arm over his chest, felt it—the faint beating of his heart; he was still alive.

James, alive. James, alive. She chanted the mantra louder and louder in her head until it reached a crescendo that obliterated everything else.

James, alive. James, alive.

She redoubled her efforts, straining against the pull of the looming darkness below.

James, alive. James, alive.

They moved, slowly at first, then faster, as though they'd been released from quicksand. The higher they rose, the faster Pine was able to go, her synadroid legs working relentlessly. She said a silent prayer of thanks to Mara for her endurance.

James, alive. James, alive. James, alive. James, alive.

They were now only a hundred feet from the surface. James's chest moved under her arms. Giddiness almost threw off her rhythm. *We're going to make it. I can still save him.*

A dark form brushed against them, scraping Pine's skin with its own.

No. no.

The form circled back, and the light of her body revealed its mottled white and brown hide, the deep gouges marring its dorsal fin. Its nostrils flared as it scented James and exposed the jagged spikes of its notched teeth.

It's fine. It's just curious. It's not like James is bleeding.

Except he was. Now that they were swimming in clear water, the lacerations on his arms and one bootless foot were obvious. If Pine could've breathed, she'd have taken a deep one.

Maybe it would leave them alone. If not, she knew what to do.

The shark circled them, wary of Pine's radiant skin, yet attracted by the diffusing blood. Emboldened by Pine's meekness, it bumped them gently with its snout.

Don't react, just keep swimming. You're almost at the surface.

Then James opened his eyes. He saw the massive shark and struggled, pushing back against Pine and kicking his legs—exactly what she hadn't wanted him to do.

Pine squeezed him, trying to get his attention before the shark attacked.

She was too late.

It swam away, out of Pine's glow, then circled back, picking up speed. She knew this species well. They weren't common here, but one or two always seemed to be testing out new hunting grounds, hungry for novel prey. They attacked swiftly and repeatedly, wearing their victims down with successive bites.

You're not going to get even a single nibble here.

Pine let go of James and swam in front of him. His eyes widened when he saw her, naked and glowing, toe-to-toe with a colossal predator. If he hadn't already regretted coming with her, he probably did now.

But there was no time to feel self-conscious. Pine couldn't yet see the shark, but it *was* coming back, and when it did, it would hit them with the force of a speedboat—a speedboat with teeth.

Well, let it try.

Pine swam as far away from James as she dared while keeping herself between him and the deadly creature. She held her arms out in front of her, her palms raised toward the oncoming attack. The shark burst into the circle of her light, and Pine counted in her head. The timing had to be just right.

Three. Two. One—

An inky substance leaked from Pine's palms, wreathing her in a black fog. The shark roared toward her, its jaws wide.

Steady.

What if it didn't work? After all, she'd never used it before. It was a one-shot chance, a last act of desperation.

No, it'll work. It has to. It—

The shark passed into the dark cloud surrounding Pine, and she closed her eyes, bracing for the impact.

It never came.

Pine opened her eyes. The shark floated before her, belly up, murderous rage in its glittering black eyes. But for the moment, it was at her mercy.

She knew just how it felt.

Pine turned and swam back toward James. They had some time, but the nerve gas wouldn't last forever. They had to get up to the surface, *now.* James stared at her as she engulfed him in her radiance. He seemed stunned. Had he struck his head when the boat went down? If he had, she couldn't worry about it now.

She pointed upward. At first, he seemed confused, but then he nodded and swam, propelling himself toward the surface. She followed beneath him, keeping watch on the shark as it sank slowly out of sight.

The closer they got to the surface, the more turbulent the water became.

The storm must still be raging. *Damn.* Pine didn't know what they were going to do when they got to the surface. She had no idea where they were—

Cold slapped her face as they broke through into the air at last. Though heavy rain stippled the waves, the clouds had opened enough in places for the moon to shine its light on the water. At the top of a swell, Pine cast around her, looking for some sign of land.

There. It was little more than a shadow, but it beckoned to her like a beacon. If they could reach it, they could find somewhere to ride out the storm.

"James! There. I think there's land—" Her words were drowned out as the downpour picked up again.

James swam toward her, reaching her as another larger swell lifted them.

As they clutched each other, Pine put her mouth as close to his ear as possible. "James, I think—"

This time, her words were torn from her by a behemoth of a wave, a wave that was wholly unnatural.

It curled around them and the world ceased to exist.

SEVENTEEN

James had been hit by a train. Or at least, that was what it felt like. Every single inch of his body shrieked in agony as he rolled over onto his back and opened his eyes.

Where the hell am I? What happened?

The sun shone down on him, warming his skin; the storm was over. The ground under his bare arms was damp and gritty, and laced with something cold and oddly fleshy. Creeped out, James tried to sit up, but he was barely able to lift his head off the ground and even that small movement caused the world to spin.

The boat. The boat had sunk. He'd been drowning and then…darkness. Then Pine must've fixed his mask and…

Pine.

She'd been naked and glowing with an ethereal purple-blue radiance. Even her eyes were alight, blazing golden in the dark. It was strangely beautiful and utterly alarming.

And there'd been a shark. It had attacked them. She'd done something to it, paralyzed it.

James shuddered as he remembered the strange black haze seeping from her palms. Whatever it was, it had knocked out the biggest shark he'd ever

160

seen.

And then they were swimming toward the surface, and...and now he was here.

But where was Pine?

James gritted his teeth and pushed himself onto his elbows, his back screaming in agony. Even turning his head was torture. He lay on a yellow-sanded beach, the fleshy mass under him a dark green, podded seaweed. He craned his neck, searching for any sign of her. Behind him, a few hundred feet up the beach, was a densely packed tree line. The sand stretched for a mile on either side of James, but he could see the curve of the shoreline even from where he was.

An island. He was on an island.

Great. There were only about six hundred off the coast of Foxwept.

Where the hell was Pine? She wouldn't have left him, would she? He didn't think so, but—

A figure rose from the now-calm water of the ocean, and Pine emerged.

Naked.

So that *had* been real. He swallowed, hard.

His eyes were drawn to the delicate slope of her shoulders then down to her small, perfectly rounded breasts, down over the gentle curve of her waist and hip, the smooth strength of her abdomen...

She was no longer glowing. Had James only imagined that part? Maybe he *had* hit his head—it *was* pounding, and there was a tender spot just behind his ear.

She sloshed toward him, the water churning around her and ropes of seaweed hanging from her hands. Once on land, she placed the tangled vegetation carefully on the ground and knelt next to him.

Pulse racing, he forced his gaze down to the sand.

"James? Are you okay?" Her tone was concerned, but there was something else. A reservation that echoed her first weeks in Portfade.

"No. But I will be." He groaned and forced himself to sit up. "You?"

"I'm fine." She sat back on her heels.

"Uh, Pine? You're...naked. And normally I wouldn't complain—" Normally, he most certainly would *not* complain. "But there might be other people on this island."

She pressed her lips together, but not before he caught her smile. "Really? This beach seems pretty empty."

"But—" He gave up as she snorted. "*Fine.* It's distracting. Very distracting. And painful." How could he be in such agony and still be aroused? "*Please.* Take my shirt."

He began to peel off the still-damp piece of clothing. Halfway off, it got stuck. Pine snickered as he twisted around, trying to free his head. "A little help?"

As she pulled the rest of the shirt free, the warm air caressed James and eased some of the tension in his shoulders. "Oh wow. That actually feels better."

"Looks better too," Pine said, giving him a mischievous grin. Her gaze lingered on him, wandering over his bare skin and warming him more than the sun.

Maybe they would get lucky, and this island would be uninhabited after all. *Seriously, James?*

Pine stretched the damp shirt over her head and tugged down the hem. "How's this?"

It wasn't demure by a long shot, but at least it covered all the basics. Except where the damp fabric clung to her, of course. *Damn it, Pine.* But it would have to do. He tore his gaze away from her and looked out to sea. "What the hell happened?"

"We capsized then we were attacked—"

"No, I remember all that. I mean, what happened with you? Did I— I mean, was what I saw real? Were you...glowing?"

Pine scrunched up her nose. "Yes. That's why I took my clothes off." She gestured to her bare legs. "Once we got recommissioned to aquaculture, they imbued our skin with a bioluminescence. It made us easier to keep track of while we were working in the deeper water."

Okay, that James could accept. It made sense. But the other stuff? The dark substance that had come from her hands? "What did you do to that shark?"

"It's a nerve toxin. It didn't kill it, just paralyzed it for a time." She began peeling the outer skin off the seaweed.

"They *armed* you?" James was incredulous. She *had* saved his life, but— "You're carrying around a *nerve toxin?*"

At first, she gaped at him then her coral eyes narrowed. "How do you think we defended ourselves, James? Do you think that shark is the only dangerous creature in the ocean? Or do you believe we should be defenseless?"

James shook his head, confused. "No, it's just that—" A *nerve* toxin, for goodness' sake. She was virtually a walking weapon. As if her other abilities weren't enough. His old paranoia sank its teeth into him again. "And they didn't strip it off you when you were...sold?"

She glanced down at the palm of her hand. "They left it in because it's very specific. It can only be released if the sensors in my skin detect certain electrical signals—like sharks. Plus, it only works in water, and we only get one dose at a time." She turned her hand over. "Why does it bother you so much?" Her brows drew together; she probably knew where this was going. "What? Did you think we might use it against humans?" She glared at him. "That's what you were thinking, wasn't it?"

He hesitated a fraction too long. "No." But it was *exactly* what he'd meant.

She picked up the seaweed she'd harvested and threw it down next to him. "Here. I thought you'd be hungry." When he didn't move, she stood up. "Don't worry, it's not going to kill you." She started to walk along the surf.

"Pine! Come back." He struggled to his knees. "I'm sorry. I didn't mean that. I'm just shaken, that's all. What happened— Pine, I've never even been *in* the ocean before. And then—" James fell over, hitting the sand with a teeth-rattling thud.

"James!" Pine sprinted back. "Are you okay?" She put her hand to his forehead.

He groaned and rolled over. "Everything hurts."

She sighed. "I think there might be a town beyond the trees." She cocked her head. "At least, it *sounds* like there might be." She gazed down at him. "I can help you walk there—if you don't think I'll poison you, that is."

James nodded, too miserable to argue. With Pine's help, he staggered to his feet.

As she positioned herself under his shoulder, his arm across her chest, she peered up at him, concerned. "We're going to draw attention looking like this."

"Maybe this happens all the time and we'll fit right in." He paused. "Do you have any idea where we are?" Now that he was a bit more awake, there was something familiar about the island.

"No." Pine turned to peer back out over the ocean. Several other islands dotted the horizon. "But I don't think it was an accident."

"I don't like the sound of that." Then it occurred to him. "But hey, if we ended up here, maybe Joseph did too." It was a long shot, but they'd been tossed here during a storm, right? And if that wave wasn't natural… Eagerness to get to the town buoyed him. Joseph could be sitting there right now, drinking a cocktail in the sun.

Pine hung back as he began hobbling toward the tree line. "James? Maybe you should go to the town by yourself. I'll wait here." She started to lift the shirt back over her head.

"What? No way, Pine. We need to stick together." Why had she gotten cold feet? Was she afraid of the town? Or was it something else?

Pine hesitated then, resigned, pulled the shirt back down. She didn't look happy. "Do you need me to help you walk?"

James took a few more steps, testing his weight. His legs were shaky, but they would hold. Adrenalin and anticipation would carry him, at least to the nearest bar. "No, I think I'm all right actually." With every passing minute, the pain eased from his muscles, leaving behind a bearable stiffness. "But as soon as we hit the town, we should find a café or somewhere and sit down, get our bearings." He groaned again as a fragment of shell pierced his bare foot. "And maybe a shot of whiskey. Or two."

EIGHTEEN

At the edge of the clearing, Pine faltered. She *really* did not want to go into the town. She couldn't put her finger on exactly why, but something about the bustling, too-shiny hub filled her with dread.

James looked questioningly at her as she dragged at his hand. "Pine? Are you okay?"

How could she tell him that they shouldn't go in there? What other choice did they have? And if there was even the slightest chance that Joseph might be there... "Yes. It's just...it's a lot of people."

The town was small, but it was full of people, hurrying back and forth between vendors, haggling over prices in loud voices or slinking off to dark corners to peer under the lid of a reinforced case. It was a strange mix of high-tech and rustic living, with most of the stalls and residences beyond made from wood and thatch, while the items that were showcased and the people dealing in them would've been right at home in the most ultramodern epicenters in the Blackmoth.

But what alarmed Pine more than the swarm of activity was the synadroids. Though there weren't nearly as many as there were humans, there were more than she'd ever seen in one place outside the

166

aquaculture farm. And it wasn't just the number of them that was so staggering.

Some were missing limbs, hobbling on crutches or squatting on the fringes of the stalls. Their eyes looked strange to Pine—lifeless and dull, like the eyes of synadroids before they were carted off, never to be seen again. Others had been made to look less human, their difference emphasized by colorful hairstyles and exotic clothing. Some wore colored-coded collars around their necks, their eyes downcast as they ferried items back and forth or followed closely on a human's heels. Still more disappeared behind sliding woven doors, a lasciviously grinning human at their backs.

It was everything the synadroids had whispered about in the dark when the humans had left for the day. Rumors and tales that she'd feared but not truly believed. Yet here it was, as true and tangible as the tattoo engraved into her wrist.

She turned to James, expecting him to be as distressed as she was. To her chagrin, he didn't even seem to notice. Instead, he was shading his eyes with his hand, scanning the busy marketplace.

"I see a café with tables, just over there." He pointed. "Come on, let's go grab a seat and come up with a plan."

They slid into a booth. James perused the menu then typed an order into the terminal. "I'll have to credit it to my account—that shark didn't get me, but I think he got my comms."

"What is this place?" Why hadn't she heard of an island of broken synadroids before? Was it common knowledge? Was it something James and Joseph had intentionally neglected to tell her?

"It's called Deserter's Island. I've been here a few times, but I didn't recognize it from the other side—

I've always come in the front door." He inspected the bottom of his foot. "Which is much more hospitable than the way we came in, even if I *was* blindfolded."

"*Blindfolded?*"

"Yeah. This island is kind of…secret. A lot of the goods sold here are illegal or experimental, or even political. Visitors like myself are escorted in and out. I can't imagine they'd be too happy to find out we'd just wandered in from the ocean."

"They wouldn't be, and you didn't." A woman stood before them, blocking the sun and forcing them to squint. "You didn't actually think that wave was a coincidence, did you?" Dressed in lightweight coveralls the midnight green of the ocean that had nearly claimed them, she was peculiarly familiar to Pine, although she couldn't quite remember ever meeting the curvy young woman with azure eyes and hair the rich green of the aurora borealis.

Azure eyes.

"Blue?"

The young woman winked. "Is it so obvious? Damn." She slid into the seat next to Pine. "I'll be asking Crow for a refund."

"We saw your headstone." Guilt gnawed at Pine again; it was her fault Blue had had to leave.

"I'm glad you got the message. I wasn't sure you would." She jabbed a thumb at James. "This one's not always the best with cryptic messages."

James let out a humorless laugh. "We didn't actually *get* the message. We didn't have time. Pine here got out of prison this morning. Or was it yesterday now?"

He relayed the last twenty-four hours to Blue, stopping only to gulp from the drink deposited on the table by a human waitress. Pine fidgeted when he got to the part about her glowing and fending off the shark. He told it now with her in the hero's role, a stark contrast to the way he'd looked at her on the beach. Blue laughed with delight, slapping Pine on the back.

But when James was done with their tale, Blue's face again grew serious and she slumped back in her chair. "I can't believe it…Joseph, gone, just like that."

"He's not dead," Pine insisted. "Only missing." And she was going to bring him back.

"I'm sure he is," Blue reassured her. "He's tough as old boots. Look, I'll help you. If Joseph is out there, we'll find him."

"Thank you," Pine said. Her relief was almost painful. "But…after what happened at the cemetery…did you have to leave because of us?"

"Yes and no. I mean, that trash Todd and Tabby nearly led the police right to my door, but it was time to move on anyway."

"I did tell her that," James interjected.

Blue gave Pine a wistful smile. "I did love that old mausoleum, though. And being right under the law's nose like that gave me a certain joy."

"And after that, you still want to help us?" Pine couldn't help but ask, although she dreaded the answer. If Blue said no, Pine wasn't going to give up, but she suspected the mysterious young woman had more than a few helpful tricks up her dark green sleeves.

"Of course. Joseph has always been a good friend and mentor to me. And I'm also doing it for you, Pine. I have a feeling we're going to be seeing a lot of each other, and I'm looking forward to it."

James looked as surprised by her admission as

Pine herself was. "You are?"

"Yes. Now, James, if you come with me, I think there's a woman who might have some information about what happened to Joseph."

They looked at each other, Pine certain James's troubled face mirrored her own.

This time, he spoke first. "Are you sure that's a good idea? I mean—" He glanced around, discomposed, as though seeing the island anew.

Finally, he was detecting how wrong this island was.

"So you *have* noticed what seems to be happening with the synadroids here? Or is it only a problem now *your* synadroid might be involved?"

James reddened at her cutting tone. "No, I— I'm sorry, Pine. It's just that I've been here several times before, and I'd—"

"Gotten used to it?"

"No! I just..." He lowered his voice. "This is not a good place, Pine. It's a means to an end. And what happens with the synadroids on this island is not *right*. But it is *legal*. Probably the most legal thing on the whole damn island." He gave her a hard look, his face serious. "And you need to remember that while we're here. Don't look. Don't make a fuss."

So she should just stand by and keep her mouth shut? *I thought James's opinion of synadroids had changed, but they haven't.* Only about *her*. The hope she'd held onto about James, about Joseph, deflated, leaving her hollow.

"He's right, Pine. You're under my protection while you're here, but I, too, am a guest—my protection extends only so far. This disgusting place," she gestured broadly at the marketplace, "is a problem we *can* do something about eventually.

But not *now*."

That Pine could accept, though it stung. "Why are they even here, those synadroids?"

Blue's mouth twisted. "You know when synadroids get damaged, or malfunction, or become obsolete? What did you think happened to them?"

"I thought...I thought they were fixed, or retired, if they were too badly damaged." Because that was what she'd been told, and it had never occurred to her it was a lie. *Naïve idiot.* Clearly, she still had a lot to learn.

"I'm afraid that's not quite true. If the repairs are minor, then yes, patch 'em up and get 'em back out. But if repairs are more expensive than that synadroid's worth...well, they get what they can for them, if it's more than they'd get for their scrap."

"So their bodies are worth more than their actual lives?" Why was she surprised? Just when she'd thought human attitudes toward synadroids couldn't get more callous, they proved her wrong.

"Unfortunately, yes. For now, anyway."

Pine's first instinct was to let them see her anger, to let them all see it, penalties be damned. She was fed up with the casualness of it all, the inconsequence. To the two people seated with her, she was *not* inconsequential. Yet how could they accept the treatment of these synadroids but somehow think she was special?

James and Blue took her silence for assent and moved on with the conversation. "Right, so *will* Pine be safe here on her own?"

"Oh hell, no," The Blue Fairy scoffed. "But I'm renting a bungalow down the road. She can wait there." She beckoned for Pine and James to follow her and they set off through the southern part of the market.

"That's perfect. Right, Pine?" James tried to grasp her hand as they passed out of the market district and into a more residential quarter.

She snatched her hand away. "Do I have a choice?"

"I agree it's not ideal. But taking you with us would be more dangerous than leaving you behind." Blue led them up the path to a bungalow whose plain wood-and-thatch exterior copied all the others.

"Why? Afraid someone will make an offer on me you couldn't refuse?"

Blue let the red line of a bioscanner slide down and back up her face then turned to give Pine a grim smile. "They wouldn't even make me an offer. We go only with what we're willing to give."

Blue's living space was spartan, the walls the pale gold of the beach sand, the floor the same tawny sanded wood as the house itself. There was nothing other than a desk littered with junk and rigged out with top-of-the-line computing tech that indicated her presence here; no pictures, no knick-knacks, not a single personal touch.

"It does the job," Blue said, noting Pine's surprise. "I never was much for sentimentality." She disappeared into an adjoining room and returned with some folded clothes in her arms. She handed them to Pine. "Here. You don't want to be walking around here like *that* for too long." She glanced at James. "And this one needs a shirt where we're going."

James and Blue turned around while Pine shimmied into the t-shirt and cargo pants. They were made from a fabric so fine and soft she couldn't help lifting a corner of the shirt to rub against her face. "They're lovely, thank you." She tossed the shirt over to James. "Here. It's pretty much dry now."

He looked faintly disappointed as he took in her new clothes and slipped his shirt over his head. "We'll be back soon, Pine." Like that was supposed to make her feel better.

A few minutes later, she watched out the small round window as James and Blue walked away.

Pine wished desperately for something to distract her, but there was nothing. Nothing to do but think about what she'd been avoiding.

James.

While away, she'd spent a disconcerting amount of time thinking of him. When he'd asked her if she was happy to be home, she'd been able to answer yes truthfully. What she hadn't added was that he was part of that, more than he would ever know.

In truth, she *wanted* him. But how could she have feelings for someone who was still clearly uneasy with what she was? Was it just because he'd rescued her? Because he was finally throwing her some crumbs of kindness? Or was it *him*?

Every day she was at the docks, knowing he and Joseph were only a few miles away, had been torture, forcing her to think about him, and her future. If someone had told her when she'd first arrived at Joseph's that she would grieve for it in a matter of weeks, she'd have suspected it was an issue with her programming. But when she'd seen them in those rare early mornings when they came to meet the docking supply boats, it had taken everything in her power to conceal herself, trying to guess from James's body language how he felt about her absence.

If the tiredness of his pale eyes and the set of his mouth was any indication, he was *not* glad she was gone. Delight buoyed her at first, but then, as she relived their last few days together over and over—James standing over her in the marketplace, smiling into her hand as Blue put her back together—time slowed to a crawl, and the end of her sentence seemed painfully far away.

It was made so much worse by the fact that she *could* have seen them. Paloma had offered once or twice to arrange a clandestine meeting, but Pine had refused, worried it was somehow a trap, that Paloma was testing her. She just couldn't take the risk.

Then, when the day of her release had come, and she'd stepped out of the police station...there he was. "He's been waiting there for hours, bless him," the officer behind the counter had said. And they'd gone home and...he'd almost kissed her.

As to what it all meant, she had no idea. Just when she'd thought he'd changed his mind about synadroids, he proved her wrong. Would she ever be enough to truly change his feelings?

She peered out the small round window into the shade-dappled street. A woman stood across from Blue's, her face hidden in the shadows. When she saw Pine's face in the window, she beckoned to her.

Pine stepped back, Blue's warning fresh in her mind. A moment later, the alert on the door sounded.

"Hello?" The voice on the other side of the intercom was female.

"Go away." Pine pressed and released the comm button.

"I need to talk to you."

The temptation was brief. "No. Go away."

There was a long pause on the other side of the door. Had the woman left?

She hadn't. "I— I heard you were looking for someone. A man who disappeared a few days ago."

"So?" Despite herself, Pine's interest was piqued. But she still wasn't going to open the door. *See? I'm learning.*

"I might have some information you'd find useful."

Pine snorted. "You expect me to just open the door and let you in? A few months ago, I may have been gullible enough to do that, but not now. Leave. Please." Yet she still couldn't tear herself away from the door.

"I understand you've probably had some problems with humans. Believe me, you're not the only one. But I'm a synadroid too. You can trust me, can't you?"

That gave Pine pause. Surely she could trust her own kind? Still, she hesitated.

"We know about the freak storm that took him. If it *was* a storm." The synadroid's voice dwindled as she moved away from the door. "But if you don't trust me..."

"I *don't* trust you," Pine said, opening the door. "But I do want to talk to you. What do you mean, it might not have been a storm?"

Pine's caller had the same build as herself, and she smiled as she sized Pine up. "I think we worked in adjoining sectors. Ghostlight 46A-D?"

Pine nodded. "That's right." 46A had been one of her least favorite sectors. The foreman there had always looked at the female synadroids in a way she didn't like.

"I thought you looked familiar when I saw you in the market." She narrowed eyes the rich green of the seaweed they used to cultivate. "Well, come on."

"Come on where? I can't go anywhere with you." Pine stepped back into the bungalow, her hand curving around the door edge. "Why can't you just tell me what you know?"

"I have to *show* you," the synadroid replied, flicking her tawny braid over her shoulder impatiently.

"No. I'm sorry, I can't—" She'd made the mistake of slipping out on James before, and look where that had gotten her.

"Paloma sent me." The synadroid's voice had dropped so low, Pine barely heard her.

"You know Paloma?" She shouldn't have been surprised; Paloma had intimated on several occasions that she had connections to a lot of synadroids.

"Yes. She heard some information about Joseph. She sent me to find you."

That was a bit suspect. "How did she know I was here? *We* barely knew we were here."

"The boat you borrowed has a tracker on it." Her voice had a disdainful edge, as though it should've been obvious to Pine. "When you capsized, she made a best guess where you would end up."

Pine wavered then made her decision. "Okay, fine, I'll come with you. But I can't be gone long." She really didn't need the chastisement. Plus, she didn't want James and Blue to think she'd run away out of spite.

"It won't take more than a few minutes, I promise. My name is Ash, by the way."

"Pine." The moment she stepped onto the road, doubt seeped in. Was this going to be the same as

Todd and Tabby? Was she being foolish, yet again?

As though Ash could read her mind, she glanced over and smiled. "We sentient androids have to stick together, right? If we don't help each other, no one else will."

NINETEEN

"Well, that was a waste of time," James complained. "She didn't tell us anything—and took her sweet time doing it." The old woman had simply toyed with them for her own amusement. Witch. Hell, she'd practically cackled as they'd left.

"Ugh, I know. I'm sorry. I thought if anyone had heard anything about Joseph's disappearance, it would be her. She has eyes and ears everywhere, and Joseph is well-known." She tucked her green hair into her hood as a crisp wind rose. "Still, at least we know nothing intentionally bad happened to him. *That* she would've known about."

"Yeah, small consolation," James grumbled, frustrated and tired. "Pine's going to be so disappointed."

"You think so?"

"Yes, why wouldn't she be?" It had been her idea to search for Joseph, after all.

"Well, her life and future are completely reliant on him. Even as kind as he is, that's still got to frustrate her."

"Yeah, but she's got a pretty good deal, compared to so many others of her kind—" The synadroids on Deserter's Island had made that

178

grotesquely clear.

"You think that makes her captivity okay? How would you feel, James, having all the sentience you have, but not being in control of your own destiny?"

"Yeah, but are *any* of us—"

"Don't try to bullshit me, James. You know damn well it's not the same."

He did. "I know. I know it's difficult for her, but I'm going to do everything I can to make things better." He just wasn't sure *how*, yet.

"If that was true, you'd stay away from her."

"What?" That surprised him. He and Blue had been friends a long time, and she also seemed to genuinely like Pine.

"I saw the way you looked at her when I was fixing her. And now. Something is different between you two. Be honest with yourself. You like her, don't you?"

"Of course. I mean, I'll admit, I had my doubts—"

"No, I mean you *like* her. Don't try to deny it."

He opened his mouth to do just that. And shut it. He'd be lying if he'd said it hadn't crossed his mind. Things *were* changing, but he still wasn't sure what that meant.

"So what if I do?"

"Seriously? What do you think could happen? That she would become your girlfriend? A girlfriend who has the same social status as a pet goldfish? Are you ready for that kind of judgment?"

"I— *If* something happened between us, we'd figure it out then."

"Yeah? And what say would Pine have in all this?"

"What do you mean? She'd have a choice whether to be with me or not."

"Would she? I wonder. I mean, she's bound to do what's in her best interest for survival, right?"

What did *that* mean? No, if he and Pine ever...*if* they ever got to that point, she would be with him because she chose to be.

"And what are you going to do if she breaks? You know they don't make synadroids anymore. What if you couldn't repair her? Would you simply scrap her?"

How could Blue even think that? The idea was abhorrent. "Of course not."

"Put her in another android body then? One that would give her an emotional lobotomy? So that you can still have her body even if her personality is gone? What about when you become an old man? Or what if you decide you want to have children?"

"Blue, *stop*. Where is all this coming from?" He didn't want any part of the doubt she was sowing in him; he had enough of his own.

"James, you and I have known each other a long time. I knew you before the Perimeter, and after. I just want you to think carefully about this. For both your sakes. She's going to have a difficult enough time as it is, without the constant worry of you changing your mind or—"

"I wouldn't." That, at least he could be sure of.

"Really? I know how you felt about sentient androids when you came back from the Perimeter. You were so against everything they stood for. You questioned their humanity." She bent to dig a rock from her shoe.

"Pine isn't like those other synadroids."

"Why? Because you don't *want* her to be?"

I don't want to talk about this anymore. "Blue,

Pine and I aren't even together, so this is all just theoretical. I don't know how she feels about me."

"Well, all the more pity for her if you *do* have feelings for each other. Look, I'm going to tell you something, both for your good and hers, because there's still time for both of you to change your minds without too much pain."

"There's nothing you can tell me that will change my mind." Was there? Damn Blue and her doubt.

"Glad to hear it. You know Paloma, the harbormaster you said took Pine under her wing?"

"Yes."

"She's a sentient android sympathizer."

"So are you." What was she getting at? Given the Emancipation, there were lots of synadroid champions out there.

"She smuggles synadroids out, James. She helps them *escape*."

"Okay. I mean, I'm surprised, but what does that have to do with Pine?" It wasn't like *she* was trying to escape.

"Doesn't it seem a bit convenient to you? The day Pine gets released and Joseph goes missing, Paloma just happens to lend Pine her boat in the middle of a massive storm?"

Taking expensive kit to sell at the Field of Miracles without telling Joseph. Her quiet composure and new confidence when she was released. Being so close to Joseph and James without once contacting them. Her friendship with Paloma. Her thoughtlessness about his safety. Her insistence on going into the storm. But still, all of that didn't mean— "You think she's trying to escape?"

Blue shrugged. "Wouldn't you? Would your

feelings for one person, someone not of your kind in a world that doesn't recognize *you* as a person, be enough for you to give up any chance at freedom, no matter how uncertain that freedom may be?"

"I—" When he took everything into account, it made sense, but he still couldn't believe Pine was planning to run away. Once, maybe, but not now.

Blue wasn't done. "Would you feel safe? Would you be able to love them whole-heartedly?"

James turned it over in his mind, truth battling with hope. Honesty won. "No," he admitted. "I would always be worried about my place, about trust."

"So in Pine's position, do you think it's in her best interests to stay and hope for love with you? Or escape and try to find a life and love as a free person?"

"The latter."

"Then can *you* trust *her*?"

No. He couldn't. How could he have been so foolish? He'd known better. His own experience had taught him differently. Everything he'd believed about Pine from the beginning was still true—she was a synadroid, and an even more unpredictable one at that, and always would be. Blue was right. If they ever did have feelings for each other, what would their future look like?

Do we even have one?

He'd thought he knew Pine, despite their differences. But maybe he was wrong.

As they neared Blue's bungalow, James found his pace quickening. He just needed to see her. All he had to do was look at her, and he would know. His heart would tell him the truth.

Blue had to trot to keep up, and they arrived at

her front door only minutes later. "I wonder what Pine's gotten up to while we were gone. I probably should've told her how to turn on the wallscreen or something," Blue mused as the bioscanner traveled over her face. She turned to James as the door opened. "I know that was a dead-end, but I've got a few more ideas up my proverbial sleeve."

The living room was empty.

"Pine?" James called. "Where are you?" He peered into the tiny kitchen before raising an eyebrow at Blue. "Any other rooms?"

As she shook her head, her sympathetic expression told him what he didn't want to believe—exactly what she'd predicted had happened.

Pine was gone.

TWENTY

It was going to be fine. Ash was her kind. Besides, she didn't have anything worth stealing this time. And if there was any chance of finding Joseph... "Where are we going?"

"Down to the beach." Ash glanced over her shoulder. "There's something down there I have to show you." Her stride was long, her arms swinging feely as they walked.

"So what do you do here?" Pine tried to be polite. Maybe if she knew more about her, she wouldn't be as nervous.

"This and that. Mostly, I work for Paloma, helping other synadroids." They passed through the scrub brush that crested the slope onto the beach.

"Helping them? To do what?"

"*Escape*, of course." Her expression turned incredulous. "You mean you don't *know*?"

"Know what?" Had she missed something?

Ash stopped and put her hands on her hips. "Are you sure you know Paloma?"

"Of course I do. I just don't—" Maybe there were two Palomas and this was a misunderstanding. But Ash *had* mentioned Joseph.

"Maybe she just didn't trust you." Ash sniffed

and kept walking.

That stung. "But she lent me her boat."

"And look what happened." At the crestfallen expression on Pine's face, Ash relented. "I'm only teasing you. Paloma never told you because she wanted to be sure she could trust you. That's where I come in—*I'm* the one who gets to tell you."

"Tell me *what*?" Annoyance bit at her. What did this have to do with Joseph? James and Blue wouldn't be gone much longer. And if she wasn't there when they got back, James would have a conniption.

Ash sensed her irritation. "Okay, sit." She flopped down a few yards from the water's edge and patted the patch of sand next to her. She took a microcomm out of her pocket. "It's almost time."

This time, Pine refused to ask. She crossed her arms over her chest and glared out to sea.

"Okay, *fine*. You're not much fun, are you?" She leaned back on her palms. "Paloma helps secrete sentient androids like you and me away from here."

Pine gawked down at her. "She does *what?*" Harbormaster Paloma was a synadroid smuggler? That was news to her. She'd never given anything away when Pine was with her.

"You heard me. Now *sit down*. You'll draw attention to us if you stand there with your mouth hanging open like that."

Pine sat and scanned the beach around them. Save for themselves, it was empty. "Why *aren't* there guards out here? I thought this island was supposed to be a closely guarded secret?"

Ash smirked. "They believe their barrier is impenetrable. That no one can get within thirty miles without them knowing."

"And can they?"

Ash smiled. "Of course. The *right* people, anyway."

Pine's annoyance flared again. "Now tell me about Paloma. And what do you know about Joseph? What did you drag me down here for?" She would give Ash two minutes then she was leaving, regardless of what the synadroid had to say.

Ash gave a dramatic sigh. "Which do you want to know about first? Which one's more important to you?"

Pine didn't miss the sidelong look Ash gave her. This was not an innocent question. She decided to be truthful. "Joseph."

"His boat *was* capsized in that storm. There were marks on it, huge gouges. She believes he was eaten by a shark."

The reverberation of the ocean rushed into Pine's ears, deafening even the breaking of her heart. The dream swallowed her again, this time lucid and agonizing without the protective fog of sleep. She was choking. Joseph was dead, and it would drown her. He'd promised he wouldn't leave her. A frail human's final betrayal.

"Pine? Pine, are you all right?"

Pine looked up into Ash's concerned face. *When did I lie down?* "Joseph's dead." She needed to say it out loud.

"I know, Pine. And I'm sorry. I truly am." To her credit, she did look it.

"But if Paloma knew, why didn't she tell us? Why let us take the boat?" None of what Ash was saying made any sense.

"She was helping you escape."

"Escape? Why would I need to escape?"

"Because Joseph is *dead*. What do you think will

happen to you?"

"I— James would help me. I know he would." Out of loyalty to Joseph's memory, if nothing else. Wouldn't he?

"The man from the market? Are you *sure* about that? Are you willing to stake your life on it?"

"My life?"

"Think about it. On the same day you get out of prison, Joseph goes missing. Not everyone will think it's a coincidence."

"But he was on his way to come get me." Surely no one would think she'd done anything to him. How could they?

"Maybe, maybe not. Who knows what people will believe? I mean, you have only *one* assault on your record, right?"

"Yes, but I—"

"And then you steal a boat and disappear..."

"But he was my *father.*"

"So what? You think you can bat those doe eyes at a jury and they'll believe you? Do you think you'd even *get* a jury? *Or a trial?*" Ash sneered, an ugly, human curl of her lip. "You know how nervous we make people. And I know you've heard the stories out there about us."

Pine *did* know, because James was one of those people. The very thing he'd worried about happening was exactly what people might believe *had* happened.

"And this James, how far do you think he's willing to go to defend you?"

They'd only just stopped fighting each other, and at the end of the day, she *was* still a synadroid, and always would be.

Ash pressed her advantage. "And even if you do manage to prove your innocence, how long do you think your relationship—"

"We're not in a relationship," Pine protested.

"Not *yet*. But it's obvious you feel something for him. Do you actually think he feels anything for you? A synadroid? Will he fix you when you break down? Or send you to the junkyard? Or here?" She gestured carelessly over her shoulder toward the town. "The law doesn't care, so he can just toss you out the minute he grows tired of you.

She paused and gave Pine an apologetic half-smile. "I'm sorry, Pine. I'm not trying to hurt you. But I think you've forgotten your place among these humans. For now, they treat you like a person, but for how long? What if they don't like the way you react to something? Don't forget who the enemy is."

"Why are you doing this?" The barrage of missiles had hit home. James wasn't her enemy, not any more. But if Ash had wanted to force Pine to shine a light on all her doubts, she was doing a fantastic job.

"Because I want you to understand how precarious your situation is, Pine. I'm offering you a way out. An escape to a safe place. But if you can tell me, honestly, if you are one hundred percent confident that this James has your best interests at heart, that he will always protect you, then I'll go now, and I'll never contact you again."

Pine could've lied. But the truth seemed obvious now. Ash was right. She couldn't trust James with her future. The way he felt about synadroids, the way his world saw her...that couldn't change overnight. And it was *her life* at stake. "I can't."

Ash nodded, satisfied. "Then come with me, Pine."

"But where? Where are you going?" The only

place Pine wanted to go was somewhere quiet, where she could think everything through. She just needed a bit of time to digest everything Ash had said, to decide what she wanted to do.

"It's another island, called Bonehearth. Synadroids are *free* there, Pine. To live however they want. We'll have all the rights of citizens, because we *are* the citizens."

"Have you ever been there?" Pine had never heard of Bonehearth.

"No, but that doesn't matter. It's not just an island for us, you see. It's a *movement*. Toward our freedom. I've helped nearly two dozen synadroids get there, and now it's finally my turn." She pulled the device out of her pocket and checked it again. "Any minute now, the boat will be here. Are you coming?"

"I— I need to talk to James first. I need to tell him about Joseph." She would be able to read her future in his reaction.

Ash snorted. "Pine, of course he's going to tell you what you want to hear. He's—"

Two shapes converged on Ash and Pine at the same time—the first a speedboat, bearing down on the island, the second a man barreling down to the beach, screaming Ash's name and a command that sounded like a safe word.

But Ash didn't freeze; she scrambled to her feet. "Luckily, Paloma thought of everything." She shoved Pine's shoulder. "We have to go, *now*."

But the man was on them long before the boat reached the shore.

He pushed Pine aside and grabbed Ash's arm. The boat was only a few hundred yards away now and gaining. A man stood on the bow, a shotgun cradled in his arms.

Ash and the man grappled with each other, slamming into Pine and knocking her to her knees in the sand. The man was much larger than both of them, thickly muscled, and *angry*. Pine had never seen anyone in such a rage. He twisted Ash's arm behind her back and forced her onto her knees next to Pine.

"Where do you think you're going?" he roared, his breath fetid with the scent of alcohol and something sweet.

"Away from you," Ash shrieked.

A single shot rang out from the ocean. The man froze, bewilderment passing over his face as he looked down. A dark crimson stain spread just underneath his sternum, soaking into the grease-stained t-shirt. He dropped to his knees and the three of them stared at each other as the sand beaded with blood.

Ash was the first to recover. "Pine, come on. Now. We have to get to the boat. This is our only chance."

"But we have to help him— And James. I have to—" She stared at the body of the man, now facedown in the sand. In the distance, an alarm sounded.

"This man is a terrible person, Pine. You can't imagine what he did to me. If you don't come now, the same thing might happen to you. You can't be sure that it won't."

No. I can't. The truth filled her lungs, threatening to crush her from the inside. *I can't.*

As the boat sped away, Pine gazed back at the rapidly shrinking island. Ash had been right, as had Pine's own heart—there was no future for her here. There never would be. She would finally have the freedom she'd always wanted. No longer would she be a possession, her fate clutched in someone else's hand.

So why then did she feel more trapped than ever?

TWENTY-ONE

"James, I'm so sorry." Blue bit her lip.

"It doesn't mean what you think," James said, though the words sounded hollow even to him. "Maybe she's just gone for a walk."

"Well, we can find out." Blue switched on the screen at her workstation and brought up a camera feed.

"You're spying on her?" In truth, he wouldn't have expected any less. Old habits died hard, it seemed.

"No. But I *am* spying on anyone who comes to my front door. Can't be too careful, James, especially on an island of criminals."

"*You're* a criminal."

"That depends on your perspective. I like to think of myself more as a decent person who has to do bad things to make good things happen."

James couldn't disagree with that. It really *was* all a matter of perspective.

Like Pine. Everything Blue said made sense to him, playing on the doubts he'd already had—not only about Pine's true nature, but about himself. Even so, he wasn't quite ready to give up.

Come on, Pine. Prove Blue wrong.

Blue fast-forwarded the recording and James

watched as he, Pine, and Blue raced up to the front door, their movements jerky in the lapsed frames. There was no mistaking the scowl on Pine's face at being left behind. After Blue and James had sped off down the path, the front stoop remained empty. James breathed a bit easier—Pine clearly hadn't run off the moment his back was turned. That was something.

See? And to think you—

A woman appeared across the street, and Blue slowed the recording to normal speed. The woman stood there for a few seconds, watching the house, then beckoned to someone inside. As she raised her hand, James saw the unmistakable tattoo on her wrist.

Another synadroid.

No. Pine didn't know any synadroids here. Did she?

The woman walked with confidence up to the door and spoke.

"Isn't there audio on here?" James tried unsuccessfully to read the woman's lips.

"There *should* be." Blue tried several different commands. "*Damn.* It's been scrambled." Her frown ratcheted James's apprehension up several more notches.

Pine appeared, standing on the stoop next to the woman. The two synadroids talked for several minutes then Pine turned and looked reluctantly back into the house.

Go back inside, Pine. Walk back through the door.

But she didn't. She left without another backward glance.

Walked away, under her own free will.

It seemed Blue was right, no matter how much

James didn't want to believe it.

"Maybe it's a synadroid she knew from before. It wouldn't be the first time she's run into one," James said. "Maybe they've just gone for a walk to catch up." It was a leap, but one he was desperate to take.

"Maybe," Blue said, but she sounded troubled. "That synadroid seems familiar. Now what?"

"Now we go and find her. Your contact might've been a dead end, but that doesn't mean we're giving up." Not on Joseph and not on Pine.

"James—"

"I know what you're thinking, Blue. But until I know for sure she's not just chatting with an old friend, I'm going to give her the benefit of the doubt."

"Any idea where they might've gone?" Blue reset the camera and stretched in her chair.

If I was Pine, where would I go? The answer was obvious. "The beach. They don't eat or drink, and they probably wanted privacy."

"I wonder why they didn't stay here then?" Blue mused.

James pressed his lips together. "Let's just find her. Then we can worry about the whys."

"We'll take the most obvious route down to the beach." Blue locked the door behind them. "Maybe we'll run into them on their way back."

They were just skirting the plaza when an alarm in the center of the market began to wail. People scattered in a calm, methodical way, melting into the background until only a few vendor fronts were left, hawking their legal wares of food and drink to the several men and women who now lounged casually around the square like tourists on a secluded getaway.

"That's not a good sign, is it?" James asked.

"No, it's not."

A group of people jogged past. They wore civilian clothing, but James had been in the military long enough to discern how evenly they kept pace with each other. *Security.* As they ran, they retrieved weapons from various parts of their clothing. They were headed in the same direction as James and Blue—the beach.

No, no, no. And despite hating himself the moment it came to his mind, James's first thought was: *Pine, what have you done now?* He would find out soon enough. James and Blue clambered down onto the beach just after the security team. A crowd was gathering around a prone form lying on the sand.

Pine was nowhere to be seen. Was that good or bad?

"Stay here." Blue elbowed her way through the throng, disappearing.

What the hell happened? Please, please, don't let Pine be involved. James caught the odd word floating up from the huddle...*female synadroid...shot me...a boat...silver...* Just as he lost patience and was about to follow Blue, she broke away from the crowd and jogged back to him. Grabbing him by the arm, she steered him away and back up to the plaza.

"Blue, what happened? Was Pine involved?"

But Blue shook her head and held a finger to her lips. *Not now.* It was only after the door to her bungalow had locked behind them that she spoke.

"Right. First thing to do is delete the footage of Pine and that other synadroid, Ash. If we're lucky, she won't have been recorded on camera anywhere else, not if Ash is as savvy as I think."

"What did they do, Blue? Please, tell me." If Blue was destroying evidence, it was worse than he'd thought.

Blue started, as though she'd forgotten James was there.

"What happened?" he repeated.

"She's gone, James. She and Ash are gone."

"But how?"

"That man on the ground? That was Ash's owner. She drugged him and slipped out then came and found Pine. Do you think Pine knew her from before?"

"I have no idea. Like I said, it's definitely possible." His mind spun. Had she mentioned anyone who fit the synadroid's description?

"Regardless, they're involved now. After Ash's owner woke up and realized what had happened, he rushed out to find her. He said she'd been acting oddly lately. Anyway, someone said they'd seen her heading down to the beach with another woman who matched Pine's description—although I don't think they realized she was a synadroid." She pulled up the footage of Pine again. "So he ran down there to claim her and found them just as a boat arrived. He grabbed Ash, trying to stop her, and there was a struggle."

"Did Pine—"

"No, nothing like that. But whoever was on the deck of the boat *shot* him."

James dreaded what was coming next.

"Then Pine and the other synadroid boarded the boat."

James had to ask, although he was sure he already knew the answer. "Did— Were they threatened into it?"

"No, James. I'm sorry. The guy said they

couldn't climb aboard fast enough. And that Ash actually hugged the man—although I do wonder now if it *was* a man or a synadroid—when she got on deck."

James sat heavily on the lone rattan chair. He ignored the warning creak as it protested his weight.

I can't believe it. All this time. She was planning her escape. I thought we— Was pretending to care for me all part of her plan? To make me drop my guard?

"I feel like an idiot."

"Don't, James. How could you have known she wasn't being genuine?"

"You did."

"Not really. If all I had to go on was the way she looked at you, I wouldn't have questioned her, but there've been rumors of this kind of thing happening a lot recently...and when you consider the way most of these synadroids are treated... And then when you mentioned Paloma, well. It was a possibility, anyway."

"The signs were there," James agreed. "I just didn't want to see them."

"What now? Shall we go after her? We'll have to keep it quiet, because if she's in any way connected to that shooting—even if she didn't pull the trigger, you know what'll happen."

James considered. What should he do? Drag her back here? And for what? To break Joseph's heart? She'd obviously never cared about the old man.

Or him.

"No. Leave her. You were right, Blue, about everything. It's better to let her go." He hoped Blue couldn't hear the lie.

If she did, she didn't show it. "I'm still sorry.

Look, I'll cover her tracks the best I can. Or do you want her to get caught?"

James was hurt, but he wasn't vindictive. "No, of course I don't. I'm..." *What, James? Devastated? Heartbroken? About something that hasn't even happened?* "...disappointed, I'll admit it, but you were right about another thing. These synadroids...we don't do right by them. If she can have a chance at happiness and freedom, I want her to have it. She never would've had it here, and I know that now."

Blue put a kind hand on his shoulder. "I know you're more than disappointed, but it's probably for the best. I'm glad you're still the man I know, James, after all this." She hesitated. "Do you mind if I do some digging? Something about this whole thing just doesn't sit right with me."

James waved in dismissal. "Sure, do what you want, though I don't know what difference it'll make." He and Pine were still who they were, and nothing would change that.

"What are you going to do now?" She peeked over her shoulder at her screen; she was obviously anxious to get back to work.

"Go home. Keep the search for Joseph going. And the sooner, the better." James needed to get away from this place. He'd already detested this island; now he downright hated it.

* * *

A week later, and the hunt for Joseph continued to turn up nothing. James had gone straight from Deserter's Island to the Portfade harbor to check on its progress, even offering to join the search. He'd been turned away gruffly, his lack of experience with the sea an unwanted handicap. He'd tried to make an appointment with Paloma, hoping she would help him, but he was told she'd taken a leave of absence and wouldn't be back for several weeks.

So every day he returned and waited around for a few hours, helpless, his mind clouded with Pine and Joseph, before retreating to clear his head with some sleep and a hot meal.

Joseph's house was cool and dark when James finally pulled up out front that night. He couldn't bear the thought of going to his apartment; he needed comfort, and he wouldn't get it there in the tiny, impersonal room. When Pine was imprisoned, he and Joseph had grown even closer, James no longer returning home every night, but instead sleeping in one of the guest rooms. Joseph had even dropped subtle hints that James should simply move in, but he hadn't wanted to impose, a decision he now couldn't fathom.

But even here, there was little comfort with Joseph and Pine gone. He gazed wistfully at Mara's beaming smile as she peered up from her work at him. It was just the two of them now. "I'm so sorry, Mara. I've let you down. I've let everyone down."

Mara dipped her head back down to her work.

Rebuffed, James stretched out on the couch and dropped his arms over his eyes.

It was true. He'd let everyone down, Pine and himself most of all. He'd only told Blue half the truth when he'd said he wanted her to be happy. He did, but he wanted her to be happy here.

James rose from the couch and climbed the stairs to Pine's bedroom. The bed was still covered in brightly-wrapped parcels; they'd been in such a hurry to find Joseph that opening presents had been the last thing on their minds. She'd seemed so concerned about him then, so genuine. James shook his head. She'd simply been planning her escape.

But Blue had also mentioned the way Pine looked at him. And the way she'd been acting...Pine could lie, but she hadn't had a lifetime of practice at it like most people. If she *had* been pretending, it was the finest performance he'd ever seen.

Here, in the room where it had seemed like a new beginning for them both, James's doubts began to turn in on themselves.

When she'd walked through the door that first day, James had already decided what she was. He'd never even wanted to give her a chance. But everything she'd said and done since, everything that had been done *to* her...

More and more, he'd gotten an inkling of what life was like for her, although he would never truly understand. He took his status and freedom for granted, and yes, he was guilty of accepting the lot of sentient androids without much thought, because that was just the way it was. But he was starting to change.

Not fast enough. Not in the ways that really mattered.

And yet, she'd still trusted him. Had let him help her. Had stood in this room with him and...

If he let her go now, he'd be letting her down again. With every thoughtless thing he'd said about synadroids, everything he still accepted—even the way he still treated her at times—he'd failed her, showed her that a life without him was freedom, was a better choice. The only choice. Perhaps if he'd been stronger, she would've seen her freedom here. But she'd followed the truth her heart had told her.

James stood.

It was time he followed his own truth. He didn't know what the future held, but he wanted her in it, in any way she could be. More than that, he couldn't leave things the way they were between them, her thinking he'd failed her. Maybe she would still see him as the enemy and never truly forgive him. Maybe, but he had to try.

He was going to find her. He was going to ask for her forgiveness and offer her a choice.

Now that she was free, she could make that choice. She could choose to stay where she was, free among the refugees of her own kind, or she could come with him and face an uncertain future—but together.

TWENTY-TWO

Pine sorted the ocean-scoured stones into glossy, colored-coded piles. It helped her think. Her first few days at Bonehearth had been eye-opening. The small island was inhabited entirely by androids, both sentient and non. They were free to do what they liked, amuse themselves as they wished, and answered to no one.

Pine had felt an initial burst of euphoria, the gaiety of a dream finally realized, but it had been short-lived, almost anti-climactic. After those first few hours, unease had unexpectedly rippled inside her again, just like when she'd been sent back to the Ghostlight. Why wasn't she happy? This *was* what she'd wanted, wasn't it?

Was it because of the boat ride here? Still shocked by what had happened on the beach, Pine had distanced herself from Ash the moment they'd arrived, trying to sort out her feelings. The synadroid who'd pulled the trigger was called Sebastian, and after they'd climbed aboard, he'd embraced Ash then turned and sat down, barking orders to the android driving the boat. He hadn't looked back at the man he'd just shot, not even once.

Nor did Ash seem disturbed. She chatted to the other synadroids on the boat easily, as though they were out on lovely afternoon of boating, rather than speeding away from a possible murder.

After several minutes of excited gossip, Ash had noticed Pine's silence. "What's gotten into you? Don't tell me you're upset about Jonty."

Was that his name? "No, of course not." But she was, though she doubted he'd have felt the same had it been her who was shot.

"This one thinks she's *human*." Ash laughed, pointing Pine out to the others. "She's even got herself a genuine boyfriend."

As the other synadroids whooped, Pine ignored them and gazed out over the water. She laid her head on the side of the boat, pressing her cheek to the cool metal. A shadow fell across her, and she peered up at a non-sentient android standing in front of her. It was a model she'd never seen before, similar in build to herself and the other synadroids, but without the aesthetic 'human' touches.

Whereas Pine was covered with synthetic skin that felt as real as a human's, this android had its metal skeleton and molded silicon flesh on display. Every articulation, the complicated mechanics of every movement, were laid bare. Its eyes were set deep in its metal skull, flat and dull over a mouth that was little more than a hole in its bare face.

The android disturbed Pine on a profound level. She'd never seen one so like her, yet so different. Was that why so many humans were uncomfortable around synadroids? Was it like looking at their reflection in a distorted mirror?

It stared back at her, dumb, and revolting. What was it doing here? Androids were built to a purpose, one that was usually clear in their design.

A similar android stood behind the controls of the boat. *Ah.* They were the crew. Maybe this island *was* going to be what she'd hoped, if even non-sentient androids had a place there.

I wonder if I'll have a job too. I mean, we must do something all day, even if we're free.

Still the android stared at her.

"Hello?" She didn't really expect a response, but it seemed rude not to at least acknowledge it.

"*Run.*"

Pine started. Had it just spoken to her? She glanced around, but no one else seemed to have heard. The android's mouth hadn't moved, and yet—

"*Run.*"

"What's going on here?" Sebastian appeared at the android's shoulder.

Something like panic flashed in the android's eyes before they went lifeless again.

"Nothing," Pine said, glad she could lie. "I've just never seen an android like this before. It's fascinating."

"Slightly better than useless," he replied, and struck the android between the shoulder blades with the butt of his gun. It dropped to its knees and stayed there.

Pine leaped to her feet. "Why did you do that?"

Sebastian narrowed his eyes. "Why do you care? They're not like us, you know. They don't *feel* anything."

Pine became aware of the others on the boat, now silent, watching the exchange. She slowly lowered herself back into her seat. "I know, but still...what if you break it?"

"Plenty more where he came from." Sebastian shrugged and pushed the tip of his gun into the android's shoulder. "Get back to work."

The android stood and tottered back into the cabin, disappearing from Pine's view. Sebastian also returned to his post, but his eyes kept returning to her for the rest of the ride.

There were others like that android on the island. They seemed to be tasked with maintaining the island and answering to the synadroids, and they contributed largely to her disquiet. *But why?* Perhaps in a few days, when she'd gotten used to the place, she would feel differently.

But she didn't. Again and again, she returned to the beach to sort stones and try to figure out her feelings. Was it the island itself that was disturbing her?

Yes. Part of it was the island. It was beautiful, a true paradise of lush vegetation and crystal water. It was well-stocked with everything a synadroid might need, but there was something not quite right. It was *too* idyllic, too much like a fairy tale.

The first day, Sebastian had echoed what Ash had told her, and explained to all the newcomers that they were now part of a new movement, the beginning of freedom for all synadroids. They would join the recruitment efforts, with the island serving as their base.

Supplies were brought in daily, boats going in and out of the tiny bay, but how was it all sustained? Where was Paloma getting the funds to support all this? And although Sebastian could spin a fine story about the future, his details on what would happen after all the synadroids had been recruited were vague. But no one else seemed to care; they were all too grateful.

So yes, the nagging questions about the island were part of it. But the other part, the much bigger part, was that she'd made a huge mistake. This didn't feel like freedom anymore.

To her, freedom was being home with Joseph and James, laughing in the backyard as James tried to uproot the enormous weeds clinging stubbornly to the ground.

It was leaving the police station to find James waiting for her. The look on his face when he'd seen her standing before him.

Joseph, rushing out to collect her with no thought other than to see her the minute she was free.

Arguing with James, the heat rising in her not unpleasant.

That was the freedom Pine wanted. It wasn't perfect, but it was real.

And already it was slipping through her fingers. Joseph was dead. That she couldn't think about, not yet. She packed Joseph away, to be taken out later when she could face it with her eyes open. *One heartbreak at a time.*

James.

Had he really given her reason not to trust him, or to think he would abandon her? Confusion clouded her mind like squid ink. Only a couple of days ago, it had seemed so clear—James could not be trusted. He didn't—couldn't—understand what it was to be in her position, how terrifying the tenuousness of it was. He'd said things offhand, not realizing how upsetting they were to her.

And how could he? He believed what he did based on his own experience, coupled with the lens through which most humans saw. But he was changing. His behavior toward her proved that.

She twirled a lock of hair around her finger. The hair James had given her. He'd come for her when she was in trouble, had saved her. He may have done that for Joseph, but sitting for hours with her as Blue fixed her up, holding her hand even as she'd nearly crushed his, could only have been done for her. He'd put all his faith in her when they'd gone out in that storm, trusting her with his life.

She'd said she trusted him, but fear had made her a liar.

She let both of them down. She'd given up her chance at a future she never expected. A future she wanted.

She had to do it. Tell James everything, and give him a choice—to trust her, as she would trust him. To face an uncertain future with her rather than the empty one she now saw stretching before her.

Together, they could decide.

Her mind made up, Pine was restless for action. *How do I get off this island?* She needed to go *now*. There must be a boat leaving for the mainland soon. And even if it didn't go to the mainland, any one of the islands would work. Maybe she could get back to Deserter's Island, to Blue. Or somewhere else where she could hitch a ride.

Pine was so engrossed in her plans, she hadn't noticed Sebastian approaching her.

"Pine. Come with me." The light glinted off his bald head and shadowed his angular cheekbones.

"Sebastian." Her eyes adjusted to the brilliance of the sun behind him. "I need to talk to you."

"That works out then, doesn't it?" His voice was oddly without inflection, and a chill pooled around the base of her spine. "Walk with me."

She obeyed, her feet sliding on the pebbled beach as she spoke first.

"Sebastian, I would like to leave. On the next boat, please." There was no reason to delay.

Whatever he had to say to her, he could tell her while she waited for her ride.

"Leave? Whatever for?" He turned to study her, his eyes as disturbingly flat as his voice.

"I made a mistake in coming here. Don't get me wrong, it's a lovely place, and I'm so grateful that I came. But before I know if I can stay here, there's something important I have to do."

He walked a few yards in silence then, "No."

"No? You can't— I thought we were free here."

"You are. *Here*. For as long as you live."

Pine's temper swirled about her like a whirlpool, rising fast. "You can't keep me here. This isn't freedom." She stopped, and after a few steps, he stopped too and regarded her, his dead eyes sparkling at last. The last time she'd seen eyes like those were on the shark that had tried to kill James.

Pine backed away, treading softly. Sebastian matched her pace for pace until her heels touched water.

There was nowhere else to go.

Unless, of course, you'd lived most of your life underwater. Pine cursed herself. Why hadn't she thought of that before? Why hadn't she just slipped out of sight, quietly, in the night?

If they were human, she would have.

Slowly, she stepped back, one foot then the other, her gaze trained on Sebastian's face.

When she was thigh-deep, she took her chance, twisting around and pushing with her feet, her body arcing into a dive. She sliced through the water, gaining speed, her arms propelling her faster and faster from the shore.

But not fast enough.

TWENTY-THREE

James opened the front door to find The Blue Fairy shivering in the light rain, her hand raised to the doorbell. He'd nearly worn a groove in the floor, pacing as he waited for her to arrive.

"Thanks so much for coming. I need your help."

"Yes, you do. More than you know."

James didn't like the sound of that. The moment he'd decided to find Pine, he'd called Blue. If anyone could help him track the missing synadroid down, it was her. After their conversation on Deserter's Island, he'd expected some resistance when he explained he wanted to find Pine, but she'd agreed before he could even finish asking. That alarmed him. What had she found out?

"Come in." In anticipation of her arrival, James had hot drinks ready and waiting. Blue slid off her coat and wrapped her hand around one of the mugs, taking an appreciative sip.

James shifted his weight from one foot to another, trying to be patient. He didn't have to wait long.

"Before we do this, James, I need to ask—why do you want to find Pine?"

James answered simply. "Because I need to know if we have a future."

"If? So you're giving her a choice?"

"Of course I am. If she's happy where she is, I'll never bother her again. And I know Joseph, when we find him, will feel the same. It'll break his heart, but her happiness is of paramount importance to him."

"I'm glad to hear it."

"You are? I thought you were so against—"

"I was, but only because I knew you hadn't thought it through, and I didn't want to see either of you get hurt, especially Pine. But now you have. I'm good with it."

James gawked at her. "Are you kidding me? I—"

"Needed to get things straight in your head. And you did." She held up a hand as he opened his mouth again. "James, we don't want to waste time arguing about this, believe me."

He snapped his mouth shut. "Tell me."

"Okay, first things first. I managed to retrieve the audio from my front door. I heard what Pine and Ash were talking about."

"And?" James held his breath.

"And it looks like I was wrong." Blue dipped her head in apology. "They weren't talking about escaping at all. Ash told Pine that Paloma had sent her, that she had information about Joseph. Something she needed to show her."

"Oh, Pine," James groaned. Yes, this was evidence that Pine did care for Joseph, but— "She knew better."

Blue drained her cup. "Yeah, well, Ash is of her ilk. In Pine's current state of mind, could you blame her?"

No, he couldn't. "So if she wasn't planning to run away, how did she end up on that boat?"

"That I don't know. But Jonty—the man who was shot—made it clear that Pine had nothing to do with it. She even wanted to help him, he said. My guess is she probably panicked."

"I'm not surprised, after what happened with Todd and Tabby." James swore. "But still, that's good news, right? She doesn't have to worry about coming back."

"*If* we can get her back. James, I've been doing some digging and—"

"I'm going to need to sit down for this, aren't it?" Blue rarely took so long to get to the point. Whatever it was, it must be bad.

Blue winced and nodded. "Yes. It looks like I was wrong about Paloma too. She's *not* a sentient android sympathizer. She's a— Well, I don't even know what to call her."

"Blue, please. I can't stand the suspense." Every minute that passed was one he could be using to find Pine.

"I know, I'm sorry. I just don't know how to describe it. Rumor is—and these rumors come from a source I believe—that she lures disenchanted synadroids to a remote island, promising them a utopia where they're free."

"That must've made Pine's decision to get on the boat a little easier." In fact, given everything that had happened to her up until that point, it must've seemed like a gift. How could he compete with that?

"But it's a total lie. Apparently, she gets them to this island under the guise of a recruitment camp. Once there, they get a taste for what they think their freedom will be. And it tastes *good,* as you can imagine." Blue focused on a spot above James's head. "So for a few weeks they trot out like good little missionaries to find new recruits and regale them with tales of paradise to lure them in. Then, on their final mission, they're taken away and dismantled instead." She met his gaze and shook her head. "Their components are worth a small fortune since they've stopped producing them. In fact, that's one of the main reasons the government is considering giving them personhood at all."

James's stomach felt like he'd sailed over a colossal waterfall in a raft made of sticks. He dropped his head between his knees. "But that means—"

"That Pine is in mortal danger. We need to move fast."

He was already lacing his boots. "You know where they are?"

"Yes, but it won't be long before they know I know. And then they'll move. And god knows if I'll be able to find them again."

"How did you find them this time?"

"Ash's owner had a tracking chip put inside her when she was in for repairs. She didn't know about it, and so Paloma didn't either."

James was already yanking his coat over his shoulders. "Right, how do we get there?"

"The Owl and The Crow have a boat waiting for us down at the docks. James…"

What was she waiting for? James didn't want to be rude, but they were wasting time standing around.

"We might be too late."

James closed his eyes then snapped them open again as images of Pine lying on a cold table, her face terrified as impersonal hands tore her apart swept over his lids. "It doesn't matter. We have to try." He dashed back into the living room and over to Mara's portrait. "I'm going, Mara. I'm going to get Pine back. Then, we'll bring Joseph back, together."

Mara just looked up at him and smiled.

* * *

James had never been on a boat as fast as *The Avenoir*. "Is this even legal?" he shouted, the wind tearing the words from his mouth.

"Technically, no." Blue grinned, tears streaming down her cheeks as she faced the wind. "But we had to make a choice, and we chose speed. And that's not all." She gestured to The Owl, and the boat slowed, evening out at only a few miles per hour. "Watch this."

The Owl checked the control panel in front of him and gave Blue a thumbs-up. The small ship shuddered, and a translucent pod closed over the open deck, encasing the entire vessel.

"It's a submarine too." Blue's voice boomed in the sudden silence.

As they glided beneath the surface of the water, James's old panic gripped him. Although he was glad for the camouflage the sub offered, he wished the damn exterior was opaque. The last thing he needed was his nightmares unfolding before his eyes while he was trying to rescue Pine.

But at the thought of Pine, his panic subsided. The ocean wasn't the monster here. Paloma was. Pine had loved this ocean, had feared the land and world he lived in much more. James walked to the front of the boat and stood on the prow, facing the water rushing past head-on. Shapes sped past him, some large and dark, others small and flashing. He welcomed them all.

Blue at his elbow made him jump. "Okay, we're almost there. Here—" She grabbed his arm and turned it over before stamping something onto his wrist.

It looked like a synadroid tattoo. "What's this for?"

"From what I've been able to tell, they rely on their obscurity and above-water observation rather than alarm systems, so I can get us onto the island undetected through a hole in the island that functions as a lagoon." She showed him her own tattoo. "But after that, we need to blend in if we're going to try to find Pine."

That makes sense. Okay, James, breathe.

"Blue?" The Crow called. "Owl says we're heading just under the island now."

The four of them stood silently as the sinister phantom of the island passed over them. Owl navigated the sub through the dense catacomb of the island's body, checking and rechecking his course through the shadowed water toward the small tunnel that would lead them up to the surface.

Dark rock pressed in on them from all sides, and James's resolve began to slip. Just as the panic reared its head again, light broke through the top of the sub's dome. James let out a shaky breath and wiped the slick sweat off his forehead with the back of his hand.

They hovered beneath the surface and waited. "Have you got that synadroid's location?" Blue asked The Crow.

He checked a few coordinates on a nanocomm he'd drawn from his pocket. "Yep, we're good. Let's just hope Pine is somewhere near her."

Still, they held back.

James's pulse pounded in his ears. "What are we waiting for?"

"You didn't expect just four of us for this rescue mission, did you?" Blue grinned.

Well, yes, I did. "So who—"

"The authorities, of course." Blue chuckled as James gaped at her. "What? Sometimes we work together. I tipped them off about this island and what Paloma was doing. I put a significant emphasis on how the synadroids were victims here, how they were being exploited. The government's having enough problems right now with the emancipationists. Could you imagine if something like this became public? And that the government knew and did nothing?"

James whistled in admiration. "I'm sure that's *exactly* how you explained it to them."

"Pretty much. I mean, I may have added a few incentives, such as a timed exposure. They may be able to look the other way on certain gray areas, but this isn't one of them."

James swept Blue up in a tight embrace. "Thank you."

For a moment, she submitted then pushed him away. "Fine, whatever." She checked her comm. "Right. They'll be here soon. Let's get a head start. Our goal is to get in, get Pine, get out. Leave the rest for them." She put her hand on James's arm "We're counting on you, so get your head straight."

"Me?" He'd thought Blue was in charge.

"You're the military man, Lieutenant. This is what you used to do for a living."

James exhaled slowly. He had trained for this. He just wished Blue had told him sooner. He'd have spent less time worrying about Pine and more coming up with a plan. Well, he'd just have to manage.

"Going up." The Owl raised the submarine, breaking the surface of the water. "The coast is clear for the moment, but I don't know how long it will last. I'll wait here, just under the surface." He held out his arm to stop Blue as she passed him. "*Try* to give me a few minutes warning."

Blue smirked. "We'll *try*." She picked up an oddly-shaped bag and tossed it at James. "Here, you carry it."

He grunted as he caught it. "What is—"

"Your shining armor and your white steed." She grinned. "Ready to go rescue the princess?"

If he lived a thousand years, he'd still never see every side to Blue. But he *was* ready, readier than he'd ever been for anything.

They made it to the edge of the lagoon undetected, before ducking into a copse of trees as the hull of the sub sank out of sight. The Crow brought out a tiny compass-like device. "According to this, she's only a few hundred feet away. In that direction." He pointed south.

They crept through the foliage at James's signal, trying to make as little sound as possible.

"I think we should just stand and walk normally," James said. "I mean, we're trying to fit in, right?" No other synadroids were likely to be creeping about in the bushes.

"Good point." Blue straightened up and double-checked her synadroid tattoo. "And this is why you're the leader. I'm not used to going in the front door."

"Speaking of which," The Crow said. "*There's* the front door we're looking for."

About fifty yards ahead sat a stark, rectangular

building. It was clearly modern, all thick steel and reinforced concrete. The closed door had a keypad to the right of it and judging by how long the android entering the code stood there, a complex cipher.

"Damn," James whispered. "Did you know about that?" Codes were *not* part of his particular training. Maybe the time for being subtle was over.

Blue gave him a look of disgust. "What do you think I am, an amateur?" She pulled yet another tiny device out of her pocket and held it up. "*This* is for *them*." She pointed at the two synadroids guarding the door. They each wielded a shotgun. "And them." Several other synadroids milled around near the building. "In fact, it *should* work on the whole island. Well, anyone outside the building, that is."

"Do the authorities you're working with know you have that?" James indicated the device. "'Cause I'm pretty sure that's good for ten years in prison."

Blue looked unconcerned. "Meh. We're making it easy for them. Don't ask, don't tell." She pulled an amplifier out of the bag James carried and plugged the gadget into it.

Satisfied they were ready, he nodded at Blue, and the three of them stepped out of their cover in unison.

They didn't fool anyone. Tattoos or not, to the sentient androids, they were instantly recognizable. The two guards at the door lifted their weapons, their mouths opening to sound the alarm.

"Blue, *now*."

Blue lifted the amplifier overhead and activated it. An invisible wave of electromagnetic power rolled in all directions across the island. For a few seconds, nothing happened, then the synadroids dropped like puppets with their strings cut. Blue waited a few more seconds then tossed the device back in the bag.

The Crow looked impressed. "That worked even better than I thought it would."

James peered down at the nearest synadroid, a young man in too-large clothing. "It won't hurt them, will it? How long will they be out?"

Blue bent and gently stroked the synadroid's forehead and scalp. "It's so mild it won't do any permanent damage, but it will take time for their systems to unscramble themselves." She smiled at James. "I'm so glad you care."

James ignored her and strode toward the building. Pine was here; he was sure of it. *We're coming, Pine.*

At the door, he examined the keypad. "You said you had something for this, right?"

"It'll be as scrambled as the synadroids now. We should be able to pry the doors open." She reached into the bag hanging off his shoulder. "Want to do the honors, Lieutenant?" she asked, handing him a crowbar.

James stuck the flat end between the two doors and leaned heavily on it, trying to get leverage.

The doors didn't budge. James swore under his breath.

"Let me try." The Crow nudged James out of the way.

"Seriously? No offense, but—" James wouldn't have called Crow scrawny, exactly, but his physique was definitely more geared to electronic wizardry than prying open steel doors, even if their locks *had* been nullified.

The Crow ran his fingers down the crack in the

door then eyed the length of the metal bar. He mumbled a few words to himself then gave a slight jerk of his wrist.

The doors popped open. Not all the way, but enough for three bodies to slip through.

James stared at him, dumbfounded. "Where did you learn—"

The Crow shrugged. "Physics."

"You guys? We don't have a lot of time…and we don't even know if Pine is in here. So can we…" Blue gestured impatiently toward the space between the doors.

They opened into a narrow hallway as austere as the building exterior. Crow checked the tracker in his hand and held it up for the others to see. "Ignore the rooms on this corridor and take the right at the end. The room we're looking for is all the way at the back. Got it?"

"Got it. All right, Blue, let's see what goodies you brought me." James tugged the bag off his shoulder and unzipped it. He groped around for a moment before pulling out a neo-hand cannon. He checked the chamber. Explosive rounds. Perfect.

James hefted the gun in his hand, feeling the familiar weight. He'd thought a gun would feel foreign to him after all this time, but it sat naturally, even comfortably. He could do this. "I hope you've got lots of ammo."

"I'm *always* prepared. Here." Blue tossed a small kit to Crow. "I'm sure you know what to do with these." She also fished out three masks and passed them around.

Crow opened the kit and grinned. "Yes, ma'am, I do. Savage choice." He bowed.

Blue lifted a shock rifle out of the bag then pulled it over her own shoulders. She turned the charge all the way up. "I'm ready when you are, Cricket."

James pressed forward. He kept close to the wall, his eyes darting back and forth as he scanned the hallway and adjoining rooms for movement. He motioned for Blue and The Crow to follow.

No one stood in their way.

"Thank God for Paloma's arrogance. We might actually have a chance," Blue whispered behind him

"Don't get cocky," James warned her. "It's what's *in* the room we have to worry about."

In less than a minute, they stood outside the door. *Please, please, let Pine be in here. Please, don't let us be too late.*

"Okay, Crow, it's your turn." James had no idea what The Crow had in his pockets, but he was a master at getting in and out. This was going to be interesting.

The Crow took a set of tiny nodes from his kit and placed them around the door. As soon as he was done, James motioned for him to take up position on one side of the door. James joined Blue on the other side, and at his signal, they all slipped on their masks.

James fought to keep his breathing steady. *Okay, here we go.*

A scream split the air.

Pine.

The Crow pressed the button.

TWENTY-FOUR

Pine's eyes were open before her brain had fully engaged. Confused, she stared at the furrows of the waves molded into the ceiling plaster. Where was she?

I told Sebastian I wanted to leave the island. He refused. He—

He attacked me.

I'm lying down. Pine tensed, trying to sit up, but wide bands across her body kept her immobile—even her head was firmly strapped down. She wiggled her fingers with relief. *At least I'm not paralyzed.*

Voices rose from the opposite end of the room. Pine tried to turn her head, even just a little, but had to be satisfied with straining her eyes instead.

Four figures—two men and two women—stood around a long table, peering down at the pile of metal on it.

Two of them had their backs to Pine. From their movements, they appeared to be human. Of the other two facing Pine, one was Sebastian.

The other was Paloma.

A quick rush of relief cut through Pine's confusion. *Paloma is here. She'll know what's going on. She'll help me.* Just as Pine was about to call out to her, the man and woman stepped away from the table and Pine finally saw what had held their interest.

A sentient android lay on the table, its eyes wide and mouth locked open in horror. Pine couldn't tell if it was male or female, alive or dead. Its skin had been peeled from its head and body, exposing its complex metal skeleton and synthetic musculature. Although it was immobilized, to Pine's synadroid eyes, it seemed to vibrate.

The androids. The androids that staffed the island. The android that had warned her on the boat. They'd been made here, from sentient androids. Synadroids like Pine.

Run.

Terror, purer than anything Pine had felt before, burned through her body like jellyfish venom. *It was all a lie. There is no freedom for us.*

As Pine watched, Paloma peeled the last part of the android's skin down and off its foot, like she was taking off a sock.

"Ha!" She held it up triumphantly. "Perfect. This'll net us a fortune. Did you see how I did that? *All* of them need to be done like that, not like the butcher job you did on the other one, Sebastian."

Sebastian smirked. "He struggled."

Paloma raised an eyebrow. "That's why you use the safe word, Seb. Fine if you want to leave their pain sensors on and have some fun, but at the end of the day, we're here for the product, not your depravity."

"I'll make it up to you later." He winked suggestively, and Pine didn't miss the lewd look that passed between the human couple. They moved away to stand together against the wall while Paloma and Sebastian strolled to the next table, Paloma twirling her scalpel between her fingers.

A strangled cry tried to force its way from Pine's throat.

Paloma's gaze snapped up, her scalpel poised over the skull of the next hapless synadroid.

Don't move, don't move, don't even move your eyes.

"Ana, could you please just check the cameras for me?" Paloma pointed to a small control panel near the door.

"Of course." Ana passed her gun to the man, squinted at the screen, and pressed a few buttons to rotate the view. She frowned.

"What is it?" Paloma asked sharply.

Ana pulled back from the screen. "Nothing. I'm just still not used to how *human* they seem."

"But they're not. And never forget it." Paloma bent back over her work.

For once, Pine was glad she couldn't cry. Nothing in the world would've stopped the tears from forcing their way out of her eyes and giving her away.

James. I'm so sorry. First Joseph, and now me. I've only just realized what it means to be alive.

Had Ash known what Paloma was? Was she here? Pine strained her eyes to the side again and could just make out Ash on the table next to hers. Her head, arms, legs, and torso were all secured by wide metal bands. Ash's eyes were open, and Pine made the tiniest of sounds to get her attention. It worked.

Frozen, Ash couldn't meet Pine's gaze. Her eyes were wide, like Pine's, and terrified. And there was something else in them, a kind of disbelief, a betrayal.

She didn't know.

Sebastian had, though. Had not only known but had made it happen. How could he betray his own kind like that? What was in it for him?

Paloma and Sebastian worked their way down the line tables, taking turns stripping the skin from each of the prone synadroids then hanging it on a hook on the wall, like a macabre boiler suit. By the time they were two androids away from Pine, she understood what was in it for him.

Obviously, he had a relationship with Paloma. They stood in each other's space the way lovers did, and once she even drew the back of the scalpel playfully over his lips.

But it was more than that—he was a sadist. Somewhere along the way, the emotions he'd been given were corrupted, made hungry for a very particular type of stimulation. He spoke quietly to the synadroids under his breath as he pressed the knife to their flesh, grinning as their eyes flashed and their bodies and minds fought to react to the pain and couldn't. Everything Sebastian murmured to them, every twist of his hand, every bite of cold air hitting their exposed insides, they could feel. And Pine had only to glance below Sebastian's waist to see the effect it had on him.

How can I escape?

It would have to be at the last minute, just as the blade sunk into her. They would need to remove the restraints, and she would have a split-second to— To what? Try to take out four people, all of whom had much more experience with violence than she did?

She had to try. If James ever found out what had happened to her, at least he'd know she'd tried. She focused on that thought, suppressing the more logical one that James would *never* know what had happened.

Then they were beside Ash, and Pine's terror almost overwhelmed her. It took everything in her power not to scream, to fight her restraints. She had to stay still; she'd only have one chance. *Hold steady. Think of James.*

Ash's survival instinct started to overcome her programming when she saw Paloma and Sebastian looming over her. Sebastian watched her twitch for a few seconds, fighting against her paralysis, and laughed, a rumbling from deep in his belly that made Pine's circuits want to short out. *What happened to him?*

"Fanavitae."

Ash froze again, though her mouth snapped open in a soundless scream. Gathering her hair in one hand, he sliced off the top of her scalp in one swift motion.

"Sebastian," Paloma admonished him. "We want the skins as whole as possible."

Every sickening rupture of Ash's skin separating from her frame wormed its way into Pine's soul. She couldn't block it out, couldn't turn away. She didn't even dare shut her eyes for fear they would catch her.

It seemed like only seconds until they were done, Paloma hanging the skin while Sebastian ran his hands over the slick metal of Ash's exposed form, digging his fingers into pressure points until one of the pupils in her green eyes blew.

Then he turned to Pine. Leaning over, he spoke to her in a deep, almost hypnotic voice.

"I told you you wouldn't be leaving here. Not alive, anyway. I'm still not sure what we're going to do with you. Take you apart completely, or just fix you up a little—get rid of that nasty human side." As he spoke, he retracted the bands from around her.

The sudden release of pressure made Pine feel like she would float off the table. *Not yet. Keep still.* She tried to gauge where everyone in the room was. This attempt might be futile but focusing on it was the only way to stop her mind from imploding.

Paloma loitered near her feet, running her finger down the smooth skin of Pine's legs. Sebastian stroked her hair back from her face and poised the scalpel over her forehead.

Pine rolled off the table.

Sebastian stared at the empty slab, his hand hovering in the air. Then he looked at Pine and his face distorted in a vicious snarl, his lips pulling back from his teeth like a wild animal.

"*Pearlvitae!*" Paloma screamed, her face twisting in astonishment as Pine backed up to the wall. Ana and the other guard stared dumbly; obviously, this was the first time a synadroid had gotten off its deathbed.

Sebastian pushed the table out of his way, advancing on Pine. The crash of the upturned table spurred Ana and her companion into action, and they lifted their weapons toward Pine.

"Don't shoot her," Paloma shouted. "Don't damage the—"

The door blew off its hinges, slamming into one of the stripped androids and toppling its bench.

After a moment of stunned silence, Paloma pointed at the door. "Ana, Pol! Go. Now!"

They obeyed, running to either side of the doorway then leaning against the wall and checking their weapons. Pol nodded to Ana, and they stepped out together, their weapons sweeping from side to side in the empty hallway. Confused, they took a few more paces, clearing the doorframe.

A figure reached out from the shadows and shot one then the other before they'd even realized she was there. They fell to the ground, convulsing, a white froth gathering at the corner of their mouths.

A man burst into the room, his weapon trained on Paloma. A dark-haired man with eyes the color of home.

James.

He'd come for her. Despite everything she'd said to him, despite how she'd left him, he'd come for her.

I was right. We are right.

"Put your hands on your head, Paloma." He stepped closer as she obliged, her mouth distorting into an ugly smile. "Where is—"

He saw Pine then, but not before Sebastian took advantage of her distraction and captured her in a chokehold, the scalpel pressed to the base of her neck where her spine met her skull.

"Drop the gun," he said to James, his voice low and nauseating in its calm. "Or I'll sever her nervous system."

James readjusted his grip on the gun but didn't lower it. Beads of perspiration formed on his forehead, but his hand was steady.

"I said, *drop it.*"

The Crow came up behind James and put his hand on his shoulder. "It's okay, James."

James jerked his shoulder as though trying to shake off an annoying fly. He kept the gun and his gaze trained on Sebastian.

"James, please."

He grimaced and lowered the gun. Rage and fear

burned in his eyes.

Sebastian laughed, taunting him. "I'm still going to kill her, you know."

Several tiny forms scuttled across the floor. *What are those?* They looked like tiny insects. James kept his gaze on Sebastian, but The Crow subtly tracked the minuscule figures, a slight smile quirking his mouth.

As Sebastian and James stared each other down, daring each other to make a move, the insects reached Pine's feet and crawled up Sebastian's pant leg. Even when one of them climbed up the skin of his arms, he didn't glance down.

The coward had turned his own sensors off.

Then one of them scrambled into his ear. "What— What's going on?" He kept his arm around Pine but dropped the scalpel and brushed his hand against his ear. "What the f—" His eyes widened, and he pushed Pine away from him.

"No—" His head canted oddly to the side and one hand curled into a claw. He stared at Pine, uncomprehending, as both his pupils blew, like Ash's had, the iris blackening as he dropped to his knees.

"You all might want to take cover," The Crow said, ducking behind the overturned gurney as Blue spun back through the doorway.

James snatched Pine around the waist and knocked her to the floor, curling his body around hers.

"Pine, I—"

The air sucked out of the room as it filled with a strange hum, a low drone that swelled into a whine before splintering into dazzling shards of glass that pierced Pine's skull and drilled into her brain. Just as she began to feel herself coming part, it stopped.

Air rushed into the room again, a vortex that was at once silent and deafening. After a few minutes, James moved away from her, and she fought to sit up.

James and The Crow stood over a body on the floor. Pine, unable to stand yet, crawled to them.

"I'm a bit disappointed, to be honest." Crow wore an almost childish pout. "I expected it to, you know, explode *out*...not *in*."

James squeezed his shoulder. "It's still a victory."

"He's dead?"

James crouched as he turned, and Pine crawled into his arms. "Are you okay, Pine?"

"Yes, I thought my head was going to explode." *And it still might, but only because I'm so happy you're here.*

James gave her a curious look.

"Didn't you hear that? That— Is that Sebastian? He's dead?"

"He's dead."

"I want to see." She *needed* to.

"Pine, are you sure?"

"Yes. I want to see the end of this. I want to remember it." James shifted to the side, and she finally saw the synadroid who would've happily taken her life.

The ruins of his face looked so unlike the man she'd met she couldn't remember what he'd looked like. "How could he do it, James? What—"

The bark of a loudspeaker assaulted the island, followed by the undulating wail of a siren.

Blue stuck her head through the doorway. "Time to go, everyone. The cavalry is here, and we're not supposed to be."

"What about Paloma?" Sebastian might be

dead, but Pine wanted the harbormaster to pay.

Blue dismissed her with a flick of her wrist. "Leave her." She placed more nodes on either side of the door after they'd passed through, and a horizontal band of pale blue light flared. "She's not going anywhere."

Outside the compound, the sun was beginning to set, the sky a riot of red and gold. "Red sky at night, sailor's delight," muttered The Crow as they ran.

Pine's shadow followed her through the brush and the thicket of trees, over the comatose bodies of her kin. What had happened to them? Were they dead? "James—?" She pointed to the bodies on the ground.

"They'll be okay, Pine. We had to knock them out to get past them, but they're not hurt, not permanently."

So why do I feel like a traitor, leaving them here? "But what if Paloma—"

James gripped her hand tighter. "Don't worry about that. Listen." The keening of the siren had been replaced by the rumble of many pairs of boots. "Paloma won't be able to hurt them."

They came to the edge of a lagoon, the water still—and empty. How were they planning to escape? One glance at James's calm expression told her this must be part of the plan, but—

Blue's hand moved in her pocket, and a few seconds later, a translucent shell, iridescent like abalone, broke the surface of the water.

A submarine.

They must've come up through the bottom of the island.

I wish I'd known. I could've saved us all. She closed her eyes. No. *They never would've come.*

Unlike you, none of the others had anything worth going back to.

The hatch opened smoothly, and The Owl stood in the doorway, waving cheerfully. "Right on time!" He gestured grandly to Pine. "Welcome aboard."

She didn't move, her mind a blur as doubt tried to grasp her around the throat again. *What's going to happen now? Once we leave this island, then what? With Joseph—*

Then James's arms were around her and she let him guide her aboard the vessel.

As the sub navigated back through the island's catacombs, Pine clung to James, her head against his chest, absorbing the soothing rhythm of his heart. It echoed through her until she could almost believe it was her own. She closed her eyes. Whatever had happened didn't matter now and she could deal with whatever the future held. She was on her way home.

TWENTY-FIVE

"She told you Joseph was *dead*?"

"Yes. She said Paloma knew, but that she let us think he was still alive as a cover, so I could escape." The bewildered look on her face tore at James's heart. If he'd ever had doubts about her feelings for Joseph, they were now quelled. He'd never seen grief looking back at him so starkly before.

"Is that why you got on the boat?" *Or was it because of me?* But he couldn't ask the latter, afraid the answer would crush the careful happiness growing inside him.

Pine buried her head in her arms. "Partly, yes. If he was gone…I didn't know what would happen to me."

"Pine, look at me." When she tightened her arms around her face, he gently pried them away. "Please."

Her strange eyes shone as he cupped her face in both hands and rubbed his thumbs over her cheekbones. "Listen to me. If anything happened to Joseph, I would take care of you. I will always take care of you. And not just because of him." He gripped her shoulders. "You believe me, right?"

She gazed at him, the war between everything

she'd thought to be true and what she wanted to believe playing out on her face.

He understood completely. A tiny part of him still hung back, wondering if she was truly here the way he wanted her to be.

The smile she finally gave him was tentative, but James was okay with that. They still had a way to go, but at least now they would have the chance.

"James? I need you to know…before you came to the island, I tried to leave. I tried—"

He didn't need to know. She was here, and that was what was important. "It's okay, Pine, I—"

"No. I need to tell you this, and I need you to believe me. I didn't want to leave *you*, James. I thought— Well, that doesn't matter now." She clutched at his wrists, holding them fast.

He gently pulled one of his hands free and cupped her face again. "I know what you thought. And I'm sorry. I had my doubts too, Pine. But I don't anymore." He hesitated then, "Do you?"

"No. I don't." And in her smile was the truth.

He smiled back, and they stayed that way until Blue coughed pointedly behind them. They broke apart, but no awkward tension remained, and James couldn't have been more grateful. He didn't know what would happen between them now, but it didn't matter. She was here, and that was enough. "Now what?"

"First thing is to find Joseph." Blue was nonchalant, as though she hadn't just helped rescue Pine from certain death. "Sorry to interrupt, but this boat is a borrow and time is ticking."

Pine pressed her face into James's hand. "But he's dead." Her voice cracked over the last word.

He ran his hand over her hair. "I think Paloma lied, Pine. Nothing has been found—either of

Joseph or his vessel. And believe me, we would've heard. Wouldn't we, Blue?"

"Yep. Even if Paloma tried to cover it up. I'm with James, Pine. I think Joseph is still alive. We just need to find him."

Pine dropped her face into her arms again, and her shoulders shook. She was weeping as best she could, and his heart ached for her. He sat back on his heels, weariness vying with frustration. "I just wish we knew where to look."

Pine's shoulders froze. She stared up at James, her misery forgotten. "The storm."

The Owl and The Crow had joined them, and James glanced around at the others. Was he the only one who wasn't following? "What do you mean, Pine? What about the storm?"

"There was a storm when Joseph went missing, right? A strange storm, the man at the docks said, lasting only twenty minutes or so." She stood and paced the length of the floor as she thought out loud. "Do you remember what I said, James, that I sometimes thought something brought the storm, rather than the other way around?"

Storm-bringing sea monsters. How could he forget? Dread surged inside him.

"What if I'm right? We synadroids always knew when a storm was coming, because we would see things, feel things before it happened. If I'm right, all we need to do is look for a storm."

"But there's no way every storm is unnatural," Blue said, although James could see her mind already surging ahead.

"No, not most storms. A small, isolated storm like the one Joseph disappeared during. A storm that isn't predicted by the weather sensors." Pine looked at them expectantly.

Blue's eyes darted around the sub as though calculating the odds. "I have no idea if you're right, but it's the best lead we have right now."

"Is it possible, Blue? Not that I doubt you, Pine." It just seemed like such a long shot.

"Absolutely. The ocean is huge, and I've seen some pretty weird things out there."

"Can you find the kind of storm she's talking about?" It was a tenuous plan at best, but if they couldn't even locate the squall, they'd be dead in the water.

Blue raised an eyebrow at The Owl.

"Of course." He looked almost offended. "Just tell me the parameters we need."

* * *

Three infuriating hours later, they still hadn't found a single unnatural storm.

"How far out are we looking?" James asked. "Like Blue said, the ocean is massive." Too massive. Whatever had taken Joseph was probably long gone. But seeing Pine so focused, he kept his mouth shut.

"Far enough."

James had known The Owl long enough not to feel slighted by his terse reply. *We're all exhausted.* Fatigue lapped at him, threatening to pull him under. "I'm going to go lie down for a while—in the cabin." The last thing he needed was to fall asleep on the deck and dream of whatever was out there, only to wake and find it staring back at him.

He squeezed Pine's shoulder. She ran her hand down his arm, distracted, as she stared at Owl's screen as though she could will the blink of a squall to appear.

James lay on the long tweed couch in the cabin's modest living quarters. Slowly, he slipped into sleep, his mind sinking through deepening layers of dreams.

Pine waited for him at the bottom of the ocean, her skin alight, her hair spreading around her shoulders like a black sail. "I knew you'd come."

"I'll always come for you." James gathered her into his arms, soaking in the scent of sun and seaweed. He inhaled deeply. *I can breathe.*

James ran his hands over her, her luminescent skin warm to the touch. She traced her finger over his collarbone, leaving a glowing indigo trail. Over his entire body she sketched, until all but a few inches of his skin were radiant.

The light covering him burned with an expansive warmth, and he tilted his head back and raised his arms, weightless. Pine brought her mouth to the few dark spaces left on him, over and over, leaving marks of brilliance he thought would blind her. But as Pine traced her lips down his chest, down his stomach, the darkness in the sea behind them expanded. Pine's skin dimmed and grew cold, and James's breath no longer came easily. "What's going on, Pine?"

"It knows we're here. All we have to do now is wait." Her luminosity pulsed once then went out, plunging James into darkness and knocking the remaining breath from his body.

"We have to get to the surface, Pine. I have to breathe. We have to find Joseph." Euphoria seeped into James as his mind grew light. He was going to suffocate.

"Don't worry, we don't have to find anything. It'll find us. It always does." Pine gave him an enigmatic smile.

Behind her, a behemoth rose, a vast, dark shape with cruel, glittering eyes and a miasma of violence. It glided toward them silently as James tugged at Pine's arm, desperately trying to get her attention.

The great mouth opened, and Pine was framed by a ring of viciously barbed, inward-turning spikes. James wanted to scream, to warn her, but Pine held a finger to her lips. "It's very old, James. Don't scare it away. Don't—"

Pine crashed into the cabin just as the giant teeth pierced her.

Startled awake, James tried to stand, his long legs tripping over each other and bringing him crashing to the floor.

"James!"

"Pine? Is everything okay? Did you find Joseph?" He sat up and leaned against the couch, rubbing his elbow where it had grazed the floor.

"Yes. No. I don't know. But we found a storm. We're heading there now, come on." She was practically quivering with excitement, nearly pulling James's arm out of the socket as she dragged him toward the deck.

The ocean beyond the translucent shell shot by them in distorted smudges, too fast for his eyes to focus on. Thankfully. "How fast are we going?" He tried not to sound disapproving.

"Again, James? Don't ask what you don't want to know," Blue answered primly. "Like when we rescued Pine, we have to go fast if we're going to get there in time."

He couldn't argue with that. James turned away from the dizzying view to face Pine. "Are you ready for this?" He rubbed his fingers over his eyes, unsure whether the blurriness was from sleep or the scenery whipping past. "What's the plan?"

"Crow kitted out a…well, I guess it's a life-pod." She wrinkled her nose, as though dreading his reaction. "When we get close enough, I'm going to drive it into the storm."

Had he misheard her? "What do you mean, *you?* You're not going without me." Did she actually think he'd let her go on her own?

"James, this is just like the storm before. You nearly *died*. You're staying here, where you can breathe." She stood on her toes and cupped his cheek. "We don't know what's down there. I'm not willing to risk your life again."

There were so many ways he could've argued. He could've ranted that it wasn't her choice. Could've put his foot down and demanded. Instead, he gazed at her and simply asked, "Would you let me go on my own?"

She stared back. He already knew the answer, but he needed *her* to know. "No. I wouldn't."

"Well, then."

Wordlessly, she brought his hand to her lips.

He cleared his throat. "Just so I'm clear, we're going to drive a tin can into a storm that's possibly the cover for a giant, man-swallowing sea monster?"

Pine gave him a pained smile. "Yes. But you—"

"Don't say it again. I'm coming." Despite his bravado, James's knees turned soft, reminding him of a jellyfish he'd once seen wash up on the shore.

Pine's voice, cutting through the dark water. "Don't worry, James, we don't have to find anything. It'll find us. It always does."

"James? Are you okay?"

"I'm fine. I just—"

"We're here." Blue's voice rinsed away the last remnants of the dream. "And it looks like we're right on time.”

* * *

The Avenoir disappeared toward the choppy surface above them. The Crow had outfitted James and Pine with trackers; they would retreat to a safe distance then come back for them when the storm was over.

Unless we disappear completely.

Pine steered the pod down onto the sea bed, where it landed with a soft thump.

“Now what?” After the way he’d felt on the boat, this was strangely anticlimactic. It had never been this quiet on the Perimeter; the threats there were always straightforward.

“Now we wait. It won’t be long.”

He believed her.

As though on cue, the water around them darkened. Sealife swam past them in the opposite direction, and James fought down the urge to demand that he and Pine do the same. *This might be our only chance to find Joseph.*

The pod lifted and bucked, and Pine bent over the controls, trying to keep them on an even keel.

Nausea roiled in James’s stomach. “Pine. *Pine.*” He clutched her shoulder, unable to say anything other than her name. What he wouldn’t give to be fighting mutated plants right now.

A shape appeared in the murky water, a shape darker than the deepest ocean. It was larger than anything James had ever imagined a living thing could be, larger than a whale, easily the size of a small cruise ship.

Pine flicked on the pod lights, igniting them into a beacon.

“What are you doing?” James fumbled blindly

at the control panel, trying to switch them off until Pine covered his hand with hers.

"Making sure it sees us. We need it to see us, James. It has to be able to find us."

"I thought—" What had he thought? That they were just going to observe?

Whatever the creature was, it saw them; Pine had placed them directly in its path. As James watched in horror, it entered the illumination of the pod's beams, moving slowly enough that they were able to get a good look.

His dream from the sub, the nightmares he'd had all his life, had come true.

It was a shark, but unlike any shark James had even heard of. It made the beast that had attacked them look like bait. It seemed to push the storm before it, the water outside the pod so cold it chilled the air inside. Even the plants anchored in the rocks of the sea floor seemed to shrink from it.

The behemoth faced them head on, drawn to their light. Its head was triangular with rounded edges, the wide, lower half studded with a circular, closed port. A large vent topped the flanks of the dorsal section like nostrils, and James made out a great, protuberant, blind eye on either side of its head. It curved slightly as it swam toward them, showing a segmented body with strange projecting gills ringing its belly. Further back, its body was encircled with ridges at regular intervals, and its fins were angular and oddly jointed.

"What the hell is that, Pine?"

"I don't know. I've never seen what brings the storm." She seemed mesmerized by it.

"Is it alive?" It couldn't be. There was no living thing like that. "It looks like a machine."

The shark gave no indication of attack, moving

toward them at a steady pace.

Maybe it hadn't seen them. Maybe—

The large circular port at the front of its face spun slowly open, revealing a single row of savage, backward-curving teeth surrounding a girdled throat that terminated in a black hole.

"Pine, what do we—"

The pod lurched and plunged forward in a vacuum, picking up speed. All around them, creatures who hadn't been able to escape hurtled alongside, end over end, their bodies slamming against the pod until James could no longer see the monster's gaping jaw.

That's probably a blessing.

The unnatural current tossed them over the teeth and down, down into the darkness.

TWENTY-SIX

"James? Are you awake?" Pine groped about in the darkness, trying to grasp something familiar. "James?"

"I'm here," a groggy voice spoke from her left. "And in one piece. I think."

Pine patted over the floor until she found his foot. "Let me see if I can get the emergency lights going." She felt her way blindly to the control panel, pressed a few buttons, pulled a lever, and waited. A few seconds later, the pod hummed into life and a dim glow flooded the interior. At least they still had power.

The exterior of the pod was plastered with a vibrant mosaic of scales and fins, claws and tentacles, and leathery ropes of seaweed so thick Pine couldn't see anything beyond them. She climbed onto the dash and pressed her ear against the cool surface. Wherever they were, they were no longer in the water.

James was sprawled on his back at the far end of the pod. "Where the hell are we, Pine?" He caught sight of their marine-life cocoon. "Oh sh— Is that what I think it is?"

"I think we're in the belly of the beast." She racked her memory, trying to pull up any information she could about a being—biological or mechanical—that could explain where they were. *Nothing.*

"Do you think that's what happened to Joseph? That he just happened to get in its path?" James rolled up his sleeve and rubbed a large bruise forming on his arm.

"I hope so, because otherwise…" What had they done? What had she done? She should've insisted he stay behind. Panic seized her. "What if this was a mistake, James? What if—"

"Shh. It's okay, Pine. He'll be here. And if he's not…at least we're together."

Pine couldn't help herself. She wrapped her arms around him. "How can you be so calm?"

"Oh, I'm not." He grinned. "I'm actually screaming in my head right now. So either my military training is kicking in, or I'm in shock. Either way, let's hope it lasts." He pressed his lips together and took a deep breath. "So now what?"

Pine squared her shoulders and gathered her composure. "Now we find out where we are." She rooted around under the control board until she found a couple of flashlights. "Here, from the survival kit The Owl insisted on." She stood and pulled the straps of the kit over her shoulders. "I'm going to open the hatch."

"But you'll flood us." James glared at the seams of the hatch as though the water had already started seeping in.

"We're not *in* water, James. Can't you feel it?"

How could he? she chastised herself. She had to remember this was beyond anything he knew.

Pine motioned to him and he stepped to her side and braced himself, one arm protectively around her. She pressed the emergency button on the dash.

"Here we go." The roof mechanism groaned then shuddered to a halt, opening only wide enough to let in the faintest whiff of bloodied, salted air. "Damn. I think we're going to have to help it along." She handed one flashlight to James. "Ready to push?"

James braced his feet and planted his hands against the pod roof. "On the count of three."

Twenty minutes later, they'd managed to open a large enough gap for the two of them to squeeze through. They found themselves knee-deep in squishy, boneless bodies and squirming, gasping beasts. The glow from the pod was barely enough to illuminate five feet, yet countless eyes shone up at them, reflecting the dim light.

"Just don't look down," James whispered, although Pine didn't know if he was talking to her or himself.

A weak light shone in the distance, but the surrounding gloom made it impossible to judge how far away it was. "James, look. There." Pine groped in the murkiness for his hand, and they treaded carefully across the writhing floor.

Twenty feet from the pod, the mass of sea life on the floor thinned out. Pine tilted her light downward to expose what appeared to be a concrete surface, discolored by damp and reeking of the sea.

James squatted, gingerly tracing his fingers over the surface. "Definitely manmade. What the hell is this place?"

Pine continued wordlessly on toward the light. As they drew closer, it materialized into a globular emergency light, marking a bulky steel door surrounded by concrete and steel-ribbed walls. "There's no way we're going to be able to shift this.

I can't see a control panel." Pine traced and retraced her beam around the doorframe.

James reached past her and tugged experimentally on the handle set into the door. To Pine's surprise, it swung open, leading into a softly lit corridor. James chuckled at her look of surprise. "Guess they're not worried about intruders."

A clanging of metal on metal sounded from further down the corridor, an arrhythmic, unmistakably human sound. Pine clutched James's arm. "Can you hear that?"

James inclined his head and waited, but the sound didn't come again. "No, I can't."

"Well, I heard something. I think there's someone down here." *Joseph*, Pine's heart pleaded. *Please, let it be Joseph.*

She strode down the corridor, hope welling inside her. It was definitely human. *We're coming, Joseph.* Unable to wait any longer, Pine broke into a run, her feet slapping on the smooth floor. Beyond the door at the end, the sound started again, this time more boisterous. *It's Joseph. It has to be.*

It wasn't.

Pine threw open the steel door at the end of the corridor. As it smashed back against the wall, a man, his face creased in shock, dropped the mallet he'd been holding.

He and Pine stared at each other until James came hurtling through the door, slamming into Pine and nearly knocking her over.

"Pine, what the hell—" He gaped at the man slouching in coveralls before him.

The man recovered first, bending over and retrieving the large hammer from the floor. "Got sucked in too, did you? Well, welcome to hell." He turned away from them and lifted the tool over his head with a whistle.

Disappointment clawed at her. She'd been so sure. "Wait!"

The man paused and squinted at Pine, as though he'd forgotten they were there.

"Where are we?" Pine asked.

The man looked faintly surprised then nodded to himself. "Ah, right. I guess you'll be wanting a tour then?"

"A tour of *what*? And who are you?"

"My name is Tunny. And this—" He placed the mallet carefully back on the ground and pointed to a door at the far end of the room. "This is the 9791 Atlas Four Holding Center. This way, please."

"9791 Atlas Four? But there's no—" James paused, as though searching his memory for the phantom Atlas. "But 9791 is a Foxwept military—"

"Is there a man named Joseph here?" Pine demanded. She didn't care what this place was. She only cared about finding her father.

But Tunny had gone on, his hands shoved deep into his pockets.

"Just follow him, James." Pine hurried after Tunny, determined not to let him out of her sight. He'd acted like they weren't the only people to get caught there—which meant there must be more people here. Missing people. Like Joseph.

The door opened into another room, this one brighter and less industrial. A dozen tables were spaced out on the brown-tiled floor, chairs tucked neatly under them. At the back was an open kitchen, shelves laden with shining pots and pans and heavy with the odor of fried fish.

"This is the mess hall," Tunny said, giving a

perfunctory wave without slowing down. "Hope you like seafood."

Pine was lightheaded as they neared the door on the opposite side of the room. *Thank goodness I don't have a real heart. It would be exploding out of my chest.*

Tunny put his hand on the door handle.

Pine clenched her hands at her sides then unclenched them. *Joseph, we're here.*

Tunny took his hand off the handle. "This is the cell block. So, you may or may not be familiar…"

Open the door.

"I, in fact, was one of the original—"

"Open the damn door!" Both Tunny and James started and turned to stare at her. "I'm sorry, I just need— James, please."

James nodded. "She's right. I'm sorry, Tunny, this is very interesting, but we're actually looking for someone. There *are* other people on this thing, aren't there?"

"Oh yes," Tunny agreed sagely. "You have some of the original prisoners, a guard or two, and of course, the few people like you who somehow manage to get sucked in—"

Pine couldn't wait any longer. She pushed past Tunny and yanked the door open herself.

Beyond was a large rectangular room, flanked on either side by two stories of steel-barred cells. Here the reek of the ocean was minimal, overlaid with the scent of mold and living people.

There were so many cells. How would she find Joseph before anticipation fried her circuits?

"Joseph!" Pine's screams echoed through the cavernous room, ricocheting off the walls and back, taunting her. "Joseph!"

Several people stepped out of their cells to see

the new inmates. Pine deciphered the expressions on their faces—everything from wariness, to hope, to despair. A few raised their hands in greeting before shuffling back into their cells to hide anything of value before the fresh faces got too comfortable.

"He's not here, James." The walls of the prison began to close around her. *He's gone. He's—* "What do we do now?" Her voice was swallowed by the cells.

"I—"

"Pine? James? Is that you?" From a unit midway down the row, a familiar figure emerged, rubbing his eyes as though waking from a dream.

Joseph.

He's here. He's actually here. Pine understood then how tenuous her own hope had been, how big a leap of faith they'd taken.

But they'd found him. Alive.

Pine reached him first and threw herself into his arms, nearly knocking him to the floor. "Father." She pressed her face against his, murmuring it over and over until she felt a wetness on her cheeks. *Am I finally crying?* She pulled back and raised her hand to her cheek. No, but Joseph was. *For both of us.*

A strong pair of arms wrapped around both of them, squeezing until Joseph groaned and began to laugh. "James."

"Is this who you were looking for?" Tunny asked mildly, his eyebrows raised. He'd ambled up behind then and was leaning on Joseph's cell door.

"Yes, this is my father."

Tunny squinted as he glanced from Pine to Joseph. "Your father, eh?" He shrugged. "Yeah, well, why not? Okay then, I'm back to work." He wandered away, stopping briefly to chat with a few of the other residents.

Joseph chuckled. "Never mind Tunny, Pine. He's been down here a long time." He put a hand on each of their shoulders and stood back, drinking them in. "I can't believe this is real, that you're actually here. How did you find me? I thought I'd be in here for years, if not forever."

"Well, we haven't gotten out yet—" James began.

"Why don't we go sit down somewhere to talk?" Joseph looked thin and frail, despite his cheerfulness. Being trapped in an underwater prison had clearly taken a toll on the older man, despite the relatively short amount of time.

"We can go into the mess hall, if you like," Joseph said, leading the way. "My cell is comfortable enough for sleeping, but not particularly good for company—the washing machine broke a few years back, I'm told." He paused before the door and hugged Pine again. "I just still can't believe it."

They chose a table in the center of the room, trying to find a middle ground between the wafting stench of raw and rotting fish on one side and the layers of grease on the other.

Joseph took the seat across from James and Pine. He was the most marvelous thing Pine had ever seen. His eyes sparkled, and his smile told her he was looking at the two things he loved most in the world. "Now, before I tell you my tale, I want to hear yours. Tell me *everything*."

So they did.

TWENTY-SEVEN

Joseph leaned so far back in his chair, James worried he would tip over.

The old man's face had run through such a range of emotions—shock, anger, sorrow, mirth—James was wrung out by the time they'd finished with their daring escape from Paloma's island.

"I can't believe all that happened while I was stuck in here. And…Oh, Pine, I'm so sorry. I never should've let my excitement get the better of me. I should've waited. I just wanted to see you so badly, to let you know you still had a home—" Tears rose again in his eyes, tracing down the creases of his face.

"No, Joseph, please—" Pine's face was pinched, her lips pressed into a thin line. Her fingers kept rearranging themselves around Joseph's hand, smoothing then squeezing then smoothing again.

James could only imagine the pain she must be feeling. Every time he thought about what she'd been through, from believing the person sworn to take care of her was dead, to fleeing from uncertainty about his loyalty, only to end up strapped to a table and nearly dismantled, his throat constricted, and his blood roared in his ears. *Never again.*

He snatched up her other hand. "Now it's your turn, Joseph." Pine leaned her forehead on his shoulder, composing herself.

Joseph smiled. "Well, you know how I ended up here—the same as you, except by accident. It should've been a short trip, but the storm took me by surprise, though I understand why, now. I jumped into my life-pod, figuring I could wait it out at the bottom then continue." He scratched his head ruefully. "It's been a while since I've driven one of those things and I ended up crashing it— nothing serious. But of course, when Alpha Four came by, I was a sitting duck."

"And the others? Tunny said some were here by accident, and some were guards and prisoners?" James's mind leaped ahead toward more practical matters, like how they were going to get out of here. He wasn't ready to give in to his relief just yet. They may have found Joseph, but they still had to get home.

"That's right. Tunny himself was the handyman."

"How long has he been here? I mean, this vessel has a military name, but I'd know if such a prison existed. It doesn't. Not on any records I know of, anyway." No matter how much James racked his brain, he couldn't remember any information regarding a shark-shaped prison swimming free around the Ghostlight.

"Ah, that's because it's not *supposed* to exist. It's a black site."

"What's a black site?" Pine glanced from James to Joseph.

James leaned back in his chair. *Now* he understood. "It's an off-the-record site for projects the government doesn't want people to know about. And it's wholly illegal."

"Then how can it exist?" Pine was still so naïve in many ways.

"The government must've decided it was worth the risk to look the other way when we almost went under martial law, just before the Goldhare Horizon disaster ended the possibility of war." James pulled at his bottom lip.

"So you don't recognize the name?" Joseph didn't seem surprised.

James ran his hand through his hair. "No, only the 9791 designation. But then again, that wasn't my branch of the military. I'd heard rumblings of a series of black prisons patrolling the waters around Foxwept, keeping high profile prisoners and collecting defectors, escapees, and insurgents. They'd been in use for about two years before the Blackmoth Provincial Autonomy was signed, and although rumors of them were leaked to the public, they were all apparently destroyed before the truth was documented. I wasn't even sure they were real."

"They were. And they were supposed to have been destroyed, like you said. Only, they lost one."

"*Lost* one?" It was unbelievable. When he'd served, he'd practically had to account for every single bullet.

"Yes. And it put them in a bit of a quandary. They couldn't exactly ask for help looking for something that's not supposed to exist, could they?"

James let out a low whistle. "No, they couldn't. But if that's true, Tunny's been down here for nearly seven years." The poor bastard. No wonder he'd been unimpressed at their arrival.

"That's right."

"Did he never wonder why no one was in contact with him? What happened to all the other people? The captain?"

"Tunny *did* wonder when there'd been no communication for nearly a year. But his superiors impressed on him the secret nature of the ship, and since they didn't seem concerned...he minded his own business, like he was paid to do. I mean, they had life-pods and everything, so they could evacuate if they needed to." He leaned back and dipped his head in regret. "Only, a few months later, a new prisoner brought a plague aboard and it swept through the prison. When it had finally run its course, only a handful of people were left, and the ship had lost all communication with the outside world. Some of them have passed on, and they've picked up a few others along the way, like me."

"What about the life-pods? I mean, I know all too well about not abandoning one's duty, but it would've been understandable in this case. So why didn't they use them?"

"The captain had apparently gone a bit...mad. He ejected all the life-pods during one of his episodes. By the time anyone realized, it was too late, and they were trapped."

"That's—" Horrible. Unbelievable. Tragic. James could barely conceive of it. What must it have been like for those people down here, the moment they realized they were virtually entombed? Nausea and pity rose in his throat.

Pressure on his hand brought him back to the present. Pine was gazing at him, reflecting his anguish. No. They would not suffer the same fate. *Think. There must be a way.* "How do they survive? I mean, what do you eat? How does the prison run?" Joseph was rough around the edges, but Tunny was what James could only call hale and hearty, and he'd kept the prison sailing all this time. Hearing Joseph's story, he was developing a new respect for the maintenance man.

Joseph made a face. "We eat whatever gets sucked in. The fish are a bit worse for wear, but it's regular. There's a water treatment tank. As for the prison itself, it's hydrogen-powered. It takes its energy right from the water. And these damn things were made to last."

"Has anyone ever tried to escape? I mean, seven *years*." Surely there'd been at least a few attempts.

"I'm sure they did, in the beginning. But from what I've been told, none managed it. It *is* a prison, after all."

That wasn't what James wanted to hear. "There must be a way out. Every place, no matter how secret, has an escape route." James drummed his fingers on the tabletop. "Is there a control room I can get into? If I can look at the schematics of the ship, I might be able to find something."

"There is. Only...Tunny says the captain's still in there. He apparently barricaded himself and the first mate in there years ago during a particularly severe bout. He'd been threatening the other inmates, so Tunny was happy enough to leave him where he is. And he just never came out. He'll be dead, of course, but I just wanted to warn you. All the other bodies were shot out into the sea."

"If bodies can leave, why can't we use the same exit?"

"The waste vents are big enough for a person to go through, but then they're still in the middle of the ocean. Without diving equipment, we'd never survive."

"There's got to be *something*. Blueprints, a manual. Will you show me where it is?"

Joseph slapped the table with both hands. "Of course. Believe me, I'm as eager to get out of here as you are."

"Should we tell the others what we're doing? One of them might have some more information." Pine glanced at the door leading into the cell block.

She wanted to give them hope, and he understood that. But they had to find some themselves before they told the others. "Not yet. We need to come up with a plan first."

Joseph bounced to his feet, sprightly as a much younger man. "Let's go find that control room."

* * *

The hinges of the control room door groaned loudly as James pushed it open.

"Strange," Tunny remarked. "The captain locked the door when he…wasn't quite right."

James groped for the light switch, flicking it up and down. Nothing. The only light in the room was the minutely less dark water outside the cockpit window. From James's best guess, they were at the forefront of the prison's triangular head.

"Pine, could you hold up the flashlight for me, please?" he asked. "We could really use that indigo glow of yours right now."

"What? I should plaster myself against the window like a naked starfish?" She left Tunny and Joseph waiting on the iron staircase leading up to the control room and lit her flashlight, holding it over her head and pointing the beam into the darkened space. "What would poor Tunny think?"

James snorted. "It would probably be the silver

lining of the last seven years of his life."

The light passed over panels inlaid with screens and dials, and what looked like enough buttons to control a fleet of ships. James had expected—given Tunny's recounting of the captain's alleged madness—to find the room in disarray. But everywhere the beam touched was fastidiously neat; even the shaft of light itself showed no motes of dust in its ray.

In the front center of the cockpit, the beam illuminated the back of the captain's chair.

"That must be him," James whispered to Pine. The captain's arms rested on either side of the chair, still clad in a crisp, navy blue uniform.

James shivered, although he wasn't sure why. He'd seen plenty of bodies before. Fresh bodies, bodies of people he'd *known*. Why would he be skittish of a years-old corpse?

"What should we do?" Pine murmured back.

"Try to get the lights going. Then we'll move the captain. I won't feel as disrespectful rooting around in his ship's system if I'm not standing two feet from his body. Besides, he deserves a proper sea burial. He never left his post or abandoned his ship."

The captain's chair creaked as it swiveled to face them. "And why would I?"

TWENTY-EIGHT

The flashlight fell from Pine's hand, clattering loudly on the floor. When the cockpit lights flared on a few seconds later, she was still rooted to the spot. Could synadroids die of fright?

The captain remained seated, his hands folded grandly on his lap. The gold-trimmed peaked hat sat in perfect symmetry atop his head, his angular face was composed, and the creases in his jacket looked freshly pressed.

Like the room, he was immaculate, unmarred by even a speck of the dusty dankness that seemed to be on every other surface in the prison, even Tunny.

"Charles?" Tunny gaped from the doorway. "You're alive."

"And why wouldn't I be, Tunny?"

"That's the captain?" Pine whispered to Tunny.

"No, just his uniform. He's the first mate."

"Incorrect. I am *now* the captain."

"I think *that's* the captain there." James pointed to a corner bordered by the consoles. The naked, desiccated remains of a man slumped against the wall, his head bowed and hands resting across his thighs.

"Correct. And in the event of the captain's death at sea, the first mate becomes the captain."

Pine had no idea if that was true or not.

"What happened to the *other* captain?" James looked as skeptical as she felt.

"He became…hysterical. He wanted to abandon our mission."

"You're a synadroid," Pine said, and James stiffened beside her.

The captain inclined his head. "Top model of my year."

"But I thought…you…I thought you were *dead*," Tunny blurted. "I've not heard a sound out of this room since the captain barricaded the two of you in here. I assumed you just…wound down." Finally, Pine had met someone as naïve about synadroids as she was about humans. She liked Tunny more and more.

"I found myself out of sorts, given recent events, and decided to power down for a short nap. I must say, I'm feeling all the better for it."

"But you've been in here for five years!"

"You jest. By my account, I've been inactive a mere twenty-eight hours."

The odd formality of his speech struck Pine. Was it his programming, a kind of naval nostalgia? In her experience, sentient androids were usually as contemporary as possible, a whimsical attempt to make them fit in seamlessly.

Or was he, as Tunny had said of the captain, not quite right?

"You've been inactive for more than twenty-eight hours." Tunny tapped the watch on his wrist.

Charles's silver eyes narrowed. "You're incorrect."

"It's true. You've been missing for nearly seven years. The other prisons have been decommissioned. And on our ship, sir, the Alpha

Four, things have…deteriorated somewhat. Nearly everyone is gone."

One corner of the captain's mouth twitched. "I don't believe you, Tunny. I would know if that were true."

"It *is* true, sir. We've been traversing this bloody ocean for years, sucking up any poor soul that gets in our path."

The captains mouth twitched again. "Felons, you mean."

"No, Tunny's right. Your duty here is *over*. We need to get back to the surface. If not, we'll all die down here." James held up his hands. "As one military man to another, it's the truth."

"Who are *you*?"

"My name is James, Lieutenant—"

"Not you. *Her.* The *synadroid*."

"My name is Pine." Her fingers followed his gaze to the tattoo on her wrist.

"Why are you here? There are no other androids aboard this vessel."

"Like Tunny told you, we got caught up in your path. We're here by mistake."

"We don't make mistakes." His pronunciation became crisper, more deliberate.

"Everything is different now. Go look around the prison if you don't believe us."

"And leave my post?" He stroked the hard-earned navy-and-gold epaulet on his shoulder. "Who are you, *really*?"

They were getting into murky waters here. "I'm no one to you. But I'm telling you the truth. We *need* to get up to the surface, now. If not, people will die. Many already have." Pine rubbed her fingers over her barcode. What should she do? There was obviously something wrong with him.

For all they knew, he'd killed his captain. They had to be careful. "I think...I think you may have had a slight malfunction, but don't worry, Joseph here can—"

It was the wrong thing to say. "A *malfunction?* That's what the captain said, right before he tried to take me out of action."

"What did you do? What happened to the captain?" James asked again.

Is this what it had been like for him on the Perimeter? This standing on a knife's edge? What was it he'd said, about the synadroids? *They hurt themselves...then one night, one of them turned on us. I was the only one who survived.*

"I disciplined him the way we did other mutineers. You can't have mutiny aboard a vessel of this sensitive nature." His lips twisted again, and his fingers dug into the leather of his chair.

James's breath rasped in Pine's ears, ragged and shallow, his face sallow in the light.

His hand moved at his side as though checking the security of his weapon, and finding none, seized the fabric of his trousers.

Pine had to diffuse the situation, and quickly. Maybe the captain would listen if it was just the two of them, synadroid to synadroid.

"James? You should take Tunny and Joseph and see if you can find another solution to our problem. Maybe Tunny has a few ideas. *Anything*, no matter how risky." She spoke low, knowing it was pointless. Charles had better hearing than a human.

"I'm not leaving you here, alone with him."

"Please, James. I need you to trust me."

"I do trust you. I don't trust *him*. Not when I know what he's capable of."

"I need you to trust what *I'm* capable of."

The muscle in his jaw leaped as he struggled to choose. "Pine—"

"Please."

He shook his head but relented. "Joseph, Tunny, I think we should go. Let the captain and Pine speak in private." James tilted his head toward the synadroid. "Captain, by your leave?"

The captain tugged on his lapels and nodded graciously back.

The set of James's shoulders told Pine how much it cost him, the will it took for him to walk out the door and close it behind him, and her heart nearly burst.

"Now it's just us," Pine addressed the captain. "You know that I can't lie. It's over. You need to do the right thing and take us up to the surface."

"The right thing? Abandon my duty?"

She feigned surprise. "You're not abandoning it. You're carrying it out."

He steepled his fingers under his chin. "How so?"

"There are still people alive on this ship, but they won't survive forever. If you take us up to the surface, they'll live. And no more people will become trapped. The people here now aren't supposed to be. They're not your prisoners."

"Do you know what will happen to me if I break protocol? I will be a defector. I will be terminated."

"But you're not. You'll be a hero."

"A hero?" He mulled it over, and for a moment, it seemed he would acquiesce. Then his mouth convulsed again, a spasm that rippled across his entire face. "And then what? If what you're saying is true, what will become of me? A secret captain without his secret ship? They'll destroy me."

"No, they won't. Look at me. We were

emancipated. We're no longer indentured to our original tasks. You can find a new life."

"Emancipated? You mean we're now considered equal?"

Pine faltered. What did she tell him? The truth? Or should she lie to save them? He didn't know she could lie; in his eyes, whatever she said was true.

The captain stared at her expectantly, his face smooth.

She closed her eyes and bowed her head. "We— No. We're not *legally* free, not yet. But—" She raised her eyes to his. "It *will* happen, I'm sure of it. It's just taking time and—"

"Then I *will* be destroyed."

"No—"

"You can't know that. I've done what they've asked of me. I fulfilled my duty more than any human, and they *will* destroy me. What else would they do with a synadroid with my history?"

"Perhaps the military can put your skills to use elsewhere? *Hire* you." But he was right. They'd retired other androids for less. Aside from Tunny, he was one of the few beings alive to know about this prison, this black site. At best, they would wipe his memory. But Pine suspected that would be more trouble to them, more uncertainty, than he was worth. Could she really, in good conscience, convince him to go to his death?

No.

"You're right," she said aloud. "I don't know what they would do with you. But I could ask Joseph to speak on your behalf. He knows—"

A clanging rang out down below, like a call to war.

The captain shot out of his chair. "What was that? What are they doing down there?"

Pine made her face indifferent. "I'm sure it's nothing. Tunny's probably just fixing something." *James, is that you? Whatever you're doing, please, hurry.*

The racket obscured the crack of the captain's fist smashing into the side of Pine's face.

TWENTY-NINE

"Joseph, we need to have faith in her," James said as Joseph stared forlornly at the control room's closed door.

"I *do*. You know that. It's just…she's—"

"Your daughter, I know. But we each have to play our part now." He put his hand on the older man's shoulder. "Believe me, I don't like it either." Leaving Pine alone in that room had been one of the most difficult things he'd ever done. He just prayed it hadn't been a mistake.

"So why are we out here?"

"Because *she's* protecting *us*."

"You mean, she's afraid we'll make the situation worse."

"Yes, that *is* what I mean." James didn't have time to sugarcoat it. "And she's right. Don't look at me like that, Joseph. She's perfectly capable in there. If he's going to listen to anyone, it'll be another synadroid."

"But what if he—"

"Don't think like that." *And don't you dare consider it either.* He put his hand on Joseph's shoulder as the older man hung his head. "Now, quickly, let's do our best to help her by finding a way out of this damn hole." James crossed his arms over his chest, resolute.

"I thought the whole point of leaving her was so that she could convince him."

"She'll do her best, but I think the captain's beyond that point. We need to be prepared for a no." Contrary to his façade for Joseph's sake, James ached to smash back through the door, barrel into the room, and snatch Pine away. If the captain had touched her, he would crush him with his bare hands—

No. She would be okay. The best way to help her now was to find an escape. But how?

"Tunny, since I can't get to the schematics, is there anything you can tell us that might help us escape?"

The custodian pursed his lips. "I can't think of anything. This place was built to keep people in, after all."

"But there has to be *something*. An emergency measure, a failsafe in case things went wrong."

"Well, I wouldn't know much about *that*. But—" Tunny became interested in a speck of dust on his coveralls.

"But *what*?" As much as he respected Tunny, the man was starting to wear on his patience.

"There is one thing. But I don't think it'll help us too much. It's risky."

"Tell us, please. Maybe we can find some way to use it." *Gently, James.*

"If there's a big fire, an engine fire, say, the ship is supposed to fill the ballasts with compressed air and rise to the surface in an emergency blow."

"Even though it's not supposed to exist?"

"It would be better for the government to rationalize the prison's existence than for even the sunken remains to fall into the wrong hands," Joseph said.

"Yeah, that's how the captain explained it to me. It should also send out some kind of warning signal to whoever's in charge, so they can get us before the enemy does—unless that's been disabled too."

"That's our solution then. We'll start a fire in the engine room, and boom, up we go." It sounded almost too easy to James.

"Except for the smoke," Tunny pointed out. "Like I said, it needs to be a *big* fire."

Of course it was too good to be true. "The smoke?"

Tunny pulled a face. "The prison will fill with smoke, toxic smoke. There's no way to vent it properly once it gets into the ducts. We could suffocate." He crept his hand up his throat as though he already felt the air thickening. "Plus, what if there's an explosion? We couldn't get out, and we might blow a hole in the sub and sink the darn thing. *That's* why I've never done it, what with the life-pods being jettisoned."

Defeat knocked the wind out of James, leaving a bitter taste in his mouth. "So that's out." Damn. He slammed his fist against the wall. *Think, James. For Pine. Think.*

"How long would it take the prison to rise?" Joseph asked.

Tunny shrugged. "Twenty-ish minutes to half an hour normally. For an emergency blow, it should take less than ten."

James raised his head. "We could get everyone into the cockpit, the highest point on this ship, block the air from coming in. We would just have to cross our fingers that we rise faster than the toxic air spreads and that the prison won't explode until *after* we get out."

Joseph snapped his fingers. "Exactly. It's a big risk, but...it might be our only option, if Pine can't convince the captain otherwise."

"Convince him of what? He'll be obsolete now that his job is over. Once he's found... He's sentient, Joseph, he knows what his fate will be." A fate, James now knew, the synadroids understood all too well.

"But couldn't we do anything? Speak to the authorities on his behalf?"

"We don't have any power, you know that. Pine was an exception out of respect for you. We can't risk her by pushing our luck."

"And yet we've left her up there, alone, with a possibly homicidal android?"

"She's buying us time, so let's use it."

Joseph hung his head. "I know you're right. I just hate—"

"Me too. But we can't make any of it right unless we do something." Galvanized, James pulled up the calm his training had beaten into him. "Tunny, where is the engine room?"

"At the back. There's a door at the end of the cell block."

"I know where it is." Joseph's back was now straight, his eyes determined.

"Okay, Tunny, here's the plan. Joseph and I are going to go to the engine room and start a fire to trigger the emergency blow. I need you to gather everyone in the cell block together and tell them what we're doing and take them to the control room. Can you do that?"

"I *can*. But I'm not sure if I *should*." Tunny's expression was apologetic.

"Why not?"

"It's about authority, you see. You want me, the caretaker, to tell them we're going to irreparably sabotage the ship on the chance we'll make it to the surface before we're blown to bits or suffocated? They like me well enough, but that's a big ask. A military man, on the other hand..." He trailed off and looked at James expectantly.

"Okay, I'll tell them. Just go along with whatever I say, yes?" Inwardly, though, he groaned. People skills were not his strongest suit.

In the cell block, Tunny beat his mallet against the steel bars. The clanging reverberated through the prison, setting James's teeth on edge. He clenched his jaw and waited impatiently as the few inhabitants of the prison made their way to the center of the room.

There were six of them, two women and four men. Who were the former prisoners and who had simply been in the wrong place at the wrong time? He couldn't tell just by looking at them. They stared at him, curious yet lethargic, the faces of people who didn't know that hope for an escape was even an option.

James cleared his throat. "Hello, everyone. I know we haven't yet had a chance to be introduced. My name is Lieutenant James Cruicéad. I am here on a rescue mission. In a few minutes, we will begin evacuation procedures. Please bring only what is absolutely necessary." Directing them to Tunny, he continued. "Please follow Mr. Tunny here. He will be taking you up to the control room, where we will gather while we ascend." He sounded like a pompous ass. *So it should be convincing enough to work.*

The inmates stared at him dumbly, slow to

understand.

"You mean, you're here to rescue us? They've found us? We're getting out?"

"We'll be making an attempt," James clarified.

"What do you mean, *attempt*?" The speaker sported a number of tattoos similar to those James had seen on inmates sent to the Perimeter. A former inmate?

"We can't guarantee the attempt will be successful." He couldn't lie to them. Whatever happened, his conscience needed to be clear.

"So we could die?" The inmate's eyes narrowed.

"Yes, but if we're successful, tonight you will be sleeping on land."

That got a reaction. They all began speaking at once, a mix of panic and hope.

"I don't want to die—"

"You'd rather die down here? Slowly, painfully? Remember what happened to Sarah—"

"I can't stand being down here another day."

"But—"

James paced in front of them, trying not to let his irritation show. After two minutes, he held up his hands. "That's enough discussion. There isn't a question of whether or not we're doing this. We are." Deep down, though, James wasn't sure if he would force ascension against their will. Hopefully, he wouldn't have to. *See if they call my bluff.*

"What if I don't want to go?" the tattooed man asked. "I won't exactly have a warm welcome waiting for me."

"You'd rather spend the rest of your life down here?" When the man didn't look cowed, James changed tack. "Look, you know as well as I do what this prison is. Believe me, the government *and* the military are going to bend over backward to make this go away. Do you have any idea what the payout on a lawsuit like this would be? Never mind a full pardon."

The man hooked his thumbs through his belt loops and chewed his bottom lip, considering. "How exactly do you plan to get us out of here? If it were that easy, someone would've done it by now." He glanced at Tunny.

James told them the plan. "So, with a little luck, you'll be eating something other than crushed lobster tonight—"

"Wait, you mean this isn't a sanctioned mission? The military isn't here to rescue us?" a scruffy young man interrupted, a note of agitation in his voice. The hair on one side of his head and face was much thinner, and even as James watched, the young man reached up and tugged a few strands free.

"No. But it's the only option we have. The military won't find us. This prison was designed to evade detection on all levels. *That's* why some of you," he pointed to the inmate next to her, "have been down here for seven years."

Everyone in the group stared at James. He stared back, his feet planted, shoulders square. "Well?" he challenged them.

An older woman with sun-starved skin and rheumy blue eyes finally broke the silence. "I'm game. Beats sitting around waiting to die." She elbowed the tattooed man. "Come on, Caleb, it'll be an adventure."

Caleb scowled, but didn't disagree further. To James's relief, the others murmured their assent and began returning to their cells to gather their meager possessions.

"Oh, and bring anything you can find that will

burn—clothes, wood, anything—and dump it in a pile by the engine room door," James called after them. He turned back to Tunny and Joseph. "What do we do about Pine and the captain? We can't send those people up there and possibly into danger."

"You won't have to." A voice spoke from the control room stairs, where Pine leaned against the railing.

James gave a strangled cry. One of her shoulders had been dislocated, and one cheekbone was vaguely caved in. "Pine." He rushed to her side. "I'll kill him."

"No need," she said wearily and sat down on the steps. "He's out of commission."

"Dead?" Could they be so lucky?

"I don't know. I hope so. Can a synadroid survive a broken neck?" she asked Joseph.

He smiled tenderly at her. "Survive, yes. But function? Not properly."

"Does this mean we can abandon this plan? Just use the sub's controls to raise it?" Hope bubbled up inside James. They wouldn't have to put those people's lives at risk.

"No. The captain made quick work of the panel." Pine touched the depression in her cheek. "I was only able to disable him because he was so focused on destroying it."

"I can't believe he attacked you." Guilt gnawed at James. He never should've left her.

"I can. He's just trying to survive, like we are." Her look said, *You can't understand*. But he did.

"I'm sorry," James said. "We never wished him any harm."

"I know," Pine replied. "I don't think he did either, not really, *but* he was the one who jettisoned the life-pods, not the captain. I think he knew more than he let on. Even before we got here, he never had any intention of leaving this ship."

Joseph ran his hands over her distorted shoulder. "I think I can fix this. It won't be perfect, but it'll do until we get home."

"I love that word." The weariness in Pine's voice made James wish he could pause time, just for an hour. He would hold her, savor every minute with her, just in case. But they didn't have the luxury. They had to do this, now.

"What about the controls? How are we going to get the hatch open if the controls are destroyed?" James hated to pile on the stress, but they had to be prepared, just in case.

"I'll have a look at them as well," Joseph said. "If all we need is to lift the hatch, I should be able to jimmy something together."

It would have to do. "Okay. Take Pine up to the control room with the others and see what you can do. I can start the fire on my own. I'd feel better if the two of you were there to keep an eye on the captain, anyway. Just in case."

Joseph helped Pine stand, and they disappeared back into the cockpit. James headed back to the engine room, passing Tunny and the inmates on the way. Their faces were strained, their steps uncertain, with none of the excitement of being so close to freedom. James wasn't surprised. They'd probably resigned themselves to their fate and now, in only a matter of hours, were placing their lives in the hands of a stranger. Life in the prison had been a certain kind of hell, but at least they were alive.

I'm going to get you all out of here. I promise.
Tunny ushered them into the control room. It

was time.

The engine room was warm, vibrating gently with the hum of the machines. James found the panels at the back, just where Tunny had said they would be.

He gazed at the blinking lights and shifting dials, marveling at their endurance. It was a testament to Tunny's skill that the prison itself had managed to survive all this time. *Seems almost a shame to destroy it.*

Bracing himself, James shoved a screwdriver into the seam of one of the panels, prying it up. When he could get his fingers around it, he tore it off and tossed it to the floor with a crash. Bundles of wires and plates of switches stared back at him.

He went back out to the cell block, retrieved everything the inmates had brought, and piled them in front of the exposed panel. If he could get all of them burning, it should be enough to trigger the system.

Here goes.

He ripped a handful of wires free and carefully selected two of them—one red, one black. Mumbling a quick prayer, he held the exposed ends over the pile of blankets and touched them together. Sparks erupted from the connection, leaping onto the musty fabric.

James held his breath.

A small wisp of smoke rose then thickened as the blankets began to smolder. James showered them with a few more sparks for good measure then stood back. Within seconds, the smoldering fibers ignited, and orange flames stretched toward the ceiling, releasing a thick black smoke that stung his eyes.

Adrenaline shot through James. This was it. *Get*

to the control room.

He shut the engine room door behind him and sprinted for the cockpit stairs. Just as his foot touched the first step, an alarm launched into a high-pitched wail, and emergency lights flashed around the perimeter of the room.

Tunny waited for him at the top of the steps. "Did a good job of that, I see."

"Yes. Sorry to ruin your years of hard work, Tunny."

Tunny clapped him on the back. "Never mind about that. You can buy me a beer when we get to the surface. They still have beer, right?"

"Yes, they still have beer. And I'll buy you a whole keg."

Tunny nodded, satisfied. "Get in then, and we'll lock the door. I think your friends have been able to make some progress on the hatch."

"Really?" James cringed as he stepped into the control room.

Joseph sat in the captain's chair, working busily among the wreckage of the console. Pine stood next to him. Her shoulder was back in place, though it still didn't look normal. Considering the damaged room, though, it was surprising her injuries weren't worse. The other passengers sat in a silent group in the center of the floor, as far away from the bodies of the captain and first mate as they could.

Pine glanced up as he came over. "Joseph thinks he'll be able to trigger the hatch to open when we get to the surface," she said brightly, loud enough for everyone to hear.

But he caught the unnatural tone of her voice.

"That's great," he said. "That'll make it so much quicker to get that first breath of fresh air."

Pine rewarded him with a grateful smile.

"Are the ducts closed? Is the room as airtight as possible?" Joseph asked.

"Everything is as snug as we can make it." Pine staggered slightly as the room rocked. "Here we go."

The room grew noticeably cooler as compressed air roared into the ballasts. The sound was deafening.

James's stomach turned queasy, his legs heavy, like they were whenever he took an elevator. *It's working. We're rising.* One look at the others told James they felt it too.

The older woman gripped Caleb's hand so tightly that the hard man winced, though he made no attempt to pull his hand away. Someone began praying under their breath, a litany of pleading that James couldn't make out.

So far, so good. He went over to Pine and wrapped his arms around her, watching out the window as the water lightened almost imperceptibly.

This might just work.

A blast from the control room rocked the sub, throwing those standing to the floor.

No, no, no. James braced himself, expected the sub to descend, sure they'd blown out the tail.

They kept rising.

The prayer chanted more fervently, and Caleb tucked the old woman's arm under his.

"Joseph? How fast are we ascending?" James tried to keep his voice from reaching the others.

"Not fast enough."

"Is there anything we can do?"

"No."

One minute passed then two. James waited for another explosion, but none came.

Three minutes, four.

The water was noticeably lighter now, changing from twilight blue to rich cobalt.

Five minutes.

The tiniest wisp of poisonous black smoke snaked through the crack in the vent.

Six minutes.

The water was now rapidly lightening into a pale sapphire, and James could almost feel the sun. *We're so close. Just a couple of minutes more.*

The wisp of smoke thickened and coiled, and James's eyes began to sting. Around him, the crew pressed whatever they could over their noses and mouths.

Eight minutes.

The prison shot out of the water like a bullet, arcing gently before its belly smacked back down onto the surface with a wave-rolling crash.

Sunlight streamed through the translucent hatch, blinding James. "Joseph, *now.*"

Joseph fumbled with the hatch controls. The mechanism groaned then stopped. He slammed his fist down on the panel, and the groan turned into a shriek as the top of the shark's head lifted at last.

Fresh, cool air bathed the dazed faces of everyone on board.

James was stunned. He turned to Pine. "We—"

The air was knocked from his lungs by the force of her hug. Her face was alight as she gazed up at him. "You did it!"

"*We* did it." Under the warm of the sun, his amazement turned to giddiness and he swept her up and spun her around, her feet narrowly missing Joseph's head.

She punched his shoulder. "Put me down before you throw me overboard." But her smile was delighted.

He complied, but he couldn't resist cupping her face in his hands. They would have their chance after all, and he wanted nothing more in that moment than her, the smile on her lips, the smile that was for him. Light slanted over the delicate planes of her face and his heart swelled at the warmth in her eyes as she gazed at him, drinking him in like *he* was her freedom from the dark depths, rather than the open sky. But in truth, she was his.

It was always going to end this way. You knew it, and that's what you were afraid of. But now, it seemed so obvious, so *easy. How could you have wanted anything else?* He traced his fingertips over the ruined side of her face. So what if she wasn't human? She was more than human. She was everything he could never even dream of.

"I love you, Pine." It was so familiar on his tongue, as though his soul had murmured it to him, night after night, until he'd finally listened.

"James—" She stood on her tiptoes and wrapped her arms around his neck, pulling him to her. Then, finally, he pressed his lips to hers and everything else in the world disappeared—every fear, every doubt, every sorrow, eclipsed by her.

Her mouth was at once hungry and reverent, parting beneath his as she stroked the damp skin on the back of his neck. "I love you too." Her whisper passed over his lips and rippled down his spine, and he willed the rest of the world away, wanting to hold on to the revelation that was her in a moment that would last forever.

As he bent to kiss her again, a thunder of applause skated over the water between them. A fleet of ships had surrounded them, their decks swarming with people, all of them cheering. Encircled by a number of smaller boats, some unmarked, others with the insignia of local news channels and networks, was a large, white military vessel. An emerald-haired figure stood on the deck, grinning and waving furiously.

Pine pulled back and turned, smiling ruefully. "Is that Blue?"

James raised his hand in greeting just as an unyielding, inhuman arm wrapped around his neck and dragged him overboard.

THIRTY

Pine had no time to react. One moment James was there, and the next he was gone, with barely a ripple to mark his passing.

"James!" Pine screamed, rushing to the edge of the open hatch. "*James.*"

Joseph grabbed her by the shoulder, his fingers digging into her synthetic flesh. "What happened? Where's James?"

"The captain," Pine gasped. "He's taken him." She peeled her shirt over her head then scrambled out of her pants. "I'm going after him." She dove off the exposed deck of the cockpit, ignoring the many pairs of astonished eyes and Joseph's hands trying to hold her back.

James and the captain hadn't gotten far. The captain's head sat at an odd angle on his broken neck, one eye gazing upward, and the other down past his shoulder to the dark depths waiting to embrace them. His arms were undamaged and locked around James, using nothing more than his own solid weight to carry them down. James thrashed in his grip, surrounding them with a haze of tiny bubbles.

Pine cut through the water like an arrow, gaining on them. The captain may have had a head start, but he was no match for a woman who'd lived her entire life in these waters. Years of immobility as he'd played at the role of captain had taken their toll, and his limbs were uncoordinated and stiff.

Her body crossed the path of the sun, and both men looked up. The captain bared his teeth in a snarl and tried to angle James's body for a faster descent.

Not here. Not in my ocean.

James stared up at her, his semi-conscious expression one of disbelief and regret. As his eyes began to close and his body grew limp, Pine's luminescence flared, surrounding her in a ball of light.

The sight of her radiance incited both men. James's eyes widened, and he struggled again, thrashing in the captain's hold as he tried to find purchase and thwart the synadroid's iron grip. The muscles in his arms corded and strained, and for a moment, Pine thought he was going to triumph, his large hand wrapped around the captain's already twisted head.

But James was human, and he needed oxygen to survive. His burst of strength fled as quickly as it had come, and he slumped over, his hand drifting lifelessly from his enemy. The captain grimaced and shoved James away from him, opening his arms for Pine.

Had he hoped to take James hostage? Or was it simply revenge? Taking the man responsible for his doom down with him?

Judging by the grin spreading across his face, it was the latter. The captain knew James would never survive in the water, knew without a doubt he would drown. *But.*

Pine grinned back, and the captain's smile faltered as he realized what she'd already figured out.

James couldn't live in the ocean. But neither could the captain.

Cloistered in his ship for years, he'd forgotten it was the human prison that had kept him alive. He'd been lulled into thinking he was of the ocean himself, as his ship had been. And in his desperation, he'd forgotten what he truly was.

His model had been created for a different purpose; it was never meant to be submerged for any length of time. Pine saw the understanding in his eyes, the sealing of a fate he'd been desperate to avoid.

He reached for her, his fingers grasping for the life she held in her hands. She could choose to save one of her kind, who'd only done what he could to survive, as had she, who'd done nothing but his duty for a thankless god. Or in seconds he would disappear, down into the dark where he would cease to exist, as though he never had.

She gazed upward to where James floated, his head bowed, arms spread. His chest no longer moved, and the only bubbles now were the ones captured by his hair. Another life that would simply disappear, a life so different from her own, that lived in a world so far from hers.

This. This is what it means to be alive. To choose. To choose to love or hate, to fear or leap, to merely exist or to thrive. The truth or the lie.

She chose truth.

EPILOGUE

It seemed to Pine lately that the rain was never going to end. She lowered the car window and reached out to let the cold drops break over her palm and run down her arm.

"James would've been very proud of you today," Joseph said from his seat next to her. "So, so proud."

She wished he'd been there. It would've brought him so much peace.

"Do you think it made a difference?" Today, Pine had stood in front of the Foxwept Provincial Court and given an impassioned plea for the legal recognition of personhood for sentient androids, and all the rights and freedoms that went along with it, including full citizenship.

She'd told the judges, the audience, the Province, and the country at large her story. She'd told them of Harlequin, of Ash, and the captain, from their births to their deaths.

She'd spoken of Todd and Tabby, Sebastian and Paloma.

She'd told them of James and Joseph. Even The Fire-eater, The Blue Fairy, The Owl, and The Crow got a mention, albeit a cryptic one.

She talked about fear and fate, about

exploitation and suffering, neglect and indifference, kindness and compassion.

About humans and synadroids.

About love.

The results had been mixed. Some were outraged she'd been given a platform, disgusted by the indulgence and its implications. Others without a personal stake simply shrugged and turned away. Some who felt a spotlight shine on them fought back, arguing about what it meant to be genuinely alive and the privilege that came with that, the entitlement which needed to be carefully bestowed and reserved for those *truly* living.

Others wept, remembering a not-so-distant past, other struggles whose lessons had been forgotten. More were moved, their eyes opened to a truth they'd felt in their hearts but had been unable to articulate in a culture where change was erratic and priorities unpredictable.

And many hearts swelled to bursting, poised on the cusp of finally being recognized, of having a voice.

Joseph patted her shoulder. "You know, Pine, I think so. The fact that you're currently the heroine of a cause célèbre certainly helped."

It was true. If it hadn't been for Blue's quick thinking—and the fact that she was a practiced opportunist—Pine never would've had had a stage at all, and synadroids would still be in the shadows. Though the prison had countermeasures to avoid detection, including tracker-blockers, the camera in Pine and James's life-pod had managed to capture the oncoming shark, its whirling, opening maw clearly human-designed, before it swallowed them whole.

Blue had secured those images, and disseminated them immediately to the media, who'd come out in droves to investigate. When the sub began to ascend, it *had* emitted a distress signal, alerting both the military and the government to its sudden reappearance. Blue, intercepting the call, was able to pin down the location, only eighteen miles from where James and Pine had disappeared.

In the eight minutes it took for the sub to rise, all the players had swarmed. There could be no denial, no cover-up. Then, with the cameras rolling, Pine had dived into the water to try to save the life of the human man she loved from the clutches of one of her own kind. The public drank it up.

The military and the government, not so much. But they had little choice other than to make a deal. In return for Pine, Joseph, and the others agreeing to pretend they were merely part of a potential tourism project that had had a mishap, they were compensated as they chose.

Pine had chosen to speak.

Joseph put his hand over hers. "*I'm* proud of you, Pine. I know that wasn't easy."

And it hadn't been. To lay the most painful, devastating moments of one's life bare and intertwine them with the most intimate and hopeful, all for public consumption, had taken its toll. As grateful as she was for the opportunity, she was glad it was over—for now, at least—and wanted nothing more than to be home.

A few minutes later, she was. She and Joseph stood together in the front yard, gazing up at the house where their life together had begun, and where it would continue.

My life.

"Are you ready to go in?" Joseph asked gently. He knew how overwhelming being in the house could be for Pine these days. But he also knew it was where she was happiest, that there was no place she'd rather be.

"Yes." They walked up the path hand-in-hand, and Pine recalled how James had once carried her over the threshold. She composed herself on the doorstep. *You can do this.*

The door swung open to reveal a hive of activity. Humans and synadroids bustled back and forth, relaying information, taking notes.

"She's here!" someone shouted, and the commotion turned into cheers as they welcomed her home. A confetti popper was unleashed, and for a moment Pine was blinded by a shower of tiny fish and blue glitter. *I'm here.*

James pushed through the crowd, scooping Pine up and swinging her around. "You were incredible! You should've seen the reactions of the crowd. Love it or hate it, *everyone's* talking about synadroid personhood and what it will mean. We can barely handle the influx of support."

Pine buried her face in his neck, pressing her face to the warmth of his skin and focusing on the secure strength of his arms around her. "I'm just glad it's over."

"We'll kick everyone out in a few minutes," he whispered, "but let them celebrate a bit first." He stood her back on her feet. "I wish I could've been there today." To Pine's disappointment, she'd only been allowed to bring one guest with her. "But I know how important it was to Joseph to be there with you."

"It was. Besides, what you're doing here is just as, if not more, important." Since the plight of sentient androids had been made so glaringly public, James had undertaken the task of documenting all the sentient androids in Foxwept and gathering support from humans interested in their cause.

In only a few weeks, the project had grown well beyond what they'd ever hoped for, and James had drafted in help. Blue, The Owl, and The Crow had gotten on board, their particular skills proving invaluable. Any synadroid who wanted to was welcomed—their owners, wary of choosing the wrong side, didn't dare deny them. Moving through the lively crowd, Pine waved at a newly-appointed Harlequin. It turned out The Fire-eater had played a role since the beginning, procuring rare components then passing them for sale to others like Joseph, the funds going into an account for this particular cause.

But despite all the support and their growing momentum, it was bittersweet. Few of the synadroids' stories were happy ones, and Pine's joy at their progress was tempered by the constant ache of empathy and the fear of what would happen if they failed.

But they were close, so close.

Joseph stood by himself amidst the hubbub, gazing at Mara's smiling portrait.

Pine leaned her head on his shoulder. "I wish I'd gotten to meet her." *What would it be like to have a mother?*

"Me too," Joseph said. "I also wish she'd been able to see today. She would be so happy—it's a time we thought would never come. Of course, then she would've made me wait until it was legal for me to marry her."

The mark by her hairline. His desire for an android daughter. His unconditional love.

"What happened to her?"

"She was one of my first successes. This was before your kind was produced on a large scale. She was one of a kind, experimental, and eventually, her technology was no longer compatible with life." He stroked Mara's cheek as she peered up from her work. "I could've tried to move her brain into a newer body, but she was ready to go. She saw it as a natural ending, as the true experience of her life. Who was I to argue?"

"I didn't know," James said from behind them.

"No one did." Joseph didn't turn. "It was safer for us that way. We could live our lives within these four walls as we wanted. As *she* wanted." He kissed Pine on the forehead. "She would've loved you."

James left them, and a few minutes later, began ushering everyone out of the house with the assurance they would pick things up first thing tomorrow morning. Once everyone had left, Joseph too made his excuses and retired to his room.

"Should we go upstairs?" James asked. He looked tired, dark circles smudged under his eyes.

They walked up the stairs together, past Joseph's room where the faint sounds of Mara's cheerful voice and Joseph's answering chuckle played and replayed. It was Joseph's ritual—and a happy one. Joyful sounds, not ones of sorrow, and Pine's heart was easy.

In the bedroom, they stood together at the window, looking out over the lights of Portfade. Tonight, and for every night of her life, Pine wanted nothing more than this. During the day, she and James would fight beside each other for her life and the lives of others, but now, these moments, were for them.

Pine couldn't see the ocean, but she knew it was there, that it always would be. Now the moon would be breaking up on the surface of the quiet water, while below, life flourished. She thought of the years she'd spent down there. Living, but not alive. She hadn't even known what it meant.

Turning away, she put her hand on James's chest, over his heart, feeling his life beating beneath her fingers. Beating for *her*.

Their love, alive at last.

ACKNOWLEDGMENTS

As always, I would like to express my love and gratitude to my family and friends. Thank you for making my life its own kind of fairy tale.

Thank you also to my beta, Anna Adler, for helping me in my eleventh hour—you're the best!

And finally, my editor Danielle Fine, for going above and beyond. I'm so grateful for you!

ABOUT THE AUTHOR

A.W. Cross is a made of 100% star stuff and writes social science-fiction and futuristic romance. She lives in the wilds of Canada with her beloved family and a deep nostalgia for the 80s.

Other books by A.W. Cross:

FOXWEPT ARRAY

Rose, Awake: A Futuristic Romance Retelling of Sleeping Beauty (Foxwept Array Short Story)

Clara, Dreaming: A Futuristic Romance Retelling of The Sandman Retelling (Foxwept Array #2)

Beauty Unmasked: A Futuristic Romance Retelling of Beauty and The Beast (Foxwept Array #3)

Lissa, Beautiful: A Futuristic Romance Retelling of The Frog Princess (Fowept Array #4)

THE ARTILECT WAR

The Seeds of Winter: Artilect War Book One

The Gardener of Man: Artilect War Book Two

The Harvest of Souls: Artilect War Book Three

The Artilect War Complete Series